So This Is Love

An Austen-Inspired Regency

Laura Hile

Copyright © 2020 by Laura Hile.

All rights reserved. No part of this publication may be reproduced, distributed or transmitted in any form or by any means, including photocopying, recording, or other electronic or mechanical methods, without the prior written permission of the publisher, except in the case of brief quotations embodied in critical reviews and certain other noncommercial uses permitted by copyright law. For permission requests, contact the publisher at the address below.

www.laurahile.com

Publisher's Note: This is a work of fiction. Names, characters, places, and incidents are a product of the author's imagination. Locales and public names are sometimes used for atmospheric purposes. Any resemblance to actual people, living or dead, or to businesses, companies, events, institutions, or locales is completely coincidental.

Scripture quotations are taken from The Holy Bible, King James Version. Cambridge Edition: 1769.

Book Layout ©2017 BookDesignTemplates.com

Cover Design: Damonza.com

So This is Love/ Laura Hile. -- 1st ed.
ISBN 979-8-6487097-8-2

Table of Chapters

With grateful thanks to fellow author
Margie Bayer
who asked for a Charlotte Lucas story

"I am not romantic, you know. I never was."

–JANE AUSTEN'S CHARLOTTE LUCAS

PRIDE AND PREJUDICE

1 Call of the Running Tide

The news would spread like wildfire, and why not? An unexpected engagement was the sort of thing gossips lived for. She had somehow convinced Mr. Collins to keep silent, but Charlotte Lucas did not trust him. Even in the best of times his resolve was weak; he was that kind of man. Her acceptance of his proposal was too much a triumph to be hushed up. Charlotte had a few precious hours to break the news to her friend before Mr. Collins would shout it from the housetops.

It was only right that Elizabeth Bennet learn the news from Charlotte herself. After all, three days ago Mr. Collins had proposed to Elizabeth. She had roundly refused him. Mr. Collins had plenty to say about that! Nevertheless, Elizabeth was Charlotte's dearest friend. She deserved every consideration.

That morning the walk to Longbourn House felt especially long. How Charlotte longed to turn back! For in accepting Mr. Collins, she had become Mrs. Bennet's rival. When Mr. Bennet died, Mr. Collins would inherit. Charlotte would be the one to replace Elizabeth's mother as mistress of Longbourn.

This was not Charlotte's reason for marrying; she must somehow make Elizabeth understand. The specter of spinsterhood was far more compelling than any inheritance Charlotte might gain.

It was too early for a social call; Charlotte felt the mortification of this keenly. The housekeeper answered the door with a sniff of disapproval. "The family is at breakfast, miss."

Thus, Charlotte was left to wait in the drawing room, a room as familiar as any at Lucas Lodge. This morning, however, she kept her gaze fixed on the carpet. It was tempting to look around with expectation, and this would never do. Any number of things could prevent Charlotte from being mistress here. Mr. Bennet, an uncommonly healthy man, was hardly at death's door.

Elizabeth came rushing into the drawing room and impulsively reached for Charlotte's hands. "My dear friend," she said earnestly, "I cannot thank you enough for keeping Mr. Collins entertained. It has been wretchedly awkward having him remain as our guest."

How could Charlotte answer this? She felt her cheeks grow warm.

"After what happened, we hoped that he would return to Hunsford at once. A gentleman of true feeling would never have stayed on. But as we know, my cousin has no proper feelings." Elizabeth's fingers pressed Charlotte's affectionately. "Yours has been a sacrifice of true friendship, for I know how tedious his company can be."

Never did Charlotte expect to have sympathy with Judas Iscariot! Had she betrayed Elizabeth's friendship by accepting Mr. Collins?

This thought was immediately discarded. Charlotte had made her choice; she could not turn back now. Moreover, there was nothing to be gained by delaying the announcement.

"As it turns out, things have taken a little turn," said Charlotte slowly, "in a way that is altogether unexpected."

Elizabeth's dimple appeared. "Did your mother cast him out? There is nothing wonderful in that. His ceremonious compliments would enrage a saint."

"Not precisely that, no."

"You are to be commended, for he talks everlastingly. And always about himself or his noble patroness."

"He does, yes."

"But you, my Charlotte, are an excellent listener. So patient, to endure his irksome prattle. Truly, I do not see how you have borne it."

"It was not left completely to me."

"But of course it was! I thank you from the bottom of my heart." Elizabeth's tone became confiding. "Last night Mr. Collins gave us more unwelcome news. He plans to return for another visit, can you imagine? And very soon, too. Father did all he could to discourage this. Mother, naturally, thinks he plans to propose to poor Mary."

Charlotte cleared her throat. It was now or never. "Actually," she said, "I have come to tell you that Mr. Collins has proposed, and I have accepted him."

There. She had said it.

"Engaged to Mr. Collins! My dear Charlotte! Impossible!"

There was scorn mingled with Elizabeth's surprise. Charlotte was stung into saying, "Do you think it impossible that Mr. Collins should be able to procure any woman's good opinion? Simply because he was not so happy as to succeed with you?"

Elizabeth's chin came up. "I wish you every happiness."

"I see what you are feeling. You must be very much surprised; I certainly was. For truly, I never intended for this to happen. But when you have had time to think it over, I hope you will understand what I have done. I am not romantic, you know. I never was."

Elizabeth's lips compressed into a line.

Charlotte could not allow this to pass. "I have never been the object of a gentleman's interest, not even once. You know this is true."

There was no flash of sympathy in Elizabeth's eyes. Of course not; how could there be? How could this dear friend, who was so charming and beautiful, understand what it was to be plain? "Given my age and situation," Charlotte went on, "the most I could hope for was to marry a widower, in order to look after his children."

"But—"

"Yes," said Charlotte ruefully. "You are very right. There are no widowers among our friends. There is only Mr. Collins."

Elizabeth said nothing.

"I ask only for a comfortable home. By this I mean the parsonage in Hunsford, nothing more. Considering Mr. Collins's connections and situation in life, I am convinced that my chance of happiness with him is as fair as most people can boast on entering the marriage state."

There was another pause. "When do you go into Kent?"

Charlotte had her answer ready. "Sometime after the first of the year."

"In January?"

"Yes," said Charlotte. "In January."

She did not stay long after this; indeed, there was no point. During the walk back to Lucas Lodge, Charlotte had time to reflect. January was over a month away. There was time, then, to become accustomed to the idea of being a wife.

Of being Mr. Collins's wife. Of leaving behind all she had known here in Meryton, including her dearest friend.

Charlotte would have only Mr. Collins.

And a home of her own!

This was the material point. Charlotte was no simpleton. Becoming Mrs. Collins would cost her something. But Charlotte Lucas, spinster, would at last have a home of her own.

This was a sensible, reasonable goal, decided through commonsense deduction.

Why then did Charlotte feel so little peace?

2 More Than Just a Kiss

Mr. Collins returned a scant fortnight after his departure, bringing with him all the ardor of a proud bridegroom. On every occasion, with Charlotte at his side, he must bask in the glory of their betrothal. The phrase *my future father-in-law, Sir William* was often on his lips.

Moreover, Mr. Collins accepted the good wishes of the people of Meryton as if they were his due. Had he not rescued their dear Miss Lucas from spinsterhood? Charlotte thought this attitude was unbecoming.

Indeed, lately it was all she could do to maintain composure in his presence. If only she did not see so much or *think* so much!

"I have no opinion," Charlotte reminded herself. "None at all."

But she did have an opinion, and therein lay the trouble. Moreover, this opinion would not curl up or slink away, but instead chose to taunt her. It had been taunting her for days.

Just now, for instance, it was obvious that Mr. Collins had mixed up the value of the playing cards. And not just any cards, but a knave and an ace. What simpleton would do a thing like that?

In addition to everything else, must Mr. Collins be *stupid*?

Charlotte took herself in hand. There was no excuse for being petty and ungenerous. "Not every gentleman needs to play whist," she told herself firmly. "Mr. Collins has other qualities that are admirable."

Never mind that she was unable to think of even one!

Mr. Collins's gaze held an expression of shame mixed with bravado. "Whist is not often played by Lady Catherine de Bourgh," he said, as if this explained everything. "Doubtless you find my skills a little underdeveloped."

He looked at her expectantly. Was he waiting for her to reassure him? He was! Charlotte knew her duty and said all that was proper. But oh, she hated the duplicity of this. It was not as if whist were a complex game!

"Card games did not come my way during university days," he announced. "I felt it was my duty to dedicate every moment to my studies."

Was it truly duty? Or was it because he was so unintelligent that he had difficulty learning anything?

Fortunately, Charlotte did not speak this thought aloud. She sorted her cards and said mildly, "If Lady Catherine is not in the habit of playing, when she does it will be in your best interest to lose."

She was rewarded with a braying laugh.

"Shame, shame!" he chided. "You oughtn't to speak of the provider of my living—that is to say, the provider of *our* living—with such levity."

"I understand," said Charlotte. She played her card, and her father and Johnny did likewise. Mr. Collins hesitated, gazing with dismay at his cards.

"Come on, Collins," said her brother. "We haven't got all night."

"Now, son," said Sir William. "Give the man space to think."

Charlotte drew a long breath, and then watched her betrothed put down a low-ranking card from the wrong suit. Another blunder.

Johnny gave an unmannerly whoop. Mr. Collins's face took on a pinched expression.

"I can do this," Charlotte told herself. "I can manage him as husband."

And she would! She would encourage him to keep busy with his duties as rector, to practice reading aloud sermons in his study, to call on parishioners, and to cater to Lady Catherine's every whim.

If he allowed it, she would even teach him how to play cards properly.

Again Charlotte told herself what she had said to Elizabeth Bennet, for it was very true. "I am not romantic. All I ask is a comfortable home."

The game played itself out, and Johnny took on the duty of tallying the points. Charlotte knew without looking that she and Mr. Collins had lost again.

Presently she excused herself from the card table and went out.

As Charlotte stood in the vestibule, considering whether or not she should retire for the night, she heard the drawing room door open and close.

"Charlotte, my love."

She froze to silence. It was Mr. Collins, but this singsong voice was something new. She could feel his coy smile. He had been smiling like this all evening.

A feeling of dread crept up Charlotte's spine. Slowly she turned round, and when she saw how near Mr. Collins was, she took a hasty step back.

"It is getting rather late," she said. "Perhaps you ought to return to Longbourn. You do not wish to offend your relations by being always absent."

He brushed this aside. "No one minds that. I would far rather be here. With you."

She did not like the way he said this.

Mr. Collins gave a quick glance behind him and then stepped nearer. She felt his hand creep round her waist, and he drew her closer. Was he expecting—he was obviously expecting—

Charlotte knew her duty. One chaste kiss. How difficult could that be? She lifted her chin and waited. Mr. Collins did not delay.

She felt his lips on hers, but there was more. He kissed her again, this time with more intensity. He pulled her against his chest, embarrassingly close.

And then she felt his hand work its way up the bodice of her gown. His fingertips were probing, seeking—what?

His bare fingers slid along her throat and then down, beneath her gown, beneath her chemise, finding pleasure in—

No!

Charlotte pushed him roughly away. "Mister Collins," she cried. "You forget yourself, sir!"

He ought to have looked ashamed; any decent gentleman would. Instead he gave a giggle. "Only until after the ceremony, my love."

"*My love*?" she cried. "You are hardly that, sir. We scarcely know one another! Affection will grow, but it will take time and patience."

His smile never dimmed. In fact, it grew wider. Was he leering at her?

"Desire is a good foundation for"—he reached up to toy with the neckline of her gown—"the intimacy of the marriage bed."

Charlotte took several steps back. Although he was her fiancé, he had no right to say such things!

"Good *night*, Mr. Collins!" She turned sharply away, giving him no time to reply. Up the stairs Charlotte ran, skirts held high. And run she must, for what if he followed and discovered the location of her bedchamber?

She traversed the upstairs hall as quietly as she dared, and then reached her room. For some minutes Charlotte stood with her back to the closed door, trembling and listening. Was he ascending the stairs? Would he follow her here? If so, the carpet runner would give no indication. If Mr. Collins came seeking her, would he find her because of her breathing? For she was fairly gasping for breath.

He had seemed so harmless and mild and pliable. She now knew that this was not the case. Charlotte had seen farm animals. Would Mr. Collins behave like that?

The memory of his probing fingertips made her shudder.

Swiftly she moved to pull a chair in front of the door. No, this was not enough. She took the chair away and pushed the bureau, heavy though it was, before the door.

Intimacy was to be expected; Charlotte knew this. It was the duty of a wife to her husband. But somehow she had never realized how *personal* the shared bedchamber would be; to have him touching her in ways no one else had.

She must be practical; she must think this through. She and Mr. Collins would have children together. Charlotte had always enjoyed children, but what if they were like him?

No, they would not be; she would not allow it. She would teach her children to read and to think and to dance gracefully and, heavens, to play games intelligently by following a strategy instead of bluffing.

Moreover, her sons would not make jokes that only they laughed at. She would teach them to converse easily on pleasing subjects. They would learn to listen sincerely and with interest. Their conversation would not be limited to restating the obvious.

And she would teach her sons not to grope women.

For that was what Mr. Collins had done tonight. He had *groped* her.

She trusted him, and he treated her as an object of lustful desire.

To be fair, he was almost within his rights. He was her betrothed. But oh, how she wished that he were not!

Still trembling, Charlotte poured water into the basin and wet her handkerchief. She must wash away all evidence of his presence: from her lips, from her throat, from her breast—

Charlotte did not ring for Sally that night, nor did she put on her nightdress. She took up the fire iron, kicked off her shoes, and climbed into bed fully clothed. If Mr. Collins returned to Lucas Lodge with his mind set on an easy seduction, he would have another think coming!

3 Sailing to Windward

After several hours it became obvious that Mr. Collins would not return to trouble her further. Charlotte fell to thinking. In accepting his proposal, she had disappointed her dearest friend. And now, if she followed her heart, she would greatly disappoint her parents.

If she followed her heart. Here was a laughable thought. Charlotte had no heart; she had proven it. But she did have self-respect. Moreover, she also knew that no home would be comfortable if she must share it with William Collins.

Lucas Lodge fell silent as everyone slept, and Charlotte longed to do the same. But the magnitude of her decision weighed on her. Would she change her mind? Did she have the fortitude to act?

After several hours of this, there was nothing for it; she must light a candle and get to business. Down she went to the back parlor for stationery and writing supplies.

The first letter she wrote was to Elizabeth Bennet. With the furor that was to come, it was unlikely that Charlotte would be able to call at Longbourn. The second was to Miss Whitby, headmistress of the ladies' seminary Charlotte had attended. A third was to Lady Mary, Sir Hugh's wife. Charlotte had helped with the children at various times; would Lady Mary be willing to give a reference?

And then Charlotte counted out the contents of her purse. The coins made a pitiful pile, for Quarter Day would not come until Christmas. Her mother had already paid for several items of apparel. Charlotte would either be allowed to keep these, or her sisters would become the grateful recipients. Nothing in the Lucas household went to waste.

Her parents had been thrilled to see her marry well. When morning came, that joy would disappear—if Charlotte's courage did not fail.

She came down to breakfast wearing a severe black gown. Her mother lifted an eyebrow, but said nothing. When Charlotte requested a private interview, her parents exchanged glances but made no protest. Sir William took up his teacup and led the way to his bookroom. Charlotte squared her shoulders and followed her mother.

Sir William took his usual seat behind the desk and waved Charlotte into a chair. She gazed at each of them in turn. Her father was nursing another cold. Her mother waited with tranquil expectation, a half-smile pulling at her lips. So trusting, her parents were. Truly, they had no idea.

How could she wound them? Charlotte had never done anything to bring shame or reproach. Perhaps she ought to relent. Perhaps she could marry Mr. Collins after all and somehow deal with his expectations.

A memory came rushing forward: Mr. Collins's ragged breathing, hot against her neck. His probing fingers—

Charlotte put up her chin. There would be no going back. "Mother, Father," she said quietly, "I shall come straight to the point. After much reflection, I have decided to end my engagement to Mr. Collins. I have discovered that we do not suit."

Their cries of dismay were hardly surprising. It would have been easier to face a blaze of temper, but there was none of that. "Oh my dear," said her mother. "How can you do this? The banns have already been read."

Charlotte must not waver! "Then we must un-read them, Mother. I refuse to marry William Collins."

"But why? Mr. Collins is not the wisest of men; you knew that already. But his situation! Think of his situation!"

"I am, Mother."

"And what of us? We shall never live this down. Mrs. Bennet shall never let me live this down."

Charlotte bit back a sigh; her mother had a point. Mrs. Bennet's scorn would be merciless and public. At all costs Charlotte must carry her point. "Would you rather have me miserable in my marriage?"

Sir William turned aside to cough. "What of Collins?" he sputtered. "What does he say?"

"I—have not yet informed him of my decision. He is due here shortly, as he is fond of sharing our breakfast. I might add, this is after he has already breakfasted at Longbourn. I cannot abide his selfishness, Father. As to what he thinks of my decision, we shall know soon enough."

Relief washed over Lady Lucas's face. "He does not *know*?" She turned to Sir William. "Why, it is only a lovers' spat. Thank goodness. They will make it up soon enough."

"No, Mother, my mind is made up. I shan't marry Mr. Collins."

"Was it because Collins mishandled the cards last night? Burn it, you cannot end an engagement because a man ain't clever with card games!"

"It was not that, Father."

"He told Mrs. Hanchett the other day that her pudding ought to be *infamous*. Even I know that's not the right word." Sir William attempted a laugh. "Whatever he's done, Collins is sure to apologize. Best thing in the world for a man to do when his woman is upset. Otherwise, she goes about saying that everything is *fine*. Dangerous word, when a woman says it like that."

Charlotte did not wish for an apology, because she knew he would not mean it. But she could hardly say this to her father.

"Never fear, he'll come round with his hat in his hand. All will be well, my girl. You wait and see."

"I understand the seriousness of my decision. Nothing can be as it was. I have already written to Miss Whitby."

Sir William's smile disappeared. "Miss Whitby? Who is Miss Whitby?"

Lady Lucas gave a cry of surprise. "Good gracious. She is headmistress of that school in Bath. Why would you write to her?"

"She might have need of an assistant teacher. I have offered my services."

Sir William's face went red. "Never shall a daughter of mine teach in a school. What would people say? 'Look, there goes Sir William's daughter, the paltry teacher, slaving in a school.'" He broke out coughing again.

"Now look what you have done," said Lady Lucas. "For heaven's sake, William, calm down. Take a sip of tea."

Sir William did so. Presently he regained his voice. "You shame us all, girl. I can never again show my face at St. James Court."

"The gossip will be fearsome for a time, I understand that. It will be better for everyone if I leave Meryton."

"And confirm everyone's suspicion of wrongdoing?"

Charlotte met her mother's gaze. "I have done nothing wrong."

The bookroom door came open, and Sally put her head in. "Mr. Collins is come from Longbourn House, miss. He's asking after you. Shall I bring him here?"

"Indeed, yes," boomed Sir William. Once the door was closed, he added, "*Now* you shall have your apology."

Lady Lucas turned to Charlotte. "You will mind your manners, Lottie, and do as you ought. Having made up your mind to marry Mr. Collins, you are duty-bound to keep your promise."

Mr. Collins came in with a cheery "Good morning," and if he felt any shame for his behavior the night before, he did not show it. "This is a jolly meeting! Before breakfast, too." He found a chair and sat. His expression became hopeful. "Do I smell bacon?"

"Thank you for coming, Mr. Collins. I have an announcement to make."

"Oh my dear," whispered Lady Lucas. "Be reasonable."

"I am being reasonable, Mother. Mr. Collins, I must inform you that our engagement is at an end. I am unable to marry you."

Mr. Collins's mouth fell open. "I beg your pardon?" he sputtered. "Impossible! You cannot *break* our engagement. It is simply not done. Everyone expects us to marry."

"I am sorry to cause you pain, but I find that we do not suit."

"Nonsense! We are *perfectly* suited. Great heaven, what will Lady Catherine say?"

"You will do well to put the blame on my account."

"I most *certainly* shall. And with a clear conscience! After all, I have been uncommonly generous."

"Generous?"

"With great kindness and forbearance, I have overlooked your deficiencies."

Was he sneering at her? "Pray enlighten me, sir. To which of my deficiencies to you refer?"

"Very well, since you ask, I will elaborate. For one, your lack of fortune. Your settlement will bring thirty pounds per annum, a contemptible amount. For another, your father's distasteful connection with Trade. I am, after all, a gentleman with *expectations*."

Mr. Collins warmed to his subject. "Then too, there are defects of person to consider. But I shouldn't go into those."

"*My* defects, do you mean?"

Mr. Collins looked down his nose at her. "As my former schoolmates would say, you are a drab little piece, Miss Lucas, without looks or countenance. You shall certainly not receive another offer of marriage, not at your age."

"I am no beauty like Eliza Bennet, but I'll thank you to not insult me. As to the reason for my change of heart, you know precisely why."

For the first time Mr. Collins looked worried.

"I trust there is no need to *elaborate*?" Charlotte added.

Mr. Collins would not meet her eyes; he looked the other way. "Now what am I to do for a wife?"

"I suggest you return to Longbourn and cultivate a friendship—a friendship, mind—with Mary Bennet. She likes you. That is a good beginning."

"I thought you liked me."

Charlotte hesitated. "What transpired last night, sir, changed all tha—"

Mr. Collins hastened to interrupt. "Er, good day, Miss Lucas! You have said quite enough! Accept my wishes for your future happiness, such as it is." After a nod to Sir William and Lady Lucas he went out, shutting the door behind him.

A wave of relief washed over Charlotte. He was gone. She was free. Oh, the joy of it!

"Well," said Lady Lucas. "This is a fine kettle of fish. The news will be all over Meryton within the hour. I trust you are happy, Lottie."

"Oh, but I am, Mother. You have no idea. I shan't have to put up with Mr. Collins or his sneering."

"A disgraceful display. Deficiencies, indeed. He ought to be ashamed of himself."

Humility was not one of Mr. Collins's strengths. "The only thing remaining is to decide where I should go."

"Not to that school," said Sir William. "Out of the question."

"I quite agree," said Lady Lucas. "But there must be someone you can visit for a time. One of our friends, perhaps."

"I am willing to work as a companion. I shan't mind the isolation of a country place, away from everyone we know."

"Companion?" Sir William gave a crow of triumph. "I say, that's it. What about my sister Meg? She and Allen have no children; perhaps our Charlotte can keep Meg company."

Lady Lucas continued to frown. "Wiltshire is not an easy distance, especially at this time of year."

"There's no snow to hamper travel, not yet. Two days; three at most. Meg is just the thing. She enjoys young people. Had a hand in arranging a marriage for a young neighbor of hers. Vastly entertaining for her."

Lady Lucas gave a long sigh. "I dislike importuning your sister, especially during the winter months. But it appears that we have no choice."

And just like that, Charlotte's future was decided. Strangely enough, she did not mind.

"I'll write to Meg at once."

"By express, William; there must be no delay. We'll stand the expense."

4 Shake a Leg

During dinner, the footman brought a letter for Mr. Allen, along with a murmured explanation.

"What now?" he said, taking it from the salver. He then fished a pair of spectacles from a pocket and broke the seal. After spreading the letter beside his plate, Mr. Allen began to read.

His wife shook her head in disapproval, causing her diamond jewelry to sparkle. "Letters at the dinner table," she complained to their solitary guest.

Jack Blunt knew better than to smile. What a piece of ceremonial nonsense! Mrs. Allen would have a fit if she saw how he ran his house.

"This is not just any letter," explained her husband without looking up. "It came by express from your brother"

"William?" Mrs. Allen brought a hand to her breast; her bracelets jangled against one another. "Bless me," she cried. "Two from him in one week! Has something happened?"

"Lucas writes that he cannot come himself—he's indisposed with some illness or other—so he is sending Charlotte on the stage. With a maid and one of her brothers for company." Mr. Allen looked up. "He instructs me to meet them in Trowbridge on Tuesday afternoon. By Jove," he added, "that's tomorrow. Christmas Eve."

Blunt's frown descended. "He put a young woman on the stage? With all the robberies along the southern stretch?"

"Robberies?" said Mrs. Allen. "Nonsense. I've heard nothing about robberies."

"It's been in the papers." When she continued to object, Blunt pushed back his chair. "You don't believe me? I'll prove it." He rose to his feet and tossed aside his napkin.

"Captain Blunt!"

Proprieties again. Blunt turned back and made a small bow. "If I may kindly be excused, ma'am?"

"Oh very well."

Again Blunt hid a smile. "That cousin of yours!" he heard her say as he went out. "You may think what you like about your heir, Geoffrey. But I say that the Royal Navy has quite ruined his manners."

Captain Blunt returned from Allen's library with a newspaper. He folded back a page and passed it to his cousin. "A series of robberies has been plaguing a stretch of road known as Clegg's Close. That's just shy of Trowbridge."

Mr. Allen studied the article. "Plaguey nuisance, highwaymen. Aha." His finger tapped the page. "According to this, there was a robbery four days ago. That ought to tide those devils over for a bit. Charlotte will have time to get through before they need to strike again."

"Are you willing to take that chance?"

"Heavens, Jack, Charlotte is no schoolgirl; she must be almost thirty! Moreover, she is a practical woman like her mother. No die-away airs with Charlotte! But all this talk is a waste of time. Nothing will happen. It would be madness to rob the stage."

"You say there is a maid?"

Mr. Allen consulted the letter. "Lucas mentions *our faithful Sally*, whoever that is."

"What of the brother? Strapping fellow? Good in a fight?"

"Apparently it's only Johnny; Lucas says here that he hopes he won't be any trouble. I daresay he will. A twelve-year-old boy is next door to a swarm of locusts, able to eat one out of house and home overnight. No doubt that is why Lucas sent him, to give his larder a rest."

"So no help is to be had from Johnny. Late December is a difficult time to be traveling such a distance."

"Oh, but you haven't heard the *reason*," cried Mrs. Allen. "Such a tragedy! William writes that our poor niece has suffered the breakup of an engagement. She hadn't known the gentleman long, but you know how people will talk. So unpleasant, gossip. She comes to us for a respite."

"It sounds like she is well rid of him."

Mrs. Allen turned a wrist. "I would not expect a bachelor to understand."

"Try me," Blunt said to himself. Aloud he said, "I daresay I wouldn't."

"At Charlotte's age, *any* bridegroom is a godsend, Captain Blunt. She must feel the loss deeply. Truly, my heart bleeds for her. As for you, being a bachelor for *all* these years, why, the fault is entirely your own."

"I fear you are right," he said solemnly.

"It's that beard," said Mrs. Allen, warming to her theme. "If you would shave like a civilized man, women would find you more attractive."

"I—" Blunt broke off speaking. He had his own reasons for the beard, but he was not about to share them with Mrs. Allen.

"The color of your hair also works against you," she went on. "Women prefer gentlemen who are dark and romantic, not blond. I realize that this is not your fault," she added kindly. "However, it would make a great improvement if your hair were cut and attractively curled."

Mr. Allen begin to chuckle, and Blunt found his voice. "Like a confounded cherub?"

"Precisely! Why you must wear a pigtail—like a sailor—I shall never understand. This is England. It isn't as if you are aboard your ship." She gave a great sigh.

Captain Blunt fought to keep a straight face. "I am what I am, ma'am."

After his wife retired for the night, Geoffrey Allen became more expansive. "The trouble is this: my brother-in-law,

Lucas—Sir William, I *should* say—hasn't enough blunt to buy his girl a proper bridegroom. He gives her a thousand pounds and thinks it good enough. Well it isn't."

Captain Blunt shrugged. "It depends on the man."

"Not everyone has your talent for capturing enemy ships and amassing prize."

Blunt lifted his glass. "His majesty's pirate-in-a-dress-coat, at your service."

Mr. Allen gave him a look. "A fine business Lucas had; made money hand over fist. What should he do next but hanker after a title? The fool is *in love* with the idea of being a knight. He crows like a cock on a dunghill."

Captain Blunt's brows went up. "Heroic service to king and country?"

Mr. Allen gave a scornful laugh. "He loaned money to the Crown, of course. He'll never see a return. Moreover, his precious title gave him a disgust for his business. What must Lucas do next but sell the enterprise outright and buy a house on the outskirts of town. Not a landed estate with tenants and an income, but a solitary house. Lucas Lodge he calls it."

"Named after himself? That's rather singular."

"Isn't it? Imagine your Cliff House being called Blunt Barracks."

"I'd rather not."

"His fortune goes to the eldest son, who is not Johnny, by the way. But if Richard won't invest in income-producing property as I have, he'll be selling Lucas Lodge as soon as he inherits."

"As for the girl, are you able to offer help?"

"Add to Charlotte's settlement? I can't see that it would do much good; doubling her dowry won't make it enough to tempt most men. Then too, what I do for her I must do for all the others. I'd be out ten thousand when all is said and done, for there are at least three sons and I forget how many more daughters. Easy figure to bandy about in conversation, ten thousand. It's quite another thing to save it up."

Captain Blunt rotated the stem of his glass. "So for reasons of economy, your niece comes to you on the common stage. I cannot like that." He cast his gaze to the ceiling. "I knew I should have brought Ord with me."

"Who is Ord?"

"My former first officer; put ashore a year ago. Good in a crisis, Ord is."

"Let me guess. You've built him a house on that bluff of yours, haven't you?"

"Something like that. Ah well, I've been in tighter spots. I'll need the use of one of your saddle horses, Allen. And whatever pistols you can spare."

"Great Scott, man, why?"

"I'll be meeting the stage as it enters Clegg's Close, if I can. I'll ride alongside as an armed escort."

Geoffrey Allen set down his wineglass with unnecessary force. "Haven't you seen enough battles and bloodshed? Must you go looking for trouble?"

Captain Blunt's grin appeared. "Trouble finds me of its own free will. Like St. Paul's thorn in the flesh, trouble is God's way of keeping me humble." He paused, still smiling. "What say you, Allen? Care to come along?"

"With my gouty foot? No, I thank you! You are an odd duck, Jack. This isn't your concern."

"If something were to happen to your niece ..."

"Confound it, what has that to do with me? I'm not the one who put her on the stage!"

Jack Blunt sighed. "Allen, Allen. You are such a landsman."

5 Touch and Go

The stage rattled its way along the southbound coaching road: crawling up hills, splashing through shallow fords, and rumbling over bridges. To cover the one-hundred-odd miles to Wiltshire was no small feat; Charlotte endured the discomfort as best she could. The constant noise of the wheels, the driver's shouts from overhead, the blowing of the horn at each coaching inn, the stifling air inside—these were enough to drive a sane person mad.

For a time, the passing countryside held Johnny's interest. He kept up a running commentary on the game birds he'd sighted, or how handy he had become with a gun, or how many birds he was sure to bag if their mother would allow him to hunt on his own.

Charlotte rested her forehead against the window frame, a foolhardy move. The wheels hit another pothole, rewarding her with a sharp knock. She would be bruised and battered by the time they reached Trowbridge! But bruises were only part of it. Her brother had already eaten much of the food their mother sent. Thirst must be endured, for stops were determined only by the need to change horses. Passengers were left to fend for themselves.

Sally Keith never complained, bless her. This trip to Wiltshire was a treat, a chance to visit her brother's family. After each stop, once the coach was underway again, she promptly fell back to sleep. Eventually Johnny tired of watching for game birds or playing cards with Charlotte, and slept as well.

Charlotte was left to confront both the rattling silence and a smarting conscience. This wretched journey was all her fault, the consequence of pursuing the security offered by Mr. Collins. Fine security! Now what was she to do? God only knew what the future held.

And here was another thing. She ought to have prayed before making her choices, but she hadn't. Something happened when she steeled her heart to marry Mr. Collins. A coldness had settled in. It hadn't lifted.

She ought to be praying now, if only for safety! The coach was so top-heavy that it could overturn at any moment. But surely this was an unreasonable fear. The driver and his boy traveled this road often without incident. Surely they knew their business.

Instead, Charlotte focused on keeping her gown and cloak from being trodden underfoot, an impossible task. Dirt and dust could not be helped, nor could her close-fitting bonnet hide the wreck of her hair. Strands worked loose and fell across her face; Charlotte relentlessly tucked them back.

The fourth seat was now occupied by a woman who was industriously knitting stockings. Charlotte did not see how this was possible; surely the shaking and jolting would cause her to drop stitches.

"I suppose we should be thankful that it does not rain," Charlotte said aloud. Now why had she spoken? It was not as if Sally or Johnny would respond.

The woman's needles stilled. "Rain is a far cry from what lies just before Trowbridge," she said. "Clegg's Close, they call it. A lonely spot where the coaching road winds along the river. Oaks such as you never saw hang over the road, shutting out the light."

A ghoulish description! And yet this woman was enjoying every word of it.

"It's a tunnel of trouble, sure enough. A haunt of footpads and highwaymen, Clegg's Close is."

"Are you saying we could be attacked?"

"I shan't be," said the woman, "for I'm out at Bayhill. Best to hide your valuables and be on your guard." The woman's needles began to move again. "I wouldn't pass through Clegg's Close for anything."

"Nonsense," said Charlotte bracingly, with an eye on the sleeping Johnny. "This is England, for goodness' sake."

"Suit yourself," said the woman. "You've been warned."

Sure enough, when they reached the coaching inn at Bayhill, the woman gathered her knitting and departed. A thin, stern-looking man took her place. Charlotte drew as far into her corner as she could.

Outside, an argument was brewing between a female passenger and the driver. Her tone became shrill and insistent; he folded his arms in an uncompromising stance. The stern man lowered his book in order to look out the window.

In the meantime, a new set of horses was being led forward. The driver, still arguing with the woman, gestured to the sky. Obviously, he was anxious to be on his way. Another man came out of the coaching inn and joined the discussion. The driver threw up his hands and came stomping toward the coach. The door was wrenched open, and the driver put his head in. He tapped Johnny on the shoulder.

"Hallo, lad. Rise and shine," he said. "I've got a proposition. Come sit up top with me."

Johnny sat up and rubbed his eyes. "Huh?"

"My boy Billy can sit with the luggage; come take the seat beside me. It's a grand day." He wrinkled his nose. "You don't want to be cooped up in here with the ladies and an old gent, do you?" He turned to the stern man. "No offense."

"Sit beside you? That's famous!" cried Johnny. "I should like it above all things!"

"But—" said Charlotte.

"Come on, Lottie! I'm not a baby."

Charlotte could not resist his pleading eyes. "Oh very well. Mind you wear your cap and keep your coat buttoned up." She bent to retrieve a fallen glove and passed it to him. "And for goodness' sake, hold on!"

Charlotte scarcely had time to clear his seat of crumbs before the woman pushed her way inside. "Well I never," she remarked, settling herself. "I've a ticket, bought and paid for with good money. The cheats in the coaching office, they sell as many as they can and then some. I was not about to sit up top with the riffraff. The idea!"

"But—" protested Charlotte. Johnny's seat had been paid for; she did not see why he must give it up.

The woman continued complaining. "I was welcome, if you please, to sit among the trunks and parcels. As if anyone could, in all this cold. That boy will be better off in the open air. He's young and wiry. He won't be swept off, as people so often are." She nodded to the stern man. "Let the rustics sit together, I say."

"My *brother*," said Charlotte, "has kindly given up his seat for you."

The woman's response was to sniff. "I daresay he's only done as he ought."

Nothing was to be gained by conversing with a person such as this. Charlotte bent her attention to a page listing the stops. Trowbridge, where her uncle would meet them, was perhaps fifteen miles distant. Three hours would seem like an eternity.

Sometime later, Charlotte came awake with a start. Was it possible that she had slept? The stern man was in his corner, reading. Thank goodness she had not rested her head on his shoulder by mistake! The rude woman was consuming a meat pasty.

Charlotte had no way of knowing where they were, but it had been a good while since she had last heard the horn. Presently the road began to descend, and soon a river came into view. Charlotte shifted in her seat to look out. The coaching road was now overshadowed by large trees. They were massive oaks, just as the knitting woman had described.

"Nonsense," Charlotte told herself. The sun had not yet set. Highwaymen did not rob during the day, did they?

Was that fog rising from the water? No, it was only her imagination. Phantom fears, these were. Brought on from exhaustion and that knitting woman's ghoulish prattle.

Presently the road veered away from the river bottom, and the coach began a sharp ascent. There! So much for the dangers of Clegg's Close! The horses, obviously tired, slowed to a walk. Trees and undergrowth were thick along this stretch.

Wait, what was that sound? Was someone shouting? Charlotte strained to hear above the rumble of the wheels.

A gunshot was fired, quite close. There was no mistaking the sound of it. Above them, the driver began to curse.

"Highwaymen?" cried the stern man. He cradled his book over his heart, as if to protect himself from a blow.

An answering gunshot came from above. And then another from the side of the road.

"Johnny!" cried Charlotte.

The coach ground to a halt; from above came a scrambling. "Leave be, Billy," a man shouted. Was this the driver? Another string of oaths and then, "No time to reload. Git, boy! Run for help!"

Charlotte looked out in time to see a young man run off into the woodland. Thankfully, no more shots were fired.

"Halt right there, if ye wish to live," someone shouted. "No funny business, mind."

The door of the coach was pulled open. The fellow wore a flour sack over his head with eye holes cut out. If she were not so frightened, Charlotte would have laughed. "Stand and deliver!" he shouted.

Sally stirred and came awake. "Is this Trowbridge?"

"Lady, are ye daft? This is a hold up! On your feet, all of ye." He waved his pistol to emphasize his point. "Your money or your life."

"Heavens, we shall all be murdered," moaned the stern man.

Onto the road the travelers tumbled, shivering with cold and fear. One of the highwaymen unhitched the horses from the coach and led them off. This was not good.

And yet, there were surprises. She expected to see an army of horsemen surrounding them, but there was only one rider. The sack-masked fellow was on foot. Did highwaymen *walk*?

"Look lively, now!" The rider had his pistol aimed at the driver's head. "Nice and peaceable-like." The rooftop passengers began to climb down, including Johnny.

A hand was thrust under Charlotte's nose; a dirty glove with the fingers cut out. "Your val'ables, if ye please." The sack-masked fellow waved his pistol menacingly. "This here is loaded, and I ain't afraid to use it."

The gun he held was a single-barreled flintlock. But had it already been fired? Charlotte knew something about guns, but not enough to be sure. He might have another pistol on him. Then again, did not blackguards brandish loaded firearms in each hand?

Unfortunately, everything she knew about highwaymen came from books.

"But—" said Johnny.

"Be quiet!" Charlotte pushed Johnny behind her.

"Shut your mouth and hand over the goods."

"I haven't anything that would interest you."

"Sure ye don't," he jeered.

The mounted highwayman came up; he had a black scarf pulled high over his nose and chin. "Hand over your purse. I know you gots one, a fine lady like you."

Had his flintlock also been fired? Charlotte wished she knew. The rooftop passengers were busy digging in their pockets.

In the distance came an unmistakable sound: hoofbeats ringing against the hard road. Someone was coming. Was this a friend? Or another foe?

"Manny, hark yonder." There was concern in the sack-masked fellow's voice. "Do ye reckon we been followed?"

"Shut your trap. We've still time to fleece 'em." The man on horseback collected the stern man's purse, timepiece, and ring, and coins from the other passengers. Sally's guineas—her life savings, she tearfully claimed—were wrested from her.

The sound of hoofbeats grew louder.

The sight of faithful Sally, surrendering her precious coins, struck a nerve. If *Dear God* worked as a prayer, Charlotte was certainly praying now. She faced the man on horseback. "Return her money. You've no call to rob an honest woman."

The rider bared his teeth. "Now then, missy," he said. "Your purse, if you value your life."

"Miss Charlotte," begged Sally. "For heaven's sake, heed what he says."

The hoofbeats slowed to a halt, yet no horseman appeared.

Charlotte surrendered her reticule. "You are a blackguard and a coward."

The rider leveled his flintlock menacingly. "And you," he said, "are as good as dead."

"You would shoot an unarmed woman?" cried Charlotte. "Fine courage!"

A gunshot rang out, and the highwayman was thrown from his horse. His pistol fell with him. Charlotte stared in horror. Blood seeped through the front of his coat and pooled on the road.

The sack-masked fellow, his pistol still aimed at the driver, blanched white. "Manny," he cried.

"I would stay put if I were you," said a new voice. "One of you, take his gun." Johnny hurried to comply.

A man on horseback emerged from the hedgerow. Johnny ran up to him. "His flintlock's been fired, sir," he crowed. "So's the other one! It's all a bluff."

Charlotte saw the flash of a smile. The man swung down from the saddle, keeping his double-barrel flintlock aimed at the sack-masked robber. From his belt he drew a second pistol. "Take this," he said to Johnny. "Keep him covered. If he moves, shoot."

"Yes, sir."

Their rescuer wore a dark greatcoat, dark breeches, and riding boots. He could be anyone, yet he had a military bearing. Charlotte did not understand why she thought this. He was nothing like the easy-going officers of the militia.

"Who else, knave? In addition to this one?" He indicated the fallen man on the road. "Well? Speak up!"

The sack-masked fellow was trembling. "No one 'cept Brock. He lit off with the horses."

"So there is only you." The way the man said this brought a shiver.

He transferred the pistol to his left hand and made a movement with his right. Charlotte nearly gasped aloud, for he drew a sword. "I am more accustomed to using this," he remarked, strolling forward. "My flintlock is inconvenient. Only two shots, whereas with the cutlass—"

He brought the point to an exposed spot beneath the masked fellow's ear. "The opportunities are, shall we say, limitless?"

"Please, sir," the fellow whimpered.

"So now you beg for mercy?" He made a slight movement; a spot of red welled up on the robber's neck. "Return their money," he ordered. "All of it."

Coins and valuables spilled from his pockets onto the road.

The man raised his voice to address the passengers. "I apologize for the delay. That shopkeeper was informative, but he talked on and on."

Who was this person? His hair and beard were light, but his face had been tanned by the sun. And he was handsome; even Charlotte could see that.

The man's gaze never left the masked robber. "You knaves have been at this for some time, preying on innocent travelers. It ends now."

His cutlass flashed in a sudden arc. Several passengers gasped, including Charlotte. With a sickening crunch, the butt of the hilt hit the robber directly on the temple, hard. He dropped like a stone.

"There is no such thing as a *cavalier highwayman*," the man remarked, surveying his handiwork. "And our noble Robin Hood is nothing but a charming myth."

"Is he dead?" faltered Charlotte.

His eyes met hers in a frank and appraising gaze. "Merely knocked out. As for the other one, I daresay he is." He pocketed the pistol and returned his cutlass to its scabbard. "We'll have this one before the magistrate. He'll be dancing with Jack Ketch soon enough."

Did he mean a hangman? Charlotte was too shocked to answer.

The driver came surging forward to shake their rescuer's hand. "Straight through the heart you shot him! By Jove, a fine piece of marksmanship, sir. I was never more grateful in my life. I'm Rab Marlow," he added. "A pleasure to meet you, sir. A genuine pleasure."

"Jack Blunt, at your service."

Charlotte now noticed that the driver's cheek was marked with an angry red line.

"One of them bullets," said the driver, "was fair buzzing like a bee. Right beside my ear it flew! It's a wonder I wasn't hit in the face and killed. Nor was Johnny, yonder, nor my Billy."

The man turned to address Charlotte. "You must be Geoffrey Allen's niece, Miss Lucas."

He knew her name? How was this possible? Charlotte was both confused and embarrassed, but she was not about to argue with this masterful man.

6 From Bad to Worse

Of first importance was to cover the body of the dead man and restrain the fellow who was passed out. Once these tasks were complete, Captain Blunt hunted up the driver to see about moving the coach.

"My thoughts exactly, sir. You there! And you!" Rab Marlow moved among the passengers, recruiting help. "Let's go, gents. Lend a hand. We don't want a smash-up on the road."

The next task was to get a bonfire going. "You there, Johnny," called Blunt. "Come with me. We need to find dry wood. How are you at starting a fire?"

There was a tiny pause. "I'm a dab hand at fire-making, sir." Which meant that he was not. Captain Blunt was no stranger to boys who were eager to please.

"We'll do it together, then."

A walk through the woods was the last thing Blunt's foot needed, but what of it? He had progressed beyond using that curst cane, and the limp was almost gone. Time and rest, that was what the surgeon had said. Sometimes a man must settle for one without the other.

It took work to get the bonfire going, but soon the passengers were gathered round warming themselves. "Until help arrives, this should suffice," Blunt told them. "I'll be leaving shortly for Trowbridge to arrange for that."

He found Miss Lucas and her maid. "What are your plans? Do you leave the stage at Trowbridge?"

"No indeed, sir," said Sally. "I'm to stay on until Wesden, and then go on to my brother at Gloverport."

Blunt turned to Johnny, who had been following him about. "You will wait here with Miss Sally, ride the stage to Wesden, and then procure a horse for yourself. You will follow Miss Sally's party until she reaches her destination. To the door, do you understand? Then ride to your uncle in Fullerton."

"But that is quite impossible," cried Miss Lucas. "How is Johnny to know the way? He is only twelve."

Blunt had his purse out and was peeling off banknotes. "I've had midshipmen his age shoulder far heavier responsibilities. He is well up to the task. Aren't you, son?"

"Yes, sir," said Johnny reverently.

"You appear to know something about guns."

"I do, sir."

Blunt passed him one of his uncle's pistols, three banknotes, and a handful of coins. "Stand guard over the passengers until help arrives. If you are delayed on your journey, you'll need money. If the weather turns ugly, hole up in an inn until you can travel. And if you become lost" —Blunt paused to smile— "you will discover that you can easily hire a guide."

"But this is Christmas Eve," protested Miss Lucas.

"Serves to heighten the adventure, eh, son?"

"Yes, sir!" cried Johnny. "Come on, Lottie. Be a sport. I'd rather be anywhere than Aunt Allen's table. Especially at Christmas. She scolds so!"

"She will be very unhappy if you are absent."

"Pass the blame to me; I've broad shoulders," said Blunt cheerfully. "Mrs. Allen hates me already; she will positively enjoy having a new offense to add to my account."

Next Captain Blunt brought forward Geoffrey Allen's horse. "Miss Lucas, there is nothing for it. You must ride with me to Trowbridge, a matter of two miles. The alternative is to leave you here while I go for help, which could take several hours. I prefer to bring you with me on the chance that your uncle is waiting, as planned. If not, I will hire something and drive you to Fullerton myself." He patted the horse's neck. "She looks to have Arabian blood in her; she'll bear us both for a spell."

"Just a minute. Did you say *both*?"

"I'll throw you up first. Stand just here."

"*Throw* me? But Mr. Blunt, I am no featherweight."

"It's merely a figure of speech, Miss Lucas." Nevertheless, Blunt stepped back and studied her form. "There is nothing amiss that I can see. You'll do." He gathered her cloak and tucked it into the crook of her arm. "You won't like to sit on that just yet. Face me, and when you are mounted, hold tightly to the mane. I'll manage the reins."

"But this is a man's saddle."

"Sit to the side as you normally would. Here we go." He placed a hand on either side of her waist and deftly lifted her up. Blushing, Miss Lucas settled herself as best she could.

"Have you a traveling bag? Of course you do; what woman does not? If it is of moderate size, you may bring it. Johnny," he called. "Fetch your sister's bag." A few minutes later Blunt handed it up. "Hold this on your lap."

He then turned to Marlow. "I'll send word to the magistrate about these fellows, and also a team of horses for you. God willing, within several hours you'll have your boy back and be on your way."

With a nod to the passengers, Captain Blunt took the reins and led the horse down the coaching road at a walk. Once out of sight, he stopped and looked back at Miss Lucas. "The trouble is this: because of an injury my foot will not bear me the full two miles. I'll mount up behind you now, and we'll ride together."

"I'll gladly dismount and walk."

While he appreciated the spirit of her offer, Jack was not about to allow a woman to walk while he rode. "After twenty-odd hours cramped in that coach?" he countered. "Without sleep? I have traveled like that many a time; it is brutal."

"Brutal is certainly the word."

"It will be easier this way."

"Easier for your pride!"

"How well you understand me! We'll bring this off, trust me."

"I have no choice but to trust you, Mr. Blunt. I'll have you know," she added, "that although I am no horsewoman, I am not a coward."

"Assuredly not, merely worn to the bone. You gave as good as you got back there."

Blunt swung into the saddle behind her, and after a bit of adjustment, they settled in. Never mind that she was half sitting on his lap! He shifted the hilt of his sword so that it did not dig into her side.

"That was a bad business you were witness to," he remarked, as he urged the horse forward. "I regret having to shoot that fellow, but there was nothing else to be done."

"His flintlock had already been fired, hadn't it?"

"It had," he said grimly, "but at the time I did not know this. Moreover, he threatened to shoot you. From my vantage point, it was likely that he would. Barring that, he'd bludgeon you on the temple, possibly killing you."

"That is just what you did to the other man!"

Blunt hesitated. He would never make her understand. "It was the easiest way to disable him. It makes no difference; he'll hang soon enough."

He felt her stiffen. "These are not novices or innocents, Miss Lucas. They have been robbing travelers for many weeks; I cannot fathom why there was no guard today. You saw Marlow's cheek where the bullet grazed him."

"Yes," she said quietly.

"You do understand," he added, "that last week another driver was shot and killed along this same stretch of road?"

He sensed her discomfort. Apparently she did not know.

"Highwaymen are romanticized by women and fools. Any one of you might have been killed today, including your precocious brother." He paused. "Now, unfortunately, Johnny will think highwaymen rob with empty flintlocks and are easily mastered."

"Thank you," she said stiffly, "for coming to our rescue."

"You are welcome. Your uncle was, ah, disinclined to accompany me due to his gouty foot. A pity; a second horseman would have been useful."

Miss Lucas slewed round. "You *talked this over* with my Uncle Allen? Do I know you, Mr. Blunt?"

"Perhaps you have heard your parents speak of me," he said gently, "as Captain Blunt."

It appeared that she had heard of him after all. "Forgive me, but you introduced yourself as *Jack*. I have always heard you called *Jasper*."

"I prefer Jack," he said grimly.

"And I prefer *Diana*," cried Miss Lucas, "for it is a lovely name and she, unlike me, is beautiful. But my name is Charlotte. Plain, ordinary Charlotte. Wishing a thing were different does not make it so."

Blunt's response was to laugh. "There is nothing of the ordinary about you, Diana."

"That shows how little you know."

Again he laughed. Poor Miss Lucas was out of her element entirely. Now when would she realize that she was leaning against his chest?

Presently she did become aware, and she pulled herself rigidly upright. Her traveling bag made this an awkward maneuver. Jack put a hand to her shoulder and gently drew her back. "It's easier for the horse if you do not fidget, Miss Lucas."

"That," she muttered, "is an outright lie. What a wretched day!"

"It is indeed. Go ahead and have your cry," he offered. "Don't mind me."

"You are as stupid as you are ignorant, Captain Blunt," she said. "I never cry. Not in front of people."

"But there is only me. You have rightly characterized me as stupid; I cannot be said to count."

"Crying solves nothing. For me, it only makes everything worse. Besides, I am not pretty enough to cry."

"What nonsense is this?"

"It is very true. In my family, I am the sensible one. When I cry, I never get my way, nor do I get sympathy. People become upset, and sometimes they become angry."

He leaned sideways to look at her. "Angry?"

"It is easier for the horse if you do not fidget, Captain Blunt."

That scotched him! "Aye, aye, ma'am," he said meekly.

They lapsed into silence. "Look," said Jack suddenly. "Everyone cries. Even battle-toughened men on a warship. Even me, and I am as hard as they come. Not in the heat of battle, mind, but after. When I read the service for the deceased, and we send crewmen to their watery graves, I weep. We all do. There is not a dry eye on deck."

She appeared to consider this, but no tears came.

"You've had quite a day. Bounced inside that coach for hours on end, covered with dirt from the road, robbed at gunpoint, witness to a killing—"

"And deprived of food and drink," she added. "Johnny ate most of the food Mother sent."

"Did he now? Johnny deserves to be flogged."

"It is not his fault, poor boy. He is growing and is always hungry."

Blunt dug in a pocket for his flask and uncorked it. "Here," he offered. "Sip cautiously."

She sniffed it. "But this is ..."

"Cognac from your uncle's cellar. Otherwise known as brandy."

She took a tentative sip, closed her eyes, and then took a larger swallow.

"That'll do, Diana." Blunt removed it from her grasp. "Just enough to take the edge off." He eyed the flask and then took a swallow for himself.

He heard her sigh. "It's only a swallow," he protested.

"That's what they all say."

Blunt gave a shout of laughter. What an unusual girl!

He stole another look at her; her eyelids were at half-mast. "I recommend you settle in and take a nap."

Of course she was horrified; it would be no fun if she were not. "I could never! And if I did, I would fall sideways. You would have to catch me, which you couldn't do because I am so heavy. We would both end up on the road."

"Egad," said Jack, grinning. "I'd not thought of that. Stay awake, by all means."

Which meant she would be asleep within the quarter hour.

Sure enough, Captain Blunt was right.

7 You Again!

A good while later, Charlotte was escorted by her uncle into the entrance hall at Laurelhurst Manor, with a reminder that dinner would be served in an hour's time. It was with relief that she followed a maidservant to her assigned bedchamber. Her poor bonnet was bedraggled beyond repair. This was a sad loss, for Charlotte did not own many hats. The dress from her traveling bag was taken away to be pressed by her aunt's maid, Fleur. Laurelhurst was miles from anywhere; it was curious that Mrs. Allen would have the luxury of a lady's maid. It was odder still that Fleur was not French but English.

Presently hot water arrived, and Charlotte set to work. In her zeal to remove all traces of travel, she scrubbed until her skin was pink. Her hair was hopeless; there was nothing to be done but rinse it in the basin. Fleur was not happy about this. With many a huff, she brushed it out and braided it. She then pinned the damp braids to the top of Charlotte's head in a severe style.

Charlotte surveyed her reflection. The color of her hair was an attractive raven, but this would not last. As it dried, it would change back to ordinary light brown. The circles beneath her eyes served to accentuate her plainness. With a sigh, Charlotte turned away. She was not a friend of the looking glass. She hurried down to join her aunt and uncle.

And whom should she discover in the dining room but Captain Blunt! Why had no one told her that he was a house guest here? He too had changed for dinner, and the result was rather startling. In the candlelight his hair and beard shone honey-gold. Charlotte quickly averted her gaze. Scant hours ago, she had been sitting across this man's lap! She ought to have remained quiet during that awkward ride, but he was so provoking. And now he must sit across the table at dinner. She would do her best to maintain a dignified silence.

Mrs. Allen settled into her usual seat and signed to the footman to serve the first course; her rings and bracelets sparkled. "Your poor bonnet we put into the dustbin, my dear. It was quite ruined by travel, although in my opinion it was a disaster long before today. Honestly, how could you wear such a thing? What was your mother thinking?"

"It is far from being a favorite," admitted Charlotte. "I thought it best to wear something unobtrusive, out of consideration for my fellow passengers."

"My dear, a lady's first consideration, as far as apparel is concerned, is for herself. Others must make way for her. For you see, in all circumstances a lady must be pleasing to look at."

"Even while she is being robbed?" The words slipped out before Charlotte could stop them

"That is *right.* Your coach was held up by highwaymen. So thrilling."

Charlotte did not mean to exchange glances with Jack Blunt. Over the rim of his wineglass, his eyes glittered. "Women and fools," he seemed to say.

"Do tell us *everything* about it. The newspaper accounts are sure to leave out the feminine point of view. What were your impressions, your thoughts, your feelings? Were these gentlemen-of-the-road chivalrous, as highwaymen are said to be? Did they use the exciting phrase *stand and deliver?*"

"The man who robbed me certainly did. However—"

Mrs. Allen waved this aside. "I knew it! I simply adore *The Beggar's Opera,* which as you know is all about highwaymen and thieves. We saw it performed in London when I was a girl; it was an unforgettable experience. That gallant Captain MacHeath quite *stole* our hearts away. Like Robin Hood he was! A romantic adventurer, so chivalrous!" She paused. "He had a song; now what was it? Ah yes. *My heart was free; It rov'd like a bee.*"

"His heart went roving like a *what?*" demanded Captain Blunt. "A bee from flower to flower? As in, from woman to woman? I call that self-serving, not chivalrous."

"You, who have had a woman in every port, should not be bringing that up." Mrs. Allen returned to Charlotte. "But my dear, you wear no ornament. Of course the highwaymen let you keep your jewels." She smiled with simple pride. "Highwaymen are famous for their courteous treatment of women. They simply refuse to steal from them."

"Not these men. They took everything they could get their hands on, including poor Sally's savings. They even stole the horses. If not for Captain Blunt, I do not know what would have become of us."

"Hear, hear." Mr. Allen raised his glass in salute. "He has brought you safely to us. Well done, Jack!"

Captain Blunt became occupied with tracing a pattern on the table. Was that a bashful smile pulling at his lips? Charlotte had never pictured him as being modest.

"I thank you for *your* role in our rescue, Mr. Allen," she hastened to say. "Johnny is sure to relate every detail when he arrives; I shan't rob him of that pleasure. Suffice it to say that Captain Blunt risked his life to save ours, for which we are sincerely grateful."

"A very fine thing for him to do; yes, very fine," said Mrs. Allen. "You are perhaps unaware that he does this sort of thing all the time. I daresay it is nothing special. He is fond of risking his life, as some men are fond of sport." Mrs. Allen grew pensive. "Speaking of *sport*, your father was once very fond of fishing."

Charlotte could not allow this to pass. "Fishing and risking one's life are not at all the same!"

Captain Blunt rotated the stem of his glass. "They are if one is the fish."

Mrs. Allen ignored this. "And now at last, Christmas is upon us. It is *such* a pleasure to have another lady in the house. Now then, before we go anywhere, we must do something about your gown and hair."

"Courage, Miss Lucas," said Jack Blunt. "She does not approve of my hair either."

Mrs. Allen did not look in his direction. "Captain Blunt simply does *not* understand the feminine point of view. I daresay he will remain a bachelor forever."

"*A dear happiness to women.*"

But this was Shakespeare! Did Jack Blunt read Shakespeare's plays? Were they familiar enough for him to quote? Impossible! He was a sailor, not a gentleman.

"My dear, I am eager for you to become acquainted with our nearest neighbors, the Morlands. In particular, the eldest son, Mr. James."

Mrs. Allen was now beaming. "A worthy young man, who is preparing for ordination. He has a sad history that I know you will appreciate. You see, he was engaged to be married (as were you) to a vain, precocious young woman. She is the sister of a school friend; he met her in Bath. Oh, the trials she put him through! We were all taken in by her coaxing ways. However, once she learned the size of his marriage settlement, off she went to pursue another man. The minx."

"It sounds like he was well rid of her."

Again Charlotte's eyes met Captain Blunt's.

"And now our Charlotte has come. *She* is not so particular."

"Aunt—"

"Unlike Miss Thorpe, you are the daughter of a knight. That is certainly something. You also are able to live on four hundred a year, am I right?"

"Yes, but that is beside the point. I have no interest in finding a husband."

"Of course you have! Well. Mr. James is home for the Christmas holidays, and you will meet him at service tomorrow. We shall invite him to dine with us on the day following, and let nature take its course."

"Human nature, do you mean? Not a promising prospect."

Mrs. Allen was determined to ignore Jack Blunt. "James Morland has been pursuing his studies in Bath. His tutor lives there, and Mr. James boards with the family. Bath is an easy distance, a very good thing for you."

"Aunt, I really do not think—"

Mrs. Allen interrupted. "My dear Charlotte, it is providential! Your uncle's gout has been acting up. After Christmas we shall go to Bath. Mr. Allen will take the cure, and we shall have a lovely time shopping and attending the winter assemblies. I tell you, Bath is the place to get husbands."

"But not wives."

"Captain Blunt!" protested Mrs. Allen. "You again?" her glare seemed to say.

He spread his hands. "It isn't. Ask Morland."

"It is natural for a young man to choose hastily and, captivated by beauty, to make a little mistake. Now he knows better. Our Charlotte is a woman of worth. She is no pretty flibbertigibbet. In her, he shall find the companion of a lifetime."

Charlotte concealed a sigh. When she said she wished to work as a companion, marriage was not at all what she had in mind.

8 Invisible Mending

Before breakfast was no time for his pipe, but Captain Blunt was weary of being shut up in the house. He now sat on the portico—or piazza, or whatever Mrs. Allen was currently calling the veranda. Smoke from his pipe curled against the star-filled sky. The moon, just up, was a mere crescent, and Venus hung low on the horizon. He could just hear the parlor clock strike the hour. That was the trouble with this time of year; at seven it was still dark. And cold!

Jack shifted his position. He did not mean to come for Christmas, and yet here he was. Simmy's business was pressing, and he asked so little that Blunt did not like to refuse him. The weather held, so to Fullerton he came. And it was all for nothing. Wouldn't it figure that to complete the transaction, Allen needed to come to Weymouth?

And then there was the unfortunate incident on the coaching road. Blunt would need to make a statement to the magistrate, and who knew when the hearing would take place? He ought to have clubbed the fellow and been done with it. And yet he had threatened Miss Lucas and the others with death. How was Jack to know that the confounded flintlock had already been fired?

The fellow was a criminal, but shooting him brought Jack no pleasure. He had seen enough death to last a lifetime.

He drew his overcoat more closely about him. *Coldest before the dawn* was as true here as anywhere else. Along this side of the house was a row of windows; a light from within caught his attention. He'd started a fire to warm the parlor; had it blazed up? Jack went to investigate. The fire was burning nicely, but someone had brought a branch of candles into the parlor. It was Miss Lucas.

Jack leaned against the window frame and watched as she found a small table for the candelabra. She then settled into an overstuffed chair and brought out an embroidery frame. Apparently, she was planning to work.

A curious young woman, this Charlotte Lucas. On one hand, she was polite and reserved, carefully parceling out each word. Blunt found this irksome, but he understood it. A long career had taught him the wisdom of holding his tongue, though he struggled to do so. Apparently it was the same with Charlotte. When provoked, a different side of her emerged. She possessed a lively mind and a keen wit. Hers also was the freshness of youth, a thing she would not recognize or appreciate. One didn't, until it was gone.

She was up early, another point in her favor, and she had probably dressed without assistance. Blunt liked her for it. As a young man, he'd been captivated by feminine beauty and caprice, a marked contrast to the wooden world at sea. His fascination was short-lived. Adorable Annette Walker led him on a pretty dance before deserting him for a more promising offer. She'd been married to that wealthy admiral for a good ten years. Jack's lips compressed into a line. Never again would a woman play him for a fool.

Presently he noticed that his pipe was no longer lit. There was nothing new in that. Why remain out in the cold? He knocked the tobacco from the pipe's bowl and opened the door.

"Good morning, Diana. Happy Christmas." He waited, a smile hovering on his lips. Would she respond with cool politeness? Or could he provoke her to toss caution aside and speak freely?

Clearly she was startled, and she attempted to hide from him what she was working on. This only increased his curiosity. "What have you there?" His gaze held hers. "No, I'll not let you off," he added silently.

She gave an exasperated sigh, an excellent sign! "If you must know, this is a Christmas gift for you. Since you are here, I might as well learn if you like the color I've chosen."

At once Jack drew up a chair opposite hers, nearer the warmth of the fire. "It is unnecessary to give me a gift," he said, shrugging off his overcoat. "After all, I have none for you."

"What you did yesterday is a gift to us all. I do not know whether the Allens exchange presents at Christmas, but it is best to be prepared." She held out the embroidery frame. "It is only a handkerchief. It's not the most original gift. I do whitework like this throughout the year."

Jack took the frame from her. "I like it very much," he said. And he did. Against the white fabric, she was working a script *B* in white silk. He fingered the decorative hem. "This is drawn-thread embroidery, is it not? Your skills certainly eclipse mine."

Dimples appeared. Wait, she had dimples?

"Since when do *you* embroider, Captain Blunt?"

"You would be surprised at the skills we sailors possess. I mend, I sew on buttons, and I even make button-holes."

"How I loathe button-holes and mending! I am forever repairing my brothers' clothes."

"One of the benefits of my rank is that Martin does my mending for me."

Her eyes narrowed in amusement. "But you are no longer at sea."

"I have a crew, just the same. I take on former crewmen who are put ashore. They work for a time at my house in Dorset, until they find their feet. Some, like Ord and Martin and Gibby, stay on. Your uncle has jokingly called their quarters Blunt's Barracks."

"Is your house near the sea?" There was wistfulness in her voice. This was promising!

"That it is," he said. "I live ten miles outside Weymouth. When I began to have success in my career, I had a house built on the cliffs overlooking the sea."

She sighed again. "I love the sea. Years ago, when Father's business began to prosper, we took a house at the seaside for a summer."

"A happy choice."

"Oh, it was. I loved every moment of my time there. Each morning before breakfast I was up and dressed in my oldest clothes, with my hair pulled back in a braid. I walked the shore for miles. It was glorious."

He smiled. "You are an early riser, as am I."

The embroidery frame was forgotten. "Once," she confided, "there was a storm that raged all night. I waited for daylight, and then I ran like anything down to the seawall before Mother could stop me." Her smile widened into a grin. "She couldn't, being asleep. Oh, it was wonderful: the spray from the pounding surf on my face and the wind whipping at my skirts. And the scream of the gulls who soared overhead, even in all that wind." She paused. "You, of course, must have a very different opinion of storms."

"I will say this: storms are never dull."

"I suppose you prefer to be safe in a harbor. I know I would."

"In an all-weather harbor, yes. But that is not often the case. As they say, to remain in harbor is not what ships are built for."

"Yours are built to fight."

"And to defend."

"I'd not thought of that. In fact ..." She stopped.

He felt her draw back, as if she realized that she had been too confiding. Jack waited, prompting her with a look to continue.

Instead Charlotte took up the embroidery frame. "I wish you Happy Christmas, Captain Blunt," she said. "Do you attend service with us?"

This question was a mere politeness, but it rankled. She assumed, as did so many others, that he would decline.

"Assuredly. Shall we see Mrs. Allen arrayed in splendor, wearing every one of her bracelets? I daresay she would wear the diamonds to church if it were not in bad taste. But tell me—"

Jack leaned forward and took away the embroidery frame. She had made a good beginning; he would allow no retreat. Then too, if they withdrew into politeness, there would be nothing to talk about.

"Tell me, Diana. Are you of the same mind as your aunt? Do you attend church to display your fine clothes and hear the latest gossip?"

"I have no fine clothes."

A flippant answer was not what he was after. Jack lifted an eyebrow.

She caught his meaning and sighed. "Of course not. As if the worship of God has anything to do with what I am wearing."

"I am glad to hear it," he said. "Do you love the Savior?"

Her eyes widened in surprise. Yes, this was a direct question. He'd fired a shot straight across her bow. How would she respond? His gaze held hers.

"I do," she said softly. "But if you were to observe my actions of late"—there was a catch in her voice—"and hear my thoughts, you certainly would not believe this is true."

"I think I understand. You set your own course and remorselessly kept to it."

She nodded. A silence stretched between them. Apparently he had hit a nerve.

"A lonely place," Jack remarked. "Especially once it begins to go wrong."

She said nothing, so he decided to continue. "I lived in that place for many years. I made cocksure decisions, certain I was right. And I wasn't. Often I was in the wrong. Men have died because of my stubbornness and poor judgment, Diana. Men who were my friends."

She raised her eyes to meet his; he had her full attention now. "The outcome might have been the same," he said. "There is no way to know. The thing is, I never bothered to ask for His guidance or help or blessing. I, the one responsible for every soul aboard. I should have known better."

Charlotte sat, pale and silent. The clock struck the half-hour; Jack added wood to the fire. "It is now your turn to speak," he told her silently. "I will wait you out."

Then he heard a sound. Hold hard, was this a sob? He meant to make her talk, not weep!

Charlotte pressed her fingers to her lips, as if willing herself to stop. This did no good. Another sob escaped. Abruptly she rose from the chair and moved away from him. She stood alone in the corner; sobs shook her shoulders.

Jack pulled a handkerchief from his waistcoat pocket and brought it to her.

"I should have known better," she gasped out. "But I went ahead, just like you said. I never realized what it would cost me. I did not know what he was like."

He? Jack put a hand on Charlotte's shoulder and guided her back to the armchair. "Come," he said kindly. "Tell me about this man. I assume he was your betrothed?"

She nodded.

"He was, perhaps, not the best choice?"

"It was a sensible decision. But I never dared to ask if it was right."

"Thus setting into motion unintended consequences."

"Yes. Oh yes! I damaged my friendship with dear Eliza, my best friend in all the world! He is to inherit her family's estate. She refused his proposal, and then he came to me."

"Ah."

"We were little better than strangers, but he needed a wife. The woman who provides his living—he is a clergyman—told him he ought to marry, and he knew he must comply."

"Draconian."

"She thinks it is her right to order him about, and he is desperate to do whatever she says. But it was the reaction of my family—!"

"They disliked him?"

"On the contrary, they were elated; even my brothers. I know I am not pretty, and my fortune is small. But I never realized how hopeless my situation is. They had given up on me years ago. Everyone knows that Mr. Collins is self-important and a fool. Oh dear, I did not mean to say his name! But in their eyes, he was a *hero*."

"And when he broke the engagement?"

"*I* broke it, not he. I could not bear to marry him. Not after what—happened." Charlotte covered her face with her hands.

Here was the heart of the issue. "What happened, Diana?" he said gently. "Tell Papa Jack."

She shook her head.

"Have you told anyone?"

"I couldn't. What if Mother and Father excused him? Defended him?"

"*Defended* him?" Jack dropped to one knee; his face was now level with hers. "Diana, you must tell me. What did Collins do?"

She did not answer.

"This is important. Tell me."

"Ours was to be a marriage of convenience. I thought he understood."

"Apparently he did not. Did he force himself on you?" Her startled eyes met his. "I know men, you see. Will you leave me to guess the rest?"

"He kissed me. I knew it was my duty, but I never expected—" She swallowed. "His hands, he—"

Haltingly, she told him the rest. Jack muttered an ill-concealed curse.

Charlotte's head came up. "I pushed him away. Very hard."

"Good for you! Did you strike him?"

"I wish I had. My only thought was to escape. I slept with the fire iron beside me."

"A girl after my own heart! I take it Collins did not apologize?"

She smiled ruefully. "When he came the next day, he behaved as though nothing had happened."

"I can believe it. The coward!"

"And when I broke the engagement, he insulted me. And my parents as well."

"A man like that would. Did you strike him then? I would have. Kicked him, too."

"Nothing so dramatic, I'm afraid. Although he did leave before sharing our breakfast, a thing he was pining for. Never mind that he had already breakfasted with his hosts."

"So he is a swine and a glutton. You are well rid of him."

This brought a smile. Charlotte dried her eyes for a final time and returned the handkerchief. "This is one Christmas morning I shall never forget. I apologize for behaving so theatrically."

The clock on the mantelpiece struck eight. Jack returned to his chair and smoothed the knees of his breeches. "Given the weight of your burden, I'd say you were reserved. If you would like me to even the score, I can describe to you my self-important errors of judgment. In great detail."

He was rewarded with another smile. "That will not be necessary. You are right; I do feel better. Thank you." She reached for her embroidery frame. "May I have this now?"

He passed it to her. "Where did you say this Collins lives? Hertfordshire?"

"No, in Kent. His parish church is in Hunsford."

"Hunsford," repeated Jack, committing it to memory. "Let me see, Kent is perhaps two days' journey from here. I can manage that."

She lowered her needle. "What do you mean?"

The temptation to tease her was too great. "Nothing," he said, smiling.

"I do not believe that for an instant!" The embroidery frame was put aside. "You had better tell me, Captain Blunt."

"Only if you agree to use my name: Jack. After all, we are cousins, after a manner of speaking."

"We are not cousins, *Jasper.* Now tell me. What can you manage?"

Jack stretched a leg. "I've been thinking. If the magistrate delays the hearing—I daresay they'll haul in that third fellow—I'll need something to do while I wait. It is no trouble to hire a traveling chaise. I think I'll call on Collins and give him a piece of my mind."

"Jasper!"

"He owes you an apology, Diana. He abused your trust and insulted your virtue. I'll just step round and remind him of that. As I said, you are my cousin."

"We are not related at all. How, exactly, do you intend to remind him?"

Jack was betrayed into a grin.

"Yes, I thought as much. You are bloodthirsty, that's what you are."

He broke out laughing.

"And moreover, you are—"

But Jack never heard the rest of her opinion, for just then Mr. Allen came in.

"You're up early," he remarked. "Happy Christmas. Breakfast is on the sideboard. Any word from young Johnny?" He offered his arm to Charlotte.

Before she went out with Allen, she looked back at him. "I am not finished with you," her look said.

What else could Jack do but wink?

9 A Matter of Pride

Presently it was time to leave for service. Mrs. Allen joined the others in the entrance hall, talking all the way. "One's appearance is so important, dear. First impressions are just everything."

This was probably very true. Charlotte had first met Captain Blunt with a flintlock in his hand. She ought to have known then how troublesome he was.

"And now you will meet James Morland. I do wish you had a prettier bonnet, but we must make the best of it. I daresay he'll not notice. Men don't, you know."

How many times had Charlotte explained that she did not wish for a husband? But Mrs. Allen was set on making a match, and nothing would deter her. She claimed that Catherine Morland, at only seventeen, had not been looking for a husband either, and yet things had turned out so nicely for her. She was now Mrs. Tilney and happily settled.

Mrs. Allen took her husband's arm and sailed out the front door, leaving Charlotte and Captain Blunt to follow them to the carriage.

"Men do notice," he said, "but we've learned to say nothing. If we compliment a woman, and she thinks her bonnet is ugly, we're ditched. She claims we have no taste. If she agrees with us, we're also ditched. She then expects us to compliment every blasted bonnet she wears."

"So says the sage bachelor," was Mrs. Allen's reply. "To be perfectly honest," she added, as soon as she was settled in her seat, "Mr. James's fiancée was a very pretty girl. Yes, quite a beauty. However, we shall not lose heart. After we have your hair properly curled, you'll do nicely."

"Then too," added Mr. Allen, "no one has ever thought the Morland men to be handsome."

Heavens, was an unhandsome suitor a point in Charlotte's favor? She could sense Captain Blunt's ironic amusement.

"It is a bit of a trial, living where we do," admitted Mrs. Allen. "There are so few suitable unmarried gentlemen. No lord lives here, not even a baronet. Even the squire has no children."

"So it's Morland or no one," murmured Captain Blunt.

"I prefer no one," Charlotte whispered back.

"Chilly this morning, isn't it?" said Mr. Allen, as the carriage began to move. "Do you think we'll have rain?"

"My dear Mr. Allen, do not say such a thing. Rain at Christmas spoils all. We're sure to have a merry time tonight. I had Cook make three puddings, just to be safe. You know how young people can eat."

"We are well prepared for Master Johnny," said Mr. Allen.

"What can be keeping that boy?"

"Any number of things," said Captain Blunt. "Are you picturing him as cold and shivering, huddled in a ditch by the side of the road? It is no such thing. More likely Miss Sally's family has hailed him as a hero, and he is enjoying Christmas as their guest. He'll be here in another day or so."

"We're fortunate that he is not with us now," Mr. Allen pointed out. "An uncomfortable ride, fitting five into a space meant for four. Moreover, there's sure to be a crowd at church."

He was right. Charlotte was squeezed on the pew between Captain Blunt and Mr. Allen. Her aunt leaned over her husband to say, "Look there, in the second row to your left. Those are the Morlands. The dark-haired one on the end is Mr. James. Did I mention that the senior Mr. Morland is our rector?"

She had, several times. And why must she speak in such a penetrating whisper?

The organist launched into the introit, but this did not keep Mrs. Allen from turning round and waving. "I do love service," she confessed happily. "There are always so many friends to see. It is too quiet at Laurelhurst."

How could Charlotte respond other than with a smile? Mr. Allen was consulting his timepiece; Captain Blunt thumbed through his book of prayer.

After the service, the promised introductions took place. Mr. James seemed a kindly fellow, gentle and well-mannered. As Mr. Allen had said, he would never be considered handsome. But his expression was pleasant, and he did not simper or gush compliments. In Charlotte's eyes these counted for a lot.

With simple pride Mrs. Allen introduced each of the Morland children. "To know the names of all of them is certainly a feat, but they visit me often."

"For cake," said one of the younger boys. "And biscuits," said another.

It was the girls that Charlotte noticed; they simply could not keep their eyes from Captain Blunt. The sky was clouded, but even in this light his hair and beard shone golden. She had forgotten how handsome he was. Today he was quietly attired in a dark blue frock coat and fawn breeches. In uniform, this man would be a sight to behold.

There followed a whispered conference between the sisters, and presently Mr. James was consulted. He then said, a little shyly, "Do you enjoy reading, Miss Lucas? I am taking Jenny and Phoebe through Goldsmith's *Vicar of Wakefield* during the Christmas holidays. We would be happy to include you in our reading circle."

"And Captain Blunt." This was from the older sister, Jenny.

James Morland had to look up to meet Jack Blunt's gaze. "And of course, Captain Blunt," he said politely.

Mrs. Allen was beyond pleased. Amid much happy negotiation, it was arranged that the group would meet at Laurelhurst, with lavish refreshments to be provided. In the end, the group was expanded to include twelve-year-old Isabel.

"I wonder how our Johnny will like it?" said Captain Blunt later, as he assisted Charlotte to enter the Allen's carriage.

"You must be joking. Johnny loathes reading, especially something like *The Vicar of Wakefield.*"

"He might surprise you. The presence of girls changes everything."

"Not at home. He cordially dislikes his younger sisters."

"Ah, but these are not his sisters. And we cannot discount the appeal of cake."

Charlotte smiled her answer. In this he was probably right.

"But Johnny must first find his way home to us, poor soul," said Mrs. Allen. "Now then, is not Mr. James everything a young man ought to be?"

"He seems agreeable," said Charlotte cautiously.

Mrs. Allen beamed.

"He's a baby," said Captain Blunt. "He's twenty-one if he's a day! It will be years until he makes something of himself."

"Makes something of himself?" scoffed Mrs. Allen. "What sort of talk is this?"

"An honest facing of the truth." He turned to Charlotte. "You'd invest a good ten years in a soft fellow like that. Are you prepared to do this?"

"As if you know anything about it," said Mrs. Allen.

"I know men, ma'am. I've served with hundreds his age. Morland is soft. Without adversity, it will take years for him to become a man. And all the while, his wife must do the thinking for him, and then pretend that the ideas were his, just as a junior officer does when serving under an incompetent captain."

"I'll have you know that Mr. James has been educated at Oxford."

"A school for rich boys, shielding them from hardships."

"The rigors of scholarship count for something," Mr. Allen pointed out.

"These they shirk whenever possible, same as any midshipman. It is the hard choices of life and death that mold a boy into a man."

"Pooh. You and your battles. Mr. James has been promised a living by his father. In two or three years, he steps into a fine position with a parish of his own."

Charlotte hastened to say, "My dear Aunt, I am not looking to marry James Morland or anyone. Nor is he looking to marry me."

"My dear, he simply has not yet *realized* that he wishes to marry. We shall change all that."

"Now Meg, that Miss Thorpe threw him over hard. It isn't easy to rally after a loss like that."

"The surest way to mend heartbreak, Mr. Allen, is with a *new* love. Nor is he too young, Captain Blunt. You would have everyone enlist in the navy, even our dear, truant Johnny."

Again Captain Blunt turned to Charlotte. "Johnny is a middle brother, is he not? One who needs to make his way in the world? That is precisely why I sent him on that errand."

"Right at Christmas, too," complained Mrs. Allen. "So inconvenient and inconsiderate."

"I assigned him a task. I will learn soon enough if he is man enough to see it through."

"He'll miss our Christmas pudding. Such a disappointment for him."

"What he'll have is adventure."

Apparently Mrs. Allen had no use for adventure.

The carriage turned in at Laurelhurst's gates and went up the lane to the graveled sweep before the house. "Dear me, church is so fatiguing," said Mrs. Allen. "Now then, dear Charlotte, it will be a late night. I'll just go up and have a little lie-down. I suggest you do the same."

Mr. Allen disappeared into his library, leaving Charlotte in the entrance hall with Captain Blunt. She surrendered her cloak to the footman. It was then that she caught sight of the mistletoe. "Upon my word," she muttered.

Captain Blunt looked an inquiry.

"I suppose the servants did it, and we can guess by whose orders. When I arrived, there was one enormous ball of mistletoe hanging here. Now there are four."

"She must think Morland is in need of a hint," said Captain Blunt, grinning. "Where does she get these ideas?"

"Romances, probably." Charlotte removed her bonnet. "This is the only bonnet I own which has—how do you say it? Passed muster?" She gave it to the footman.

It had been a trying morning. Her aunt's continual nattering about marriage stretched Charlotte's temper to the breaking point.

Captain Blunt opened the door to the parlor for her. With nothing else to do, Charlotte went in ahead of him. "Once Mrs. Allen finishes her nap," she told him, "her maid will be summoned, and my poor hair will never be the same. Do sit down."

He did so. "You don't say."

"She thinks the front and sides need curls. This means that when it rains, or when the curls fall out, I shall look even worse. Like a bedraggled cat."

She noticed that he was struggling to keep a straight face. "It is hair," he said. "It will grow back."

"Not if things work out according to plan. I am to have limp curls for years."

"Which plan, I take it, does not include marriage to one James Morland."

"Certainly not. I am hoping Mrs. Allen will take me on as companion."

This brought a frown. "You would willingly subject yourself to someone like that? Her conversation alone will drive you mad. As will the continual clicking of her bracelets."

"A companion is a respectable occupation. It will not be easy, but I'll see it through. I cannot return home, you see."

"Why not?"

"Gossip, my dear Captain Blunt."

"Jack," he corrected. "What Collins did is hardly your fault."

"It will be laid to my account nonetheless. Even if the truth were known—which, thank heaven, it is not—there are those who will say I should be grateful for his attentions."

"Grateful? The man is a pig. And I wouldn't fret about your hair. Mrs. Allen says I should cut mine. I think cutting hair must be an obsession for her."

Unwillingly, Charlotte raised her eyes to his face. That beautiful golden hair, a thing he probably cared nothing for. She thought about hers and sighed. It was grossly unfair. "Your hair is fine," she said roughly.

And then she pulled up short. What business had she to be rude? "I beg your pardon. All this talk of marriage, and my aunt's endless hints and mistletoe everywhere, have put me out of temper."

"Is this a display of temper?" Jack Blunt sounded amused. "Shouldn't you shriek or throw things against the wall? That shepherdess on the mantelpiece is a likely candidate."

"My purse is empty enough without having to replace broken figurines, thank you." Suddenly a new thought occurred. "Speaking of my empty purse, do you play cards?"

"I do."

"Are you any good?"

Again he laughed. "It so happens that I am."

"And are you rich?"

This was an outrageous question, but she was finding it easy to say outrageous things to Jack Blunt.

"I am Allen's heir; does that tell you anything?"

"Not much. If you are not rich, there is no help for it. You must go to the moneylenders when you lose. My situation is such that I cannot accept promissory notes. Nor shall I wait to be paid until after you inherit."

He grinned, leaning forward. "A grim possibility. But, not likely."

"Good. Then I shall positively *enjoy* winning money off you."

"You, ah, do understand that we sailors play cards while at sea? Often daily? We are keen to win."

"Do *you* understand the desperation of an unmarried woman?" she countered. "One who can do little else to earn money? I am much more determined to win. The delightful thing is that with you I needn't prevaricate."

"We shall go at it hammer-and-tongs," he promised.

"With the gloves off, as Richard would say. Richard is my eldest brother."

"And when you lose? When I demand payment?"

"If that happens tonight, I have several options. I could cry, although as you know I am not skilled at crying prettily. I could manage to look sad and rather crushed. This would be even better, I think, for then everyone present would think you nothing but a heel for demanding payment." A grin escaped. "After all, it is Christmas.

"Do you know," she went on, "two Christmases ago, we entertained the squire and his guests." The words came tumbling out, but Charlotte did not care to check them. "One of them, a London gentleman, thought he would have my head for washing, er, as Johnny would say. I began carefully, showing maidenly trepidation, hesitating over my discards and looking doubtful. He was so very pleased, but by the end of the night he realized his mistake. I won four guineas off him."

Captain Blunt was grinning. "You will not object if I ask you to prove these rash claims?" He rose to his feet and brought forward a small table. "I happen to know where Allen keeps his playing cards."

Moments later he returned with a new pack. He removed the paper and passed the cards to Charlotte. "Would you like to do the honors?"

"With pleasure." On her mettle, Charlotte shuffled with a flourish and passed the deck for him to cut.

There was a new glint of respect in his eyes. How delicious! Now he would see.

"The trouble is," she confided, "that within our small circle, I must restrain myself. If I were to be paralyzingly ruthless, no one would play cards with me again, and I would have no source of income." She took up her cards and sorted her hand. "By the way, what are we play—"

She was interrupted by the opening of the parlor door. In came Mrs. Allen's maid. "Begging your pardon, Miss Lucas, but you are wanted above-stairs."

"Botheration," muttered Charlotte. "Thank you, Fleur. Tell Mrs. Allen I'll be up directly." She rose to her feet and turned to Jack Blunt with a look of apology.

"Thus the sheep is led to the shearer," he remarked, making a polite bow. "Poor Diana, you thought you would fleece me. But the tables have turned, figuratively speaking. Off *you* go to be shorn."

"Oh," cried Charlotte, torn between annoyance and amusement. "Of all the wretched things to say! Will you kindly—!"

He raised an eyebrow, a smile pulling at his lips. "Yes?"

"Kindly *pipe down*!" Charlotte turned on her heel and stalked out of the parlor.

The music of his laughter followed her all the way into the entrance hall.

10 Reddes Laudes Domino

That afternoon Captain Blunt was left to his own devices. He wandered into the library, but Allen was nowhere to be found. The newspapers here were a week old, and Allen's scanty collection of books held little of interest. Here was the trouble with civilian life: it was too tame and quiet. What did men like Allen do with their time?

Perhaps he should hunt up a copy of *Vicar* and begin reading? Jack made a face. He had no interest in that reading group, aside from taking in the lay of the land regarding James Morland.

Now why was this? It was not as if Charlotte Lucas was any concern of his. England was filled with unmarried women like her; wars had an inconvenient habit of reducing the male population. Not that a woman of her caliber would marry a soldier or a sailor!

Jack settled into an armchair and brought out his pipe. Much as he admired Charlotte's spirit, he knew the realities of life. Give her several years of drudging for someone like Meg Allen, and Charlotte would settle for a fellow like Morland quickly enough.

In truth, she would do better to marry one of his officers, like Ord or Spaulding. She deserved someone who was both competent and kind.

The clock ticked on; smoke from the pipe curled pleasantly. He had meant to travel home on Christmas Eve, but he would probably be here through the 27th. What he ought to do was write out a statement for the magistrate. Jack set his pipe aside, hunted up pen and paper, and settled in to work. Reports and log entries were once a part of his daily life and probably would be again.

It depended on Napoleon. Was the man fool enough to rebuild his navy? Only time would tell. Meanwhile, maintaining a tight blockade was not to Jack's taste. His majesty's navy was not to be trifled with, and yet there were merchant captains—Americans, usually—who attempted to slip through. Not a pleasant task, seizing the ships of neutral nations and impressing their crew. American diplomats were now rattling their swords; it could well be that the Napoleonic war would spread to the other side of the Atlantic.

Jack relit his pipe and sent a plume of smoke toward the ceiling. When this happened, he would return to sea, for his foot was out of danger and healing nicely. This was likely to be his last Christmas in England for some time.

At dinner, Jack understood the reason for Charlotte's absence. She now sported an abundance of attractive curls. He was torn; dare he admit to her his opinion? For she did look prettier in this softer, more feminine style. She looked younger as well, a thing that would appeal to James Morland.

Presently the Christmas roast beef was brought in, and Allen set to carving.

"We're to take our pot-luck tomorrow," announced Mrs. Allen, "as it is Boxing Day for the servants. I daresay that after tonight's lavish meal, we'll not be hungry."

Conversation was driven by Mrs. Allen's interest in how Christmas was celebrated at sea.

"Without mistletoe, ma'am," said Jack promptly. "There'd be no one to kiss, apart from the cat." He heard Charlotte's attempt to choke back laughter.

"In peaceable times," he went on, "we celebrate the New Year much as we do here at home: with merry-making, storytelling, and practical jokes. If we're lucky, the younger crewmen have a game of snapdragon. And if there is a fiddler aboard, which is usually the case, Commander Ord is persuaded to dance the jig and to challenge all comers."

"Ah yes, dancing!" cried Mrs. Allen. "Sailors do host lavish balls on the decks of their ships; this I have heard."

"Only very rarely and under a specific set of circumstances. Portsmouth, at the New Year, does not provide optimal weather for such an event."

"Life at sea must be quite an experience," said Mrs. Allen. "The sails blowing in the breeze, the cry of the sea birds ..."

"During the summer months, on a fine day, I agree. But it is well to recall, ma'am, that a ship-of-the-line is a fighting machine. Even in my own quarters, which we call The Great Cabin, there are a set of guns."

"Cannon, do you mean?" said Charlotte.

"Twenty-four pounders. One port, the other starboard. The starboard cannon, as I recall, was named Beelzebub." He smiled at her surprise. "As we name our houses here on land, we name our guns: Bulldog, Biter, Spit Fire. Woe to our holiday celebrations if an enemy ship is sighted."

"*England expects that every man will do his duty,*" Allen quoted.

"We give chase first and celebrate later."

"How horrid," said Mrs. Allen.

"That depends upon how you look at it. If there is prize to be captured—an enemy ship—even the lowliest crewman prospers. We are thus motivated to fight."

"I suspect that I would run like a coward," confessed Charlotte.

"Not you. You're a bonny fighter, Di—er, Miss Lucas."

"Well I never! All this talk of fighting and on Christmas too! The Morlands will be here shortly to sing for us. We'll have the puddings served in the drawing room." Mrs. Allen turned to the footman. "Are the card tables in place?"

"Ah," said Jack to Charlotte. "Opportunity for prize." She returned his smile.

Sure enough, just as the last course was cleared there came a series of urgent knocks at the main door. Presently strains of *While Shepherds Watched Their Flocks* came drifting in from the hall. Mrs. Allen clapped her hands in delight, pushed back her chair, and immediately went out to greet them.

"Come in out of the cold," she cried. "We'll have the puddings brought into the drawing room directly."

"With plenty of sauce?" piped one of the youngsters.

"Yes, Master Henry, with plenty of sauce."

Captain Blunt offered his arm to Charlotte. "Let's have another song," he called. "Mr. James, you're an Oxford man. What say you to *The Boar's Head*?"

"Yes, let's!" said Henry. Apparently even the young ones knew this carol.

The elder Mr. Morland turned to Jack in pleased surprise. "Did you attend Oxford, sir?"

"My father did; he was a clergyman like yourself."

Mr. James was looking bashful, but his father was not as shy. Without hesitation he launched into song: "*The boar's head in hand bear I, bedecked with bays and rosemary ...*"

Soon the hall was ringing with the well-known chorus:

Caput apri defero,
Reddens laudes Domino.

Before the final verse, there came another knock at the door. "Now this *is* a surprise," said Mrs. Allen. "Most of the wassailers call on the squire, not us." She signed for the footman to open the door.

Bundled in his overcoat and scarf, with his cap askew and his face sporting a massive grin, was young Master Lucas.

"Johnny!" Charlotte rushed to embrace him. "How worried we've been."

He was looking rather worse for wear, but he shrugged her concern aside. He motioned to the fellows who hung behind him. "Come on, Tony," he urged. "I'd like for you to meet my uncle."

He made his bow to Mrs. Allen. "You are truant, Master Johnny," she said, "but never mind. You've come in time for Christmas pudding."

"You needn't have traveled on Christmas, son," said Mr. Allen, "but you are very welcome."

"We rode in a pony cart pulled by a donkey, the most amusing thing! The weather held, so Tony figured we might as well come now." Politely Johnny shook Mr. Allen's hand. "This is Tony Keith; he's Sally's nephew, I think. And this is Mr. Gedge, a friend of the family. He knows Captain Blunt."

Johnny lowered his voice. "I say, sir, could you spare some dinner? We ate before we left, but that was hours ago, and we're fair starving now."

"But of course. Come along with me to the kitchen."

Mr. Gedge held back and edged his way to Jack's side. "'Tis a pleasure to see you again, Captain, and that's a fact. We served together on the *Valiant*, sir."

Jack held out his hand. "That would be at Trafalgar."

He was rewarded with a strong grip and a beaming smile. "Aye, sir, it was. Imagine you remembering me at Trafalgar. A fair hero you was, sir."

It looked as though Gedge would go on in this vein. "On that day every man was heroic, by the grace and mercy of God," Jack hastened to say. "I am glad to see you well and prospering."

"Was Captain Blunt a *hero*?" This came from one of the Morland daughters. The others gathered round.

"Indeed he was, lassie," crowed Gedge, too loudly for Jack's taste. "His name weren't in the headlines, as some of those admirals' were, but he's in the history books all right. One of Nelson's most trusty captains. Loved by his men, Captain Blunt is. Saved our lives, time and again. 'T'weren't nothing we wouldn't do for him."

"And how we fought for prize and so much of it sank," said Jack, clapping Gedge on the back. "Let's go into the kitchen, and you can tell me about your life ashore."

But Gedge was not about to disappoint such attentive listeners. "Fighting such as you never saw in all your life," he said. "Cannon fire, too. Like thunder it was, all around, with smoke, thick like fog."

As if Jack would ever—or could ever—forget. Would Gage describe the grislier sights and sounds? Scenes that even now robbed him of sleep? "And let us not forget the storm that followed," he quickly put in.

"Aye, that storm!" Gage grinned at the girls' wonder. "Twenty-two French and Spanish ships they lost that day. But we English lost nary a one."

"Damaged, but undaunted," offered Jack, with a smile. "The close blockade of French bases continues. God willing, they'll never grow such a fleet again."

"If they do," added Johnny, "we'll *pulverize* them. Grind 'em into dust! Won't we, sir?"

Jack gestured to the doorway. "Now how about that dinner?"

The glance over his shoulder was meant to be an apology to Charlotte, for he was deserting her. But her eyes were as bright as the younger girls'. All too well did Jack recognize the signs of hero worship. Blast that Gedge and his crowing!

"Might I say, Captain, the beard is fine, yes indeed," said Gedge, as Jack led him to the kitchen. "Popular with the ladies, ain't it? When I learnt you was in Fullerton, sir, I had to come. Even in a curst donkey cart on Christmas."

It was some time before Captain Blunt returned to the drawing room. Mrs. Allen was well prepared for guests. The younger children were involved with toys and puzzles, and the adults were deep into whist. Mrs. Allen's guiding hand was apparent, for Charlotte was paired with Mr. James. It seemed to him that tonight she was being her guarded self, especially since she was seated with her aunt and Mrs. Morland.

Johnny had taken himself upstairs for a wash and a change, a feat accomplished in very little time. Into the drawing room he came, eager for a helping of pudding, just as the players were moving to the next tables.

"Join us at whist, Johnny," Allen invited. "I'll sit out for this round."

It seemed to Jack that Johnny was rather stunned. "Yes, sir," he cried. "Thank you, sir."

"In fact," Allen went on, "let's have a little change. You sit here, and Mr. James will be your partner. Blunt, you sit over there and Charlotte, you will be his partner."

Jack did not bother to hide his amusement. "Here is a fine turn of events," he told Charlotte, as he held the chair. "We face one another not as opponents, but as partners. I am sorry," he added, "for the state of your purse."

Charlotte shuffled, Mr. James cut, and Jack was left to deal and reveal the trump suit. Soon play was in motion. Johnny was enjoying himself hugely, with a plateful of pudding balanced precariously on his knee. However, his mind was obviously not on the game. Mr. James was similarly hesitant.

It was not until sometime later that Jack noticed Charlotte's pleading eyes. What was she saying?

He stopped, card in hand. Did she know which one he was about to play? Her eyes held his, and she gently shook her head. Jack flicked a fingernail against the card's edge; her gaze never wavered.

What could he do but obey? He tossed down a card of lower value. At the end of the round, when the points were tallied, Johnny gave a cheer.

Charlotte took the loss philosophically.

"You'll never prosper at cards," he told her later. "You lack the proper ruthlessness."

"I couldn't. Not against Johnny," she whispered back. "He's never been invited to play with adults, not by his uncle. Moreover, I could not allow him to lose to *you.*"

"Paugh, Johnny wouldn't care."

"But he would care if, in front of you, he lost to *me*, a sister. He would feel disgraced."

"He needs to toughen up. It's a hard world. A man gets nowhere if he's soft. Losses are a part of the game."

"I suppose you are right," she said quietly.

What was this; had he hurt her? This was the last thing he intended to do! "It's like this," he told her. "You've too kind a heart, Diana."

She raised her eyes to his.

"And you're a very good sister."

"I will stand the loss," she said. "How much do we owe?"

"Allow me. It will mean more to Johnny if the money comes from my purse." Jack poured coins into his palm. Johnny came when called.

Allen noticed this. "No losses tonight," he announced. "After all, it's Christmas."

Jack smiled down at Johnny. "We'll call it a gift. You've heard the term *pieces of eight*? Here you are." He lowered his voice and held out an uneven coin from which pieces had been clipped. "Pirate treasure. Spanish, made in the Americas."

Johnny received it with wonder. "Pirate treasure! Thank you, sir! Look here, Lottie!" He passed it to her.

"Except that, I shouldn't take it, sir," Johnny added in a whisper. "I owe you a pound, sir. Tony and I went to the shops yesterday, on account of me being present for their dinner. I took the liberty of purchasing a few things, as a gift to the family."

"You did right."

Charlotte returned the coin to her brother. "Imagine, this has been all around the world, whereas Johnny and I have only been to the seaside once."

It was her wistful smile that gave Jack his idea. "I'll talk it over with your uncle, Lucas. I have some jobs at Cliff House that need doing. It could be that you can work off your debt."

"*Could I?* And people call me Johnny, sir. My brother Richard is Lucas."

"But Richard is not here," Jack pointed out. "And Johnny is rather a nursery name, don't you think? Shall I call you John instead?"

Charlotte looked surprised, but the boy stood a full inch taller. "Oh, *thank you*, sir," he said. "Nobody calls me John. Or Lucas."

"Then it is time for that to change."

Now what had he done? He'd as good as issued an invitation to his house in Dorset. Well, and why not? Since Allen had to make the journey anyway, why not bring everyone along?

11 Plain Sailing

The next morning Charlotte awoke to the sound of steady rainfall. She came down to find a cheerful fire burning in the parlor grate, with chairs pulled up before it. Beside one chair was a table with a lamp; on the seat of the other chair was a stack of folded newspapers. Between the chairs was a low table with two clean cups and a pipe.

Captain Blunt's pipe.

For a full minute she stood there, gazing down at those cups. He was not expecting Mr. Allen or Johnny. He was expecting her. He knew she was an early riser, and he knew she would come here. Instead of avoiding her (a thing she would have done), he was looking forward to conversing. Should she go away? Yes, perhaps that would be best. She had embroidery work to finish, and Jack Blunt was always a distraction.

And yet Charlotte's feet would not move. There she stood, clutching her work box and gazing at the cups. It would be hours before anyone else would awaken. Moreover, this was a holiday for the servants. Captain Blunt was a fellow house guest, but this did not excuse the impropriety of private conversation, a thing her mother would frowningly call *tête-à-tête.*

Charlotte felt her cheeks grow warm. What foolishness! He was only Captain Blunt.

Yet under different circumstances—say, if she were a guest at Netherfield—what if Mr. Darcy had set two cups, one for him and one for her? Knowing full well that he would be alone with her for several hours? There was nothing to decide! Of course she must leave.

And then the door banged open. There stood Jack Blunt with the coffee pot. "Good morning," he said with a smile. As if meeting with her before breakfast was a matter of course.

Charlotte attempted a smile, but her features would not cooperate. Surely her face mirrored what she was feeling!

"Ah," he said. "I see you have noticed the mistletoe in the drawing room. It's been multiplying again, no thanks to our busy hostess." He filled both cups, as if he expected her to take coffee. "Cream and sugar?" he inquired. "I can fetch them from the kitchen. I take mine black."

"Then I shall do likewise," Charlotte heard her voice say. She did not care for black coffee, but it would steady her. "This smells delicious," she added. And it did. But surely there was no reason to tell him so! And why was she sitting down instead of leaving? She put her work box on the table and took a tentative sip of the coffee. It was very hot.

Jack Blunt did likewise. "With Mrs. Allen's mistletoe scheme," he said, "Mr. James does not stand a chance."

"Nor do you with the Morland girls."

This caught him off guard, a thing that pleased Charlotte enormously. "You have seen how they look at you," she went on. "A kiss under the mistletoe would be heaven itself."

He set down his cup. "Blast and the devil take it! I must be three times their age!"

"Surely not. The youngest, I think, is twelve, but the eldest is fifteen."

"As if I did not have enough of this nonsense in the navy." He took up his cup again.

"Did you?"

Over the rim of his coffee cup, Jack Blunt's eyes met hers. "I've had my fill of ambitious daughters, lusting after the income and position I can provide."

"Not to mention your—"

Your handsome face.

Had she almost said this aloud? Did he guess it? Was this the reason for the sudden flash in his eyes?

And why was she gazing at him in this foolish way? Charlotte opened her work box and began sorting through the embroidery silk. "I beg leave to inform you, sir," she said lightly, "that if you wear your regimentals this afternoon, you are done for. Hearts will be broken."

By this she meant the Morland girls.

"My regimentals, as you call them, are safe in the wardrobe at home. Unless I am on official business, that is where my dress uniform will remain."

"Very wise, given the circumstances."

"Foolish girls, spinning dreams out of nothing. Rest assured, I shall avoid the mistletoe at all costs. However, not all of Mrs. Allen's ideas are dismal. May I say that your hair looks lovely? Curls suit you."

"If only they were not so much trouble! She had me sleep with my hair bound in rags, a thing I have not done since I was a girl."

"You are a girl still."

This only showed how much he knew! "I am seven-and-twenty, sir," she said crisply. "And before long, my poor hair will be falling down around my shoulders. I put it up this morning on my own, very ineptly. Today Fleur comes only to attend Mrs. Allen."

He looked openly doubtful.

"Very well, if you must know, I told Fleur not to come. She has enough to do on Boxing Day without bothering over me."

"Does she indeed."

Charlotte gave an impatient shake of the head. This was a mistake, for several pins fell to the floor and a section of hair came cascading down. "Botheration! It is just as I said, hopeless. How unkind of you to laugh."

"Would you like me to help put it up again? I am an expert when it comes to braiding."

"No! I'll manage somehow." Charlotte wound the errant curl around a finger and reached down to find a pin.

"Simple braids," she grumbled, "are much more practical."

"But not nearly as pretty." There was a pause. "Diana," he said softly. "Leave your hair be. It looks very well."

Charlotte released the curl. "Hanging down the side of my neck?"

"Your aunt told you to curl your hair, and you have. She did not say anything about keeping it on top of your head."

"That is not what she meant, and you know it. By your line of thinking, I should wait beneath the mistletoe and kiss the footman!"

Jack burst out laughing. "A brilliant maneuver. The element of surprise. Kiss the wrong man, by all means. That'll teach her."

"I have no intention of kissing the footman," said Charlotte firmly. "Or my uncle. Or Johnny. Or—"

Or you.

Gracious. What was wrong with her today?

Again Charlotte opened her work box. "If I kiss anyone, it will be one of the youngest Morland boys. And only on the cheek."

"What about me?"

Suddenly it became difficult to breathe. *Would she dare to kiss Jack Blunt?*

Charlotte set her teeth, removed her embroidery frame, and closed the box. "No kisses from me for anyone over the age of three."

He did not reply. Curiosity prompted her to glance at him. There he sat, sipping his coffee.

"You won't be missing much. The only person I've kissed is Mr. Collins, and that was not a success."

"Hmm," he said, and his lips curved into a smile.

It was a provocative, challenging smile. *Was Jack intending to kiss her?* With vigor, Charlotte pulled through a stitch. If he did, he would encounter the business end of her needle!

She stole another look at him. This was unwise, because he was still smiling.

"Are you asking for a lesson?"

"No! Are you volunteering?"

He gave a tiny shrug and spread his hands.

"Oh! You have got to be the most provoking, most vexatious man I have ever met!"

"You are not alone in that opinion. Countless others have said the same." He took another sip of coffee, and his eyes lost their challenging gleam. "You needn't look so stricken," he said gently. "I was only teasing."

So Jack would not be kissing her, nor had he ever intended to.

She ought to feel relieved. Of course she was relieved; how could it be otherwise? Now that she thought about it, as far as emotions were concerned, relief and disappointment felt very much the same. Indeed they did.

"You see," she explained, "I am not romantic, not even one bit. I never have been."

He gave a snort of derision. "How do you know? Since when are you an authority on romance?" He reached for his pipe and began to fill it.

No one had ever questioned this opinion before. "Because I am practical," she heard her voice bleat.

"Too practical to *feel*? You have enough poetry in your soul to see beauty in a stormy sea, instead of cowering beneath the bedclothes. And let us have no nonsense about how you have never been in love. I do not believe it."

"But I *haven't*! The closest I have ever been is admiration. A hopeless thing it was, for the gentleman I admired was much above my station."

He lit his pipe and sent a puff of smoke to the ceiling. "Liking from afar is certainly safe," he remarked. "I take it he was a handsome fellow?"

Was Jack annoyed? Had she provoked him? Charlotte warmed to her theme. "Very much so. He is not quite as tall as you or as broad in the shoulders, but he had all the women sighing. He has dark hair and eyes, and is flawlessly attired, always."

"My sad rags pale by comparison."

Yes, Jack was definitely put out. It could never be that he was jealous, but it was delightful to tease him.

"No one compares to him; how could they? He is not only well-educated and distinguished, but he is also extremely wealthy. His estate is said to be one of the finest in all England."

"Oho. Now we arrive at the heart of the matter, the reason for your admiration."

"Do you think I was drawn by his fortune and position? In no way! I was not born a gentleman's daughter. I know almost nothing about managing a grand mansion, and I am wholly ignorant of the social duties that come with that life. All I ask is a comfortable home."

"And were you Safe Charlotte in his presence? Or were you Devil-May-Care Diana?"

"I was my usual cautious self, of course," she admitted. "My father's elevation means that we are under observation always; we cannot afford a social misstep. My mother feels this keenly. She is more ladylike than many of the gentlewomen we know. She has to be."

"As with a new promotion; I understand. Did you catch this man's interest?"

Charlotte gave a gurgle of laughter. "Of course not! I did not love him, and it is a very good thing, too. Jasper, if I were a fly, I would have a better chance of being noticed by Mr. Darcy. Not that he is impolite. Quite the contrary; his manners are flawless. But to him I simply do not exist. Then too, he is captivated by my dear friend Elizabeth Bennet. She is beautiful and clever. You would like her."

"The one who gave Collins the heave-ho before you did? One can see why, with this paragon waiting in the wings."

"Mr. Darcy is no paragon; he is aloof and prideful. Eliza dislikes him thoroughly. At one time I thought he was in love with her, but I have changed my mind."

"Assuredly he is in love with her! A beautiful woman's scorn is a potent lure."

"I would not know," she said mildly and brought out her scissors. "There. My handkerchief for Fleur is finished. Simple pink daisies with her initial." She removed it from the frame and smoothed it.

Surprisingly, Jack leaned forward and held out a hand. "May I see?"

Without thinking, Charlotte gave it to him and, when he asked, the others as well. "Here is Uncle's, and Johnny's, and Aunt's."

"What about mine?" His provoking smile was back. "Was mine abandoned?"

"Yours is waiting to be starched and pressed."

"May I see it?"

The temptation was strong, but Charlotte stood her ground. "It is a gift. It will be given with the others."

"Please?"

Oh, the charm of that pleading smile! Others might have the strength to withstand it; Charlotte found that she could not. With a sigh, she passed it to him.

Too late she realized that he would see the difference, for he was studying his handkerchief with interest. The others had simple stitches; his design was far more intricate. It had taken hours to complete.

"It will look better when it is pressed," she explained.

"This is beautiful. Thank you." He began to fold it.

Charlotte held out her hand, but he smilingly ignored her. Into an inside pocket of his waistcoat went the handkerchief. "Close to my heart," he said, patting his chest.

She was surprised into a laugh. "It is only a handkerchief. Everyone knows what those are used for. *Close to the nose* would be more accurate."

He gave a shout of laughter. "A fellow tries to be charming, but Practical Charlotte takes the wind out of his sails."

"Now just a minute. I owe you no uncommon courtesy. You absconded with my gift."

"You could not have given it me in the presence of the Allens, you know," he said quietly. "And as much as I would like to give a gift in return, it isn't permitted."

"Save for in secret."

His smile reappeared. "Sweetens both the giving and the receiving, does it not?" He paused. "Speaking of secrets, I do have something to ask you, confidentially. It's about my hair."

He leaned forward. "This man you admired, Darcy. His hair is not long like mine, is it?"

Charlotte bit back a smile. "You won't like to hear my answer. He wears it in curls."

Jack sighed. "I knew it. Like a blasted cherub."

"Cherubic is not the impression he conveys."

"Not with dark hair he wouldn't. But I would. Is Mrs. Allen right? Should I have it cut?"

Charlotte gazed at him thoughtfully. It was something to be able to study him directly, without shyness. "Since you ask," she said slowly, "perhaps you might abandon the braid? And simply bind your hair at the nape of your neck with a plain ribbon?"

"But the braid is such an irritation to Mrs. Allen."

"A sacrifice indeed," she said solemnly.

"Here," he said. "Let's see."

But Jack was unbraiding his hair! Good heavens, he was threading his fingers through it, bringing it forward. Honey gold it was, brushing his shoulders. Charlotte was stunned to silence. It was enough work simply to breathe.

His expression became bashful. "Is it so bad?"

"Bad?" she cried. "In no wise! The word I would use is *unfair*. You have beautiful, beautiful hair, Jasper Blunt. You have no idea what some women would give to have hair that color. And I suppose you care nothing about it."

"Should I?"

"You have hair the color of spun gold, yet you see it as an irritation. Incredible!"

"It is worse at sea," he grumbled, "when I am often in the sun. It becomes downright yellow."

"Oh," she cried.

"Diana, it is the color of baby hair."

"Would you rather have hair the color of mine?" she countered. "The color of a rodent?"

"A rodent!"

"That's right, a mouse. Or a rabbit or a goat."

He began to laugh.

"And then there are my eyes. Yours are gray-blue, whereas mine are the color of mud. Plain brown mud."

"Hazel," he corrected. "You have flecks of green in your eyes."

Charlotte did not know where to look. How could he possibly have noticed this?

She heard him sigh. "Well then. Since your friend Darcy—"

Charlotte interrupted. "He is not my friend. If we met today, he would not remember or acknowledge me. I exaggerated in order to tease you. It's just that he was the most handsome man I'd ever seen."

Until you.

The truth of this crashed over Charlotte like a wave.

This man, Jack Blunt, far eclipsed Mr. Darcy. Moreover he, who was so beautiful, cared nothing about it. There was no denying the truth of what was in her heart. She was in love with Jack Blunt—and she had been for days.

"Mrs. Allen would like me to abandon the beard, but this I cannot do. It has taken the better part of a year to coax it into covering the scar."

"You have a flaw?" whispered Charlotte.

"My dear girl, I have a myriad of flaws! You, of all people, should know that."

But she didn't. At this moment Charlotte could not think of a single one.

"In naval circles, one thinks nothing of scars and disfigurement. Such things are commonplace. But ashore, they are off-putting. The beard works in my favor."

"Please," said Charlotte, "please do not cut your hair. I like it just the way it is, bound back, of course."

His smile was like sunshine. "I thank you for your honesty."

Jack made no move to rework the braid, but instead took up a newspaper and unfolded it. "Here's hoping a new one of these is delivered tomorrow. In the meantime, there must be something in here I missed." To Charlotte's surprise, he brought out a pair of spectacles.

Good heavens, this man was no less handsome with them on!

"Mrs. Allen is wrong about your beard," she said earnestly. "You are very well as you are. She and her opinions can go hang! Er, as my brothers would say. Would you like some fresh coffee? What we have must be cold by now."

He smiled at her, shook his head no, and turned a page.

The tick of the clock, the crackle of the fire, the rhythm of the falling rain. What a comfortable silence!

Charlotte sorted through the contents of her work box, scarcely knowing what she did. Here she was, alone with the man she loved. A wondrous thing! That he would never return her love did not matter. It was enough to love him from afar.

There he sat, reading his paper with his unlit pipe at his elbow, pleased to share his morning with her. This was as sweet a domestic scene as any woman could wish for. All that was lacking were their children, playing at his feet.

Heat rose to Charlotte's cheeks, and she bit back a sigh. She should not be stealing looks at him or dreaming of a future together. Such things led only to heartbreak. His hair, for instance, caressing his dear shoulders, was something only a wife should see in the privacy of their bedchamber.

Oh glory. Was this romance? It was both fearful and sublime.

Presently she grew tranquil enough to speak. "I have just the thing for your hair: a length of black ribbon."

He lowered the newspaper. "Another gift?"

Charlotte was helpless to conceal what she knew must be a very foolish smile. "I suppose you could call it that. I should let you know, however, that this is left over from a funeral wreath."

His eyes narrowed in amusement. "Appropriate, considering how we met."

When she passed him the ribbon, his fingers brushed against hers, creating a shiver of pleasure.

Heavens, she was romantic after all. Rather desperately so!

And what a man she had chosen to lose her heart to! Captain Blunt was kind, but he was not at all safe. Indeed, he was dangerous. Wasn't it curious that this should be so bewitchingly attractive? She could love this man forever; oh but she could!

At length there were sounds; the household was waking. "Jasper," whispered Charlotte.

Over the top of his spectacles, his eyes met hers. "What is it?" he whispered back.

She gestured. "Your hair."

"Ah. Best to tidy it before Mrs. Allen sees. She'd have a fit."

Smiling, Charlotte collected the hair pins from the floor and secured her wayward curls.

"A pity and a crime," said Jack, watching this process. "I like it better the other way."

How Charlotte longed to say the same about him! The secret of her love would be difficult to conceal, but she was determined to do it. His friendship was precious to her; never would she cause him to feel awkward because of what was in her heart.

He rose to his feet, went quietly to the parlor door, and propped it open. Immediately she felt cold air rush in from the hall.

"Propriety maintained," he whispered, and resumed his seat.

"Thank you," she whispered back.

Jack Blunt might be dangerous, but he had a noble heart. This alone was reason to rejoice.

12 Tell it to the Marines

Jack lasted not even ten minutes in the drawing room. Mrs. Allen was in fine form, holding forth on the benefits of the married state by using *The Vicar of Wakefield* as her text. Her message sailed over James Morland's head, but was eagerly intercepted by his sisters. Unfortunately for Jack, the girls not only drank in every word, but cast hopeful smiles in his direction.

Better to leave their silliness and flirtation to John Lucas! Charlotte was seated on the sofa beside Mr. James, a prisoner to her aunt's will. He noted that she sat as far from Morland as possible, a thing that pleased him.

Using the flimsiest pretext—he hadn't a copy of the book—he made his excuses and departed. He closed the door on a chorus of pleading offers to share one of theirs.

Without hesitation Jack went to his cousin's library. He found Allen sitting beside the desk with a stocking-clad foot propped on a chair. This did not look promising.

"Gout acting up again? Should we put off our trip to Cliff House?"

Allen responded with a grimace. "The left toe is inflamed. Not over-much, but enough. Comes of good living; namely, too much port wine and Christmas beef. I'm holed up in here because I haven't the taste for whatever Meg's got rigged up in the drawing room: a reading group or some such thing."

"An hour or two should do it."

"Longer, if she brings out those desserts." Allen shook his head. "Two hours, discussing something that could be gone over in twenty minutes. The point is to bring Charlotte and Mr. James together."

"She does not appear to have an interest." Jack found a chair and brought out his pipe.

"So I have told Meg time and again. I don't know what she is thinking. He's a full six years Charlotte's junior."

The library door opened to admit the housekeeper. "Beg pardon, Mr. Allen, but an express has just arrived."

"On Boxing Day? That's criminal. Thank you, Mrs. Hodge. I'll come right out." To Jack he said, "Someone must have a burr in his saddle to send an express on a holiday. Business is like the rising tide; it waits for no man." Allen made ready to heave out of his chair.

"You stay put; I'll sign for it," Jack offered. "What with the nasty weather, the poor fellow needs a meal and drying out in the kitchen. I'll get him settled."

But when Jack returned, he did not hand the letter to his cousin. He stood before the desk, tapping a fingernail against one of the seals.

"Well?"

"This is not good news. Hunsford, Kent, is the point of origin."

This had no significance to Allen. "And?"

"And it is addressed not to you, but to your niece. I don't know what she has told you, but Hunsford is the home of her former fiancé."

Allen brightened. "Here is welcome news! Perhaps a reconciliation is in the works."

"I don't like it. Why go to the trouble and expense of sending an express?"

"A sorrowing heart? One that is eager to apologize? You must admit, young men can be proud and stubborn."

Collins was certainly both, but Jack also had the impression that he was stingy. Why else would the man have the banns called instead of purchasing a license? Why did he now go to the expense of sending an express?

He put a question to Allen. "What would you like to do? Pass this to Miss Lucas to read on her own? Or call her here to open it in your presence?"

"If it is a love letter, I'd prefer to give the girl privacy."

"And if not?"

"You are a suspicious dog, Jack. What else could it be?" Allen held out his hand, and Jack surrendered the letter. "How do you know this came from Hunsford?"

"I asked the fellow who brought it. He identified the markings for me."

"An awkward business, young love. I'll give it to Charlotte."

"Theirs was to be a marriage of practicality, not love. Has she told you the reason for the breakup?"

"I've not heard a word. Have you?"

"Unfortunately, yes. I'll fetch her."

Jack entered the drawing room without apology. It seemed to him that the gentle James Morland was looking rather harassed. If the poor fellow had hoped to lead the discussion, he had reckoned without the determination of Meg Allen.

"To remind you," she was now saying, "and I quote dear Mr. Primrose in Chapter 1:

> *I was ever of opinion that the honest man, who married and brought up a large family, did more service than he who continues single, and only talked of population.*

"So you see, Mr. James, every man's happiest state is marriage." She gave a sidelong glance to Jack.

"Miss Lucas," he said quietly, "your uncle is asking for you in the library."

"Now?" complained Mrs. Allen.

"Yes, now."

"Of all things! Can it not wait?"

"I fear not." Jack held the door for Charlotte. Once in the hall, he explained the situation.

"An express for me? Is it from Father?"

"I should warn you; it comes from Hunsford."

What followed next was a wave of anxiety. "From Mr. Collins?"

"So it would seem."

"Why in the world would he write to me?" she whispered.

"You will discover that soon enough."

Once in the library, she gazed at the letter as if it were a snake. So great was her reluctance that he wondered if her courage would fail altogether. "Open it," he prompted. He moved to stand behind her chair, spectacles at the ready, in order to read over her shoulder.

"I don't think I can," she confessed. "I want nothing to do with him, nothing!"

"Best to get it over with," he said gently.

He could see that she longed to refuse him. But all at once she squared her shoulders and bravely broke the seals. One paragraph in, she gave a gasp. "But this is impossible. No, he cannot!"

Jack took the letter from her resistless grasp. "Breach of Contract? He dares to sue you for Breach of Contract? The swine!"

Mr. Allen gave a dry cough. "If the settlement documents were signed, he could be entitled to financial compensation."

"But they weren't," cried Charlotte. "He came for that purpose, but before he and Father could meet with the solicitor, I—that is, he—"

"Go on. Tell your uncle what happened."

She looked stricken. "I ended the engagement for personal reasons, Uncle."

"Apparently you did not make those reasons clear to Collins," Jack pointed out.

"But I did. That is, I thought he understood. Yes, he certainly understood, for he left our house quickly. He was afraid of what I could say, but didn't."

"He has had a few weeks to stew about the loss of a thousand pounds. Apparently it has gone to his head."

"Could he take that amount? All of my dowry?"

"He can negotiate for it, certainly," said Mr. Allen.

Meanwhile, Jack was reading the letter. "An arrogant piece, this Collins is. Full of himself. He refers to you as *the daughter of a paltry tradesman, elevated above his station.*"

Charlotte sighed heavily. "Before, he had nothing but compliments for Father."

The more Jack read, the more irritated he became. "Why, he is as stupid as he is selfish. He places the blame entirely on your shoulders, when it should be the reverse. Very well, if he needs it spelled out, we shall do that. Allen, have you pen and ink handy?"

"There on the desk. Why do you ask?"

"We need to answer at once, before the fellow who delivered this departs. It's raining, and he is enjoying a hearty meal in the kitchen. If we work quickly, we can bring it about. Allen, may Miss Lucas have your seat?"

Allen exchanged his chair for another, and Jack brought Charlotte to sit behind the desk.

"Captain Blunt," she said urgently, "do you mean I am to answer him *now*? How can I? For I must first consult with my father and then—"

Jack broke in. "*I* shall answer him. You will write to my dictation. Are you ready?"

She stared at him, open-mouthed.

"Diana," he said softly, "dip the pen into the inkwell, there. Write today's date at the top of the page, and then we'll begin. *Mr. Collins.*"

"Without a salutation?"

"If you wish to call him *dear*, that is your business. I prefer another term, but we'll save the insults for later."

Charlotte lowered the pen. "Should we not, in Christian charity, offer courtesy instead of insults?"

"We'll be courteous, after a manner of speaking, but we shall also be direct. Your initial response to him, in ending the engagement, was graciousness itself. You said nothing regarding his misdeeds; you simply wished him gone. He should have left it at that."

"What misdeeds?" said Allen.

Jack ignored this and focused on Charlotte. "Collins did not appreciate the kindness of your restraint," he said gently. "He now seeks to take advantage of you and demands a monetary settlement. In other words, he has become predatory. Thus, we shall *answer a fool according to his folly.*"

"But—"

"This man is a bully and a coward. You will notice that he writes to you, instead of to your father, hoping to embarrass you into committing yourself. Shall we begin?"

It was all Jack could do to keep from gleefully rubbing his hands. This was going to be fun.

Mr. Collins,
Your missive of 24th December reached me this afternoon. You can imagine my surprise at both its tone and contents. Apparently, you have forgotten the exact nature of what transpired in the—

Jack paused. "Where did this take place? And when?"

"In the vestibule of our home," she whispered. "At the base of the staircase. On Monday, 16th of December."

—in the vestibule of Lucas Lodge, at the base of the staircase, on Monday, the 16th of December. At that time, while we were yet unmarried, you saw fit to accost my person, not only with an unexpected, lustful embrace and kiss, of which I had no warning, but also by the intrusion of your greedy, lewd, and licentious hand down the front of my gown.

"What?" shouted Allen.

I have never been so treated by any gentleman of my acquaintance, and I certainly expected better of a clergyman who serves the Savior's holy church.

"—the Savior's holy church," whispered Charlotte, writing.

"This is outrageous!" cried Allen.

You may have forgotten, but I never shall,
the way your fingers touched my—

Jack stopped.

Her pen stilled. "Yes?" she whispered. "You were about to say?"

Jack told her the word to write.

Mr. Allen gave another shout.

"Jack! I cannot write that!"

"Why not? The meaning is clear. That is where he touched you, is it not?"

"But that word is so coarse!"

"As to meaning, it is precise. There can be no mistake."

"But Jack," she pleaded, "my signature will be on this letter, not yours."

"Plague and the devil take it! This is no time to be squeamish! Besides," he added, "think of the impression that word will make on Collins's bishop when he reads it."

"You wouldn't."

"Of course I would. Write a different word if you prefer, but leave the meaning in." He gave her a look. "When you interrupt, I lose my train of thought."

Charlotte dipped the pen in the inkpot. "You'll frighten Mr. Collins clear out of his skin with this letter."

"My dear girl, this is only the bow-chaser."

"The what?"

"A warning shot, fired before a sea battle begins," said Allen. "My sweet, did you tell your father *nothing* about what transpired?"

"How could I? I was afraid he would excuse Mr. Collins. I was afraid he would tell me to marry him. And oh, Uncle, I did not wish to!"

"My dear, you wrong your father. He would never force such a thing."

From what Jack had heard about the man, he was not so sure. "May we continue?" he said. "I hate to cut you short, but time is passing. We'll now commence firing the big guns."

Charlotte raised her eyes to his. "There is more?"

Jack felt his lips twist into an unpleasant smile. "But of course."

> *The choice to sue for Breach of Contract is yours. I am not afraid of you. I shall willingly testify before a court of law, giving an exact and detailed account of what you did.*

He added, "Underscore *exact* and *detailed.*"

"But I cannot respond to a lawsuit. I haven't any money."

"I'll back you."

"So shall I," said Mr. Allen grimly. "With pleasure. My solicitor is at your disposal. This scoundrel will get nothing from you."

Jack resumed dictation:

> *I shall tell the honest truth to the court, for I have little to lose. Although I have said nothing about your licentious behavior to my parents or my neighbors, slanderous conjecture and gossip have forced me to flee from my home.*

"Not *forced*, exactly."

Jack smiled at her. "Kindly refrain from interrupting."

She narrowed her eyes at him. He responded with a wink.

> *My decision to end our engagement has brought disappointment to you, nothing more. But it has cost me dearly. Even as I write this, I am making plans to support myself apart from my family as either a companion or a governess.*

Allen interrupted. "Charlotte, is this true?"

She nodded. He sighed heavily.

> *There is not a judge in all England who will be unmoved by my story, nor will he deny the rightness of my actions in defending myself against your lustful self-indulgence. I advise you to think carefully before bringing this matter to court.*

"Here ends round one," Jack told her. "Now we'll have round two."

> *This letter has been written out in triplicate. If you file a petition to sue, know that a copy will be sent to your bishop, to your archdeacon, and to the provider of your living. They deserve to know the truth of your character.*
>
> *Furthermore, an anonymous person is poised to send to each newspaper in Kent, as well as to the major publications in London, an account of your vileness entitled—*

Jack paused. "Now what shall the title be?"

"Which anonymous person?" cried Charlotte. "Upon my word, is it *you?*"

He grinned. "I've read enough sensationalist articles to be able to write one. Here we go; this'll get him."

> *—entitled 'The Shameful State of Morals Among Some of Our Trusted Clergymen.' Your living cannot be revoked, but public outrage can cause you to surrender both your parsonage and parish church to a curate, and to live in seclusion.*

Mr. Allen began chuckling. "You are a formidable opponent, Jack."

"I always did enjoy setting the terms for surrender."

In future, address all correspondence to my solicitor at this address—

Jack turned to Allen. "Have you his card?"

—who is in possession of a copy of this letter.

Charlotte wrote out the name and address given by her uncle.

"Very good. Sign your name *Miss C. Lucas.*"

"No closing?"

"Are there any appropriate to the occasion? *Yours truly? Sincerely? Respectfully?*"

"*Wrathfully* would be my choice. You are right; the closing is unnecessary."

"I hate to ask you to copy this out, but your hand is more legible than mine. Once finished, I'll take it to the fellow in the kitchen and arrange to have it delivered to Collins."

"By express?"

"Most definitely by express. The man deserves to have his answer, so we'll give it him."

Without hesitation, Charlotte drew forward a fresh sheet of paper. "If you would just look over what I've written, I am ready to make the copy."

When this was completed, she signed her name as suggested and pushed back the chair. "I thank you, Uncle, for your kindness and support. It means more than you know." She went over to Allen's chair and kissed him on the cheek.

To Jack's surprise, she next turned to him. "And thank you, Captain Blunt. I did not think so when you began, but this is the perfect response." He likewise received a kiss on the cheek.

Blast, why must she kiss him? What else could Jack do but dip his head? Looking the other way was no help, for how could he hide the blush that burned his cheeks? Not even the beard could conceal that. Kisses were not precisely in his line.

"No mistletoe required," she added softly, with a smile.

Oh, that smile.

"I'll—just take this down to the kitchen now." Confound it, even his voice sounded lame! "Best to hide out here with us until your aunt's party is over."

Now why had he said that? Shaking his head, Jack let himself out of the library.

13 Favor and Felicity

Early the next morning, Charlotte lit her candle and scrambled into her clothes. There was no reason to go down to the parlor. Indeed, she had much to do here to prepare for tomorrow's journey to Cliff House.

Cliff House by the sea. Even to think of it brought a sigh.

Tomorrow night she would be a guest in his house.

Against the wall stood her trunk and her traveling bag. Oh, the memories! She held this very bag while riding on that horse with Jack. Could it have been only days ago?

And how was it possible to completely lose one's heart in so short a time? Romances and fairy stories presented the miracle of love-at-first-sight as being commonplace, but Charlotte had never believed them. Until now.

Her thoughts circled back to the parlor. What were the chances that it was empty this morning?

On the other hand, was he already there, waiting?

This thought made breathing difficult.

Charlotte slid into the chair before the dressing table. She had once advised Elizabeth's sister, Jane, to show more affection than she felt, so that Mr. Bingley would recognize her interest. Doing such a thing, Charlotte now realized, was anything but easy!

Was there a way to cause Jack Blunt to fall as much in love with her as she was with him? Charlotte studied her reflection, wincing at her plain features and her hair bound up in knobby rags. Displaying affection had not worked for Jane, who was extremely beautiful. Such a thing would never work for her. Moreover, she had no feminine wiles, not even one.

And yet what if he were waiting?

It would be some time before Fleur could attend her, and Charlotte dared not risk her aunt's displeasure by combing out her hair. She freed a few curls to frame her face, but the rest she stuffed under a ruffled cap. What did it matter? Jack would not be there. She would go down to the parlor, put curiosity to rest, and then she would return—to do what? Pack her clothes? A thing that would take ten minutes?

Charlotte slipped on her shoes, took up the candlestick, and went out to the staircase. Down into the deep darkness of the hall she descended, scarcely daring to breathe for fear of blowing out the candle.

Were her eyes playing tricks in the dark? Goodness, could that be a line of light beneath the parlor door? Slowly she drew nearer. The door was slightly ajar, and there was an aroma of coffee.

Charlotte halted, and her heart nearly did the same. He had come. He had come for her.

How vulnerable and exposed she was! She brought no work box, no book. Yet how could she deny her heart its greatest pleasure? It was no crime to sit and talk with a man. Gathering her courage, Charlotte opened the door and went in.

At once there was a rustle of the newspaper, as Jack put it aside and rose to his feet. "Ah," she heard him say. "I was hoping you would come down."

Was it possible for one's heart to burst with joy?

Jack filled a second cup with coffee—for her. With him she would gladly drink black coffee every day of her life! Her chair before the fire was waiting.

"A fetching cap," he remarked.

"You are too kind." And he was! This cap wasn't even pretty. "I shouldn't risk Mrs. Allen's displeasure by taking down my hair. Not today, when we have so much to do. Mrs. Allen is driving Fleur to distraction over clothes. She wishes to take most of the dresses she owns and at least half of her hats."

"For a visit to Cliff House? I am honored. I think."

"For our visit to Bath," said Charlotte, smiling. "She has made Mr. Allen promise that we shall go directly there from Dorset, and we are to remain in Bath for several weeks or more. Before Fleur begins packing, Mrs. Allen must pore over fashion periodicals to determine which of her gowns is hopelessly out of style."

"Most of them, I would imagine."

What else could Charlotte do but share Jack's grin?

"By this time tomorrow," he said, "we'll need to be well on our way, as it's a good sixty miles. After yesterday's deluge, who knows what the roads will be like? It looks to be holding off for now, so that's something." He took a sip of coffee.

So this was to be their last shared coffee in the parlor. In the months to come, she would sit and picture him here in his chair, with his unlit pipe on the table. And perhaps, if he came for another visit ...

Charlotte knew better than to indulge in vain hope. He was not fond of Laurelhurst and came only when he had to.

There would be plenty of time later for sadness. No matter that she could not make Jack fall in love with her, she was determined to enjoy his company.

"Will Mr. Collins have our letter by tomorrow? Do you think he'll continue with the lawsuit?"

"You might receive an apology, via Allen's solicitor, but I doubt it. Nevertheless, Collins will be shaking in his boots at what could have happened. The threat of an anonymous newspaper article was not an idle one."

The dangerous note in his voice was back, a thing she found rather thrilling. Happily, she sipped her coffee.

"I wonder if I might ask a favor? This is my statement for the magistrate. Could you look it over and tell me if I have left anything out? I'd like to confirm that it reads clearly."

Surely Mr. Allen was the best person to advise him, yet he was asking her.

Charlotte took the paper he held out. "I am happy to do so, but I cannot critique your observations, as they are your own."

As she began to read, an idea presented itself. Charlotte was not one to ask for help, but the pleasure of his company gave her courage. "I have a favor of my own to ask, if it is not too much trouble. But only if you are driving into Fullerton itself."

"I am. How may I serve you?"

"It's an errand for Mrs. Allen. A widowed lady runs a subscription library in Fullerton, and Mrs. Allen would like me to select books. She claims there is nothing to do in Dorset."

"Nothing to do? I like that!" He leaned forward. "What about *The Vicar of Wakefield*? She could certainly read that."

"I fear she is finding it a bit too tame, for she explicitly said to find something exciting. The proprietress is fond of romances. She should be able to help me."

Was Jack rolling his eyes? "If my errand is inconvenient," she added, "you have only to say. Bert from the stables can drive Johnny and me."

"I'd be delighted. That is, as long as I don't have to choose the books."

"I have the task well in hand."

"Then it's settled. We'll take Allen's gig."

And just like that, Charlotte's afternoon was arranged.

"A gig wasn't built for three people," grumbled Johnny, as he squeezed in.

"Shall we leave you behind?" This was from Captain Blunt.

There were no more complaints from Johnny.

Jack sat between them, and although Charlotte pressed herself as far to the side as possible, it did no good. Of what use was shyness? After riding together on horseback, surely her dignity could survive sitting smash against his shoulder for twenty minutes. Her heart certainly had no objection.

After a spirited debate (for Charlotte would not be setting foot outside the library) Johnny won his point and was allowed to go along to the magistrate.

"Do you think he'll serve refreshments, sir?" Johnny was always hopeful.

"No. And if you make a nuisance of yourself, you'll regret it."

Within an hour they returned and took Charlotte up again. Jack eyed the stack of books on her lap. "You met with success, I see."

"Mrs. Jackson has an excellent selection. Fullerton is smaller than our town, and yet she has as many novels as one can find at Clarke's."

"Does sensible Charlotte read novels?"

"Those that come my way. This one is rather good: *The Captain's Cabin Mate.*"

He looked at her with raised brows. "Cabin mate?"

"It takes place aboard a ship. Most women think it is very romantic."

"If you say so," he said with a smile. "A ship-of-the-line is not the setting I would choose for romance."

Charlotte showed him the next title. "This one is a real find; it's as exciting as anything my aunt could wish for: *The Sinister Baron's Prey.*"

"The sinister who?"

"It's about a villainous nobleman, obsessed with courting an innocent and beautiful maiden."

"Who, naturally, despises him."

"Why, yes. He is a distasteful person, so we cannot blame her. In the end, he kidnaps her and locks her in the attic."

"Imprisonment is a sure-fire way to inspire heartfelt love."

"The main thing is, it's exciting. The Bennets took turns reading chapters aloud in the days before the militia came to Meryton. It kept us all in painful suspense. It is Lydia's favorite."

"That figures," said Johnny.

"Bennet," repeated Jack. "This Lydia is a sister to the beautiful Elizabeth you told me about?"

"Lydia's the youngest Bennet," said Johnny. "And the loudest."

"Elizabeth is much more than beautiful. She is intelligent and clever and musical; the quintessential gentleman's daughter."

"Acclaimed beauties are not to be trusted; they are too full of themselves. I prefer women who are lovely. That is to say, beautiful without knowing it."

Charlotte could not allow this to pass. "There is no such creature. Every woman owns a looking glass, and a looking glass never lies."

"But where is loveliness found? It is in the eyes and the smile and the laughter, I say. Not in the shape of one's face or the color of one's hair."

The color of one's hair? Was this for her?

No, it couldn't be, for Jack's tone was not at all lover-like. Then too, here sat her brother. Of course Jack meant nothing by it.

He turned to Johnny. "How did you like the reading group?"

"It wasn't as bad as I feared, sir. Mind, we'd have got on better if Aunt Allen didn't talk so much. I kept wanting to ask how that Mr. Primrose thought he could give up vicaring and become a farmer, not knowing anything about farming. If my father became a farmer, we'd starve."

"And what do you know how to do?"

"The usual. Ride horses and shoot; play card games and climb trees, even if Mother does scold about my clothes. Dancing's all right, but I'd rather play cricket."

"And then there are your studies," prompted Charlotte.

"Such stuff! Mr. Brooksby (he's the curate) proses on about Latin and calculus and the History of the Empire. They curdle my brain."

"I'll let Flynn know about the calculus. You need to use what you've learned; Flynn will give you that. He's a first-rate navigator. If there is a clear night, we'll have the sextant out."

"I would like that," whispered Charlotte.

Of course Jack heard, being so near. He smiled an answer. To Johnny he said, "And what did you think of the Morland girls?"

"They ain't near as bad as what *we're* used to, sir. Plus, there were only three of 'em. There are five Bennet sisters, and Lydia's the worst."

"The loud one."

"She used to be a fine, sporting girl, but when she turned fourteen, she became too good for us. I'm not even two years younger, yet now I'm scum."

"Women can be cruel that way."

"Once the officers showed up, there was no bearing with her. "'Oh, Captain Blunt,'" piped Johnny. "'You look so *fine* in your *regimentals.*' She'll say this even when you *don't*, sir. She's all about a red coat, Lydia is, which is the stupidest thing. Everyone knows militiamen haven't a feather to fly with. Otherwise they wouldn't be in the militia."

"It's the navy that defends the kingdom, not militiamen."

Charlotte said unsteadily, "They do drill sometimes; I think that means they march about. And I have heard them speak of practicing with guns. But most of the time they attend dinners hosted by our leading families, and take tea, and dance at assemblies and balls."

"And drink like fish and gamble away what little they have," added Jack. "Woe to the barkeep who does not keep an eye on his daughters."

"Lydia's not much better than barmaids," said Johnny. "She's pretty enough, like the rest of her sisters, but she cares nothing for what she says or does. She wears her dresses cut down to here"—Johnny drew a line on his chest—"and she's like Charlotte, so that's saying something."

"Where is her mother in all this?"

"Her mother eggs her on, sir! She's crazy about officers and sees no harm in it. Her father stays holed up in his library, mostly to escape the noise."

"Upon my word."

"Aye, sir. It's all tipsy dance and jollity. That's what my brother Richard calls it. I think it's something he got out of a book."

"Milton," said Jack. "But you were saying?"

"Lydia sashays about, squealing and giggling and giving playful cuffs to the officers. And she bends over when she shouldn't, without regard to—anything! I used to wonder what my mother meant by *decorum*; now I know. Lydia ain't got any! One of these days, Miss Lydia might have a surprise. She'll bend over low, and something will—ow!"

"That's enough," said Charlotte.

"Don't cuff me! And don't shush me neither. Especially as it was *you* who said—"

Charlotte gave Johnny's knee another thwack. "Ow!"

"Children, children." Jack turned to Johnny. "What did she say?"

"Johnny, don't you dare!"

"Merely that if Lydia Bennet wasn't careful at the card table, something might end up on the discard pile that wasn't a playing card."

Jack gave a shout of laughter.

Charlotte buried her head in her hands. Jack continued to laugh.

"My mother and sisters didn't know what she meant, but Richard and I, we knew."

Jack brought the gig to a halt. "Upon my word," he gasped, wiping his eyes. "The discard pile!"

"Aye, sir, we laughed about that one for days. She sings Miss Elizabeth's praises, my sister does, but *she's* the clever one. Within the family circle, when she doesn't care who hears. Never cross wits with Charlotte, sir. She'll best you every time."

"I am learning that."

"Johnny," wailed Charlotte, "for heaven's sake, be quiet. You're telling all my secrets. What will Captain Blunt think of me?"

"Too late for that, Lottie. As soon as you launched into shrewing at that highwayman, as he was robbing Sally Keith, Captain Blunt knew. He's no cabbagehead."

Yes, Jack knew, and this knowledge doomed any hope for romance. And yet, as long as he smiled at her in that delightful way, Charlotte did not care.

She could no more make this man love her than she could fly to the moon. But he liked her, and this was more than wonderful.

14 Twilight and Evening Bell

Jack had hired a traveling chaise for himself and his cousin, with Johnny and the others riding in the Allen's coach. Were sixty-odd miles ever covered so slowly? The weather held, and it was with relief that the ocean finally came into view. Jack smiled as he pictured Charlotte's response. He was as eager as his guests to catch a glimpse of Cliff House.

Some called it Blunt's Folly, due to the unsheltered location and extravagant number of windows, but Jack did not care. He'd spent much time sketching and planning this house. Built of stone, it was able to weather ferocious storms.

A substantial amount of prize money had been spent right here, in order to turn dreams into reality. Some would call it a waste, but not Jack. The war had brought additional prize, a reward for his many years spent at sea. Cliff House was now established and prospering. The home farm was expanding every year; the grove of trees behind the house was a respectable size.

Jack drew a contented breath. His time ashore had been healing in more ways than one. It felt good to be home.

Charlotte descended from the Allen's coach with wide eyes. Across the lane from the house lay the wide expanse of the sea, grey beneath a pink and violet sunset. There was much to take in: the cliffs, the cove with its horseshoe bay, his sloop, the *Flicka*, bobbing at her mooring, and sea birds wheeling in the winter twilight.

Charlotte turned to gaze at the house. The bow windows reflected the fading light. Inside, the lamps were lit, casting a golden welcome. Jack was drawn to her side. He must know what she thought.

"All this is yours?" she said at last. Her eyes smiled into his. "You must feel like a king here."

How did she know? "I do," he said quietly.

His crewmen had the door open; light spilled onto the steps. Ord, Gibby, and the others stood at attention.

Johnny came loping up. "I say, sir, this is famous! It's better than anything!"

"Get your gear together, son. Ronson is standing by to take you down to the Rest."

"Sir?"

"The Wayfarer's Rest is where you'll be staying." He pointed. "Beyond the stone wall lies the kitchen garden and a group of houses. You've a bunk waiting."

Johnny could not contain his glee. "Yes, sir! I mean, aye, aye!"

"We'll need to outfit you with work clothes," Jack observed.

"Can you advance me the money for them, sir? So that my debt to you is even larger? Then I will be obliged to work here for *years*!"

"You'll be obliged, my young scamp, to take up a post as midshipman and begin your career, not hide away here."

Mrs. Allen emerged from the coach with many a sigh. "I am getting too old for this. I knew we should not have come. And now I am ill." She paused to sneeze.

Charlotte gave a start and went at once to her aunt's side. "Travel is a trial for everyone, young or old. The sea air is so healthful."

"Nonsense. It is cold and damp. Especially at this time of year."

"Mrs. Allen," said Jack, "may I present Captain Ord, my first officer on the *Valiant*, and one of the finest men with whom I've had the pleasure to serve. He runs Cliff House; he will ensure that you have everything you need."

"Cap'n, dinner will be served as soon as you and your guests are ready," said Ord. "'Tis humble fare, due to the uncertainty of your arrival time, but there is plenty of it."

"No one makes a stew like Griffith," said Jack. "His crumpets, served warm, are without compare."

"Sounds wonderful," said Mr. Allen.

"We are starving," added Johnny.

Mrs. Allen sneezed into her handkerchief. "I'd prefer to have dinner brought to my room." She entered the house ahead of Ord.

"Your bedchamber, ma'am, is on the first floor," said Ord. "It faces the back garden, which is quieter."

"Thank you," she said. "No one wishes to hear the sea roar all night."

"Oh, but—" Charlotte closed her lips.

Jack could not help smiling; Charlotte's eagerness was infectious. He leaned in. "I instructed Ord to put you in a room facing the sea."

"Truly?"

"If you'll allow me, ma'am?" said Ord, and he led the way up the stairs.

"This is certainly a man's house," complained Mrs. Allen to Charlotte, as they followed in Ord's wake. "Will you look at the nautical décor? Not a Grecian adornment anywhere." She sighed. "Your uncle is much the same. He would have Laurelhurst decorated with hunting gear."

Charlotte made haste to follow. "But ma'am, the windows! So many face the sea! On a summer's day, think how splendid the view must be."

"Unfortunately, it is winter."

"We'll have a fire in your room," said Charlotte, with a pleading look to Jack, "and request that hot water be brought up right away."

"I should think so. And another thing; I won't share a bedchamber with Mr. Allen, not with his gout acting up. He won't like to catch my cold."

Charlotte gained the first floor and sent another look in Jack's direction. "I'm sure we can arrange for that as well."

"Absolutely." Jack lowered his voice. "Come," he said to her. Charlotte followed obediently. He opened a door. "Here is your room."

She pointed to the nameplate. "It has a name? *Thunder and Sunshine*?"

"That's Gibby's handiwork; he's our carpenter. He'd like to name all the rooms. Because it's on the south corner of the house, this one bears the brunt of the wind and the sunshine."

"The best and the worst." She pointed to the set of double doors. "And that room there, *The Great Cabin.* What is it?"

"My quarters. It's the name given to the captain's cabin aboard ship. I'll leave you to settle in." Jack went to consult with Ord.

"So clean this house is, miss!" he heard Fleur say. "I've never seen anything like it."

Jack hid a grin. It was always a surprise to women that men of the navy prided themselves on cleanliness.

It was not until later that Jack caught up with Charlotte. He found her in the main salon, gazing intently at his portrait. Jack began to squirm like a schoolboy.

"That was commissioned when I received my first command. It's customary." Now why had he said this? Because he did not want her thinking him a peacocky fellow, fond of his own appearance!

"It's stunning." There was a wistful note in her voice.

"It should be; I paid enough, for both the dress coat and the artist. I was about your age at the time. During what Shakespeare calls *my salad days.*"

She turned to him with a smile. "I've never understood that expression."

"It's from a line of Cleopatra's. She goes on to say: *When I was green in judgment.*"

"I see. Yes, that would be right. I often feel the same."

She moved on to the painting of the *HMS Valiant*, which was placed prominently above the mantelpiece. He felt the need to explain that one too. "A fanciful image, made to appear as we were at Trafalgar." His lips twisted into a smile. "Several details are widely inaccurate, although none but a seaman will notice."

"It's heroic," she said quietly. "This enormous ship, with so many men under your command. What a dangerous, demanding line of work!"

"The word I would use is *relentless*. The ship must keep on course, always moving ahead, no matter the condition of the sea or the weariness of the crew."

To Jack's discomfort, Charlotte circled back to his portrait. "*Man in his pomp shall not endure,*" he quoted.

"Your hair is shorter and not in a braid."

"The artist thought it would be more attractive thus. I was conceited enough to believe him."

She twinkled. "Cherubic curls, with a dimple in your chin."

"Unfair, I know."

"All the same, I like you better as you are now. Your present self is kinder, somehow."

"I'll have you know I've a reputation for ruthlessness, not kindness."

"That is where you are wrong. Your strength belies your gentleness, as your crewmen no doubt know."

Jack's first thought upon waking the next morning was for Charlotte. Had she slept comfortably? Confound it, why did it matter how she slept? He disliked having women aboard, and the same went for his house.

He rebraided his hair and pulled on what he usually wore at home: a dark knitted jersey, dark trousers, and a navy coat. Mrs. Allen would not like the braid, but what of it? She would be seeing plenty of them here. Even Johnny lamented that his hair was not yet long enough.

Griffith was already at work in the kitchen when Jack came in. At once he began making a pot of coffee. All the while a thought simmered: Would she come down? And if so, what would be the best spot to share coffee?

The Great Cabin would be his choice; it was ideal for watching the sun rise. His bed made this location inappropriate.

The kitchen table was a cozy spot, but Griffith was fond of talk. Jack wandered into the dining room, still thinking. What about the main salon? He opened the door and went across to the windows. The sky was now gray.

Out in the vestibule, there was movement. Someone came lightly down the stairs and then through to the main door. It opened and then softly closed.

Jack drew back the draperies. He saw Charlotte swing a cloak across her shoulders. She was making for the beach stair.

Back and forth in the lane she paced. Was she waiting there for him? No, for her brother. Hers would be a long wait, as Johnny was likely fast asleep.

Jack returned to the kitchen, pocketed two tin cups, lit a lantern, and took up the coffee pot. If it was the cove Charlotte was after, then the cove she would have.

The sky was clouded over, but Charlotte did not mind. There was no wind, and the air had a delicious salty tang. From the cove below came the low rumble of waves. A lovely, lovely morning to explore, if only Johnny would come. To the east the sky was gray, giving her just enough light.

Charlotte pulled on her gloves and rubbed her hands for warmth. On her head she wore a knitted toque.

Sounds were magnified in the pre-dawn quiet. There came a click behind her—a door closing? —and then footfalls on gravel. Charlotte turned. Someone was coming toward her with a lantern. Johnny? No, it was a much taller person.

"Waiting for your brother?" Jack's voice called.

Charlotte's heart skipped a beat.

"I doubt we'll see him before breakfast," he added. "When I left him for the night, he was sitting on his bunk, talking a blue streak."

What else could Charlotte do but smile? "He promised so faithfully to come. I've been longing to explore the cove."

"Will I suffice as a guide? As to the time, you've chosen well. In winter there can be an eight-foot swing in the ebbing tide. Would you mind carrying the lantern? I have the coffee pot."

"Coffee!"

"We have a tradition to maintain, you and I."

That he would think such a thing was thrilling.

He hesitated. "Hold hard, you're not dressed warmly enough."

"There is no wind. My cloak might be old-fashioned, but it is lined with fur." She turned back a section to show him.

"Fair enough, but I still say you'll be cold. Since you have the lantern, you should go down first. Have a care. Gibby put in a new bannister rail, but the treads can be slick."

"What about your foot?"

"My foot is fine," he said shortly. "I see your hair is in excellent form this morning. Down your back in a braid, like mine."

Here was another reason to smile. Over her shoulder she said, "It's a reminder of old times when I was a girl."

"Ah yes, your sojourn at the seaside. You are a girl still, you know."

"Mrs. Allen will remain in her room today, so I needn't bother with my hair. I'll pin it up later."

She reached the bottom stair and stepped onto the sand. The sky was now pearl gray. Even so, Charlotte was grateful for the lantern. A sea bird wheeled overhead.

"This place, it's wonderful. How did you find it?"

He gestured. "I was stationed in Plymouth, which lies to the south; I came exploring. The land here is not good for farming, and this parcel happened to be for sale. I was a young lieutenant at the time; with my first real prize money I purchased these acres. I was poor for many years because of Cliff House."

"You must be very proud."

"Grateful, more like. God has been merciful to me, the sinner."

Charlotte noticed a skiff pulled high on the beach. "Yours?"

"Aye, and the sloop moored yonder. If we have a nice day, I'll take you out."

Charlotte gazed at the graceful, one-masted sailing vessel in the center of the bay, rolling gently with the swells. "I would love that."

"I must warn you, this is not the time of year for a pleasure cruise. The channel is deep, and a gale can blow up without warning. I dislike this clouded sky. It promises an angry sunrise."

"*Red sky at morning*? Is the saying true?"

"For this part of the world, yes. Sunrise is at eight; we breakfast at nine. We'd best have our coffee before it gets cold." He gestured toward a group of large rocks.

Charlotte went at once to the place he indicated, careful to light his way with the lantern. What looked like a sand beach was actually a mixture. Pebbles crunched beneath her feet.

She settled herself on a comfortable rock and found a secure spot for the lantern. Jack took a seat beside her. In the east, the sky was tinged pink. She could see him more clearly now. He was not wearing formal clothes, as at Laurelhurst. In fact, he looked more at ease than she had ever seen him.

She sighed, recalling their evening meal. Jack had asked a blessing, much as her grandfather used to do. His was a heartfelt prayer of thanks and not a recitation.

It was this place, with its rugged beauty, pristine and unspoiled. It brought out the best in people.

"I heard Captain Ord talking to Fleur last night. He has been very kind to her."

From a pocket, Jack produced two cups. He filled one and passed it to her. "Ord, talking to a girl? I'd say it's the other way round: she was being kind to him. Ord is notoriously bashful. We've not had women as guests before."

The tin cup was hot and warmed her gloved hands. "He explained about the Captain's Table after breakfast, and he told Fleur that she must come right at nine, same as any officer."

"That is very generous of him."

"She said to me later that she could not believe it. She has never been treated with so much respect."

"Thomas Ord is everything that is respectful, especially when it comes to women. He was bold enough to speak, which is something. But perhaps he did so because it was required."

"Is pressing clothes required too? Because when Fleur brought down a basket after dinner, he would not allow her to use the iron."

Jack lowered his cup. "You have got to be joking."

"Her very words. 'Such an important man,' she said, 'and yet he would not allow me to press Mrs. Allen's clothes.'"

"Ord did them?"

"I think so. He'd best have a care. When a man presses clothes, or does any of a woman's work, it is the most romantic gesture ever."

"I shouldn't laugh, but upon my word. Poor Thomas."

"Is he very smitten, do you think? Or perhaps only just a little. I can see why. Fleur is quite pretty."

"If he manages to sit beside her at church today, then we'll know."

Charlotte tore her gaze from Jack and looked to the horizon. After all, this was why she had come. At the edge of the sea, the sky was now a brilliant rose pink. "Shall we see a sunrise today?"

"For a moment, as the sun clears the horizon. Then it will disappear beneath the clouds." There was a pause. "I dislike this angry red sky."

Charlotte could not agree. This was surely the most beautiful sunrise she had ever seen. But that was probably because she was sharing it with Jack.

15 The Wind's Song

After Jack and the others returned from church, Charlotte disappeared. "It's Meg," said Allen, in answer to Jack's inquiry. "She does not handle illness well. Charlotte has been a godsend."

"What about the girl with the French name? Is she not paid to attend her?"

"Fleur is not precisely a lady's maid, but she cares for Meg's clothes and personal needs, and she also maintains her rooms. I am told she's a source of below-stairs information, a thing Meg craves. Which is why you might find Fleur in the kitchen from time to time."

"Shouldn't she be the one playing cards and reading aloud?"

"Charlotte is a family connection, and she shares amusing stories of her home life. To be honest," added Allen, "Charlotte's true talent is that of being a listener.

She does not mind when Meg tells the same story again and again."

Unfortunately, this rang very true. "In short," said Jack, "she seeks to please everyone."

"Is it any wonder that Meg prefers her company?"

"Miss Lucas is your guest, but while here she is also mine. I don't dictate how she spends her time, but I'd like to think she has some enjoyment."

Geoffrey Allen looked uncomfortable. He did not have an answer for this, and neither did Jack.

Late in the afternoon he encountered Charlotte on the landing. She eyed him with weary hesitation. "Do you think Mr. Griffith knows how to make a mustard plaster?"

"I take it your aunt is asking for one?"

"Among other things. Captain Ord brought up an easy chair for her; I am beyond grateful. She has been able to sleep for a bit."

"But not enough for you to have time to yourself."

She smiled a little. "The work of a companion."

"Is the arrangement now formal? I thought you were her guest."

"Our travels have brought a change. Mrs. Allen now depends on me to keep her comfortable and entertained."

"What about her maid?"

"Fleur is not employed to run a sickroom, a thing I have done many a time."

"A sickroom! The woman has a cold, not the plague! Might I remind you that you are a guest here?"

"Fleur is not idle. My aunt is silly about clothes, and Fleur does not task your staff with extra washing. Also, she is engaged tomorrow to polish your silver." Charlotte paused to tuck back a stray lock of hair. "Is there to be a party New Year's Eve?"

"It's our tradition, as I mentioned at Christmas. I did not know then that you would be here to enjoy it with us. This year there will be enough ladies for dancing."

"How wonderful!"

"It is Ord's idea, strongly seconded by me. If the weather is decent, the vicar and his wife plan to join us. Speaking of weather, come here." Jack opened a door.

Charlotte followed until she noticed where he led. She stopped at the threshold. "But these are your quarters."

"They are," he said, smiling. "The view is better up here. Come." He went to the windows and drew back the curtains. "No doubt you've heard the wind pick up. Have you looked out to sea recently?"

"Not at all."

"Then you are in for a surprise. In fact—" Jack broke off speaking and crossed to the wardrobe. "Here," he said, removing a heavy coat. "Put this on. We'll go out onto the balcony."

With reluctance, Charlotte allowed him to place his coat over her shoulders. "What about you? Won't you be cold?"

"I've spent years in all weather; I am inured to cold." One of the tall windows was built as a door; he opened it. At once the draperies began to flap. "Step lively now."

Charlotte came out, hugging the coat to keep it from blowing off. "Jack," she cried. "The sky!"

A sharp wall of dark clouds stretched menacingly across the horizon.

Jack spoke into her ear. "A squall line, we call it. The leading edge of a thunderstorm."

"Was this what you saw in the red sunrise?"

"Only in part. I was hoping it would have rained itself out by now. We see a squall line more often in spring than winter. I haven't decided if we should put up the storm shutters."

"By all means, do so."

"But then we won't be able to see the storm. Isn't that a favorite pastime of yours?"

She turned to face him. "Jasper, you are not to put your house in danger on my account!"

Jack considered the cloud. "I doubt we'll have a gale."

"Isn't it better to be safe than sorry?"

"Careful Charlotte, how much you miss. Shall we go down and stand on the beach stair in the wind? Put Gibby's new bannister rail to the test?"

"Is it safe?"

He laughed. "Is anything in life safe? One must be daring and take risks."

"The only risk I ever took did not end well."

"Well now, I don't know about that. Would you rather be aground at Lucas Lodge, having never taken a chance? Playing cards and taking tea and suffering the company of militiamen? Without hope for a change?"

"The dear life of a spinster."

"You are far too young to be that. Risks are how we grow, Diana."

"Or descend into misery. I suppose the ending of my story belongs to God. I might as well risk being blown off a cliff."

"I won't allow that to happen." Jack looked straight into her eyes. "Do you trust me?"

"No."

Jack burst out laughing. "Baggage! This storm is not so bad. Look to the cove; do you see how each wave has a white crest?"

"I've heard those are called white horses."

"Aye, and their size is not alarming. We'll have wind and a downpour, but this cloud's bark is worse than its bite."

"If you say so."

"The true terror is when the sea is ripped white, with my ship caught in the middle of it."

Charlotte returned her gaze to the cove. "I cannot imagine."

"Landsmen think we men of the sea are not devout. They are wrong. We pray often and heartily."

"I would very much like to stand on the stair in the wind. But what of my aunt? When she wakes, she'll expect to hear more from her book. And then there is the mustard plaster." Charlotte turned and left the balcony.

Jack followed and secured the door. "You've been reading to her all afternoon?"

"As I said before, it is the work of a companion."

"Putting it to the test, are you? And what have you decided? It's not as easy as it appears, is it?"

As Charlotte returned the coat, she caught sight of her reflection. "Oh dear. My poor hair."

Jack had to grin. "A new style?"

"It was, before the wind ruined it. Fleur braided it across the crown (a thing I cannot do) and then softened it by loosening sections of hair." She sighed. "Now all of it is loose. I'll have to wear that ruffled cap you do not like."

"I never said I didn't like your cap."

"Not in words."

How could he not laugh? "Fetch that cap and your cloak. We'll set Griffith to work on the mustard plaster, and Ord can bring it up for Fleur to deliver. He'll like that."

She gave him a look. "You shouldn't tease Captain Ord."

"But the temptation is irresistible. Hold this for a moment while I get my coat."

"A spyglass?"

"It'll be dark soon. If we're lucky, we'll see lightning in that squall line."

Charlotte's eyes grew even wider. There was no trace of weariness now.

As the night wore on, the storm grew in intensity. The wind howled round the corners of Cliff House, and below in the cove the sea roared. Jack wrestled with his pillow and his thoughts. Was he right to leave off the storm shutters? Was *Flicka* secure at her mooring? Was the skiff high enough on the beach? Presently he rolled out of bed, threw on some clothes, and came downstairs. To do what, he did not know. But it was better than tossing and turning for half the night.

Of all things, there was light in the dining room. Jack padded to the threshold in stocking feet and looked in. There, fully dressed and wrapped in a shawl, sat Charlotte with her elbows on the table.

"Couldn't sleep?" said Jack, coming in.

Startled, she looked up and then relaxed into a smile. "Not a wink. I should be able to sleep; this has not been an easy day."

"At last, an honest answer." Jack slid into a chair.

"Are you calling me a liar?"

"Not precisely. *Polite* is a better description. You cannot stand all the watches on your own, Diana," he said quietly, "or you'll be no good to anyone. Four hours on, four hours off. Fleur must take her share."

She sighed. "I suppose you are right."

There came a flash of lightning and the answering roll of thunder.

"Shall I make coffee?"

"No!" she cried. "You mustn't go into the kitchen."

His brows came up. "Is something wrong? A broken window? Flooding?"

"No, of course not. It's just that ..."

Jack spread his hands. "Well? What is it?"

"I don't know what to do," she confessed. "I've been sitting here thinking and thinking. Fleur and I came down to escape the noise from the storm. She went into the kitchen, and I remained here. She has been there a long while."

"Alone?"

"That's just it. Captain Ord was there when she went in, working on the household accounts or some such thing."

"I see."

"I heard them talking for the better part of an hour, but now they are silent. What should I do?"

"Should you do something?"

"Jack, I think he might be kissing her."

Jack did his best not to laugh. He gave a dry cough; he cleared his throat; he hid his grin with a hand. In the end, a guffaw escaped.

"But what if he is?"

"I hate to disappoint you, but no."

Still, his curiosity was aroused. Jack slipped from his chair, padded to the kitchen door, and put his ear to it. Nothing, save for the squall of rain against the windows.

He dropped his voice to a whisper. "How can you tell what is going on in there?"

"If you'd been around young children as much as I, you would know what the expression *too quiet* means."

"Perhaps they are pressing clothes?"

Charlotte did not laugh with him. "Surely I am mistaken. He cannot have been kissing her for all this time."

Jack grinned and resumed his seat. "I could point out that Thomas Ord is thorough in his work. He won't be rushed, save at dire need."

"Jasper!"

"In all seriousness, Thomas is too wise to be trapped by a maritime romance."

"Maritime?"

"Or housebound, in this case. It's the same thing, really: a whirlwind romance. In which people of unlike backgrounds and character are thrown together, in a way they would never be otherwise."

"How else are people to meet? A ballroom isn't much better."

"The heart is easily misled."

"Do you think so?"

"I mean no criticism of Miss Fleur. But in my experience, there are those who, because of ambition, are not dealing in good faith when it comes to romance."

Charlotte did not answer. The silence was punctuated by rainfall and the occasional rumble of thunder. Jack brought out his pipe and began to fill it.

"She must have hurt you very much."

Jack nearly dropped the pipe. "Who?"

"The girl for whom you built this house."

This touched a nerve. Annette was not a subject Jack discussed with anyone. But he knew Charlotte. She would continue to ask questions, unless he gave some kind of answer.

"You are right to call her a girl," he said slowly. "She was an admiral's daughter with grand plans, whether I liked them or not. I was a young officer, and the connection was flattering, at first." Jack paused. Annette was eight years his junior, far too young.

"Was she pretty?"

Jack caught the hesitation in Charlotte's voice. "Very pretty," he said. "And, like most beauties, extremely demanding. When I could not measure up—or rather, *would not*, for you know how stubborn I can be—she moved on to more compliant prey."

This answer seemed to please Charlotte.

"Cliff House I built of my own accord; she never saw it, nor was she interested. I was too green to understand every woman's fondness for society and a comfortable life."

"Those are important to most, yes."

"They are to you. *All I ask is a comfortable home*, you told me."

He heard her sigh. "I have since learned that *who* I share that home with is everything." There was a pause. "It is curious that you have never married, for you obviously built this house for a family. It's your place to come home to."

Jack despised questions about matrimony, and he should have been very annoyed. Instead he said mildly, "As a warrior returns to his castle? You might have something there."

From beneath his brows Jack stole another look. Yes, she was still thinking. At all costs he must turn the conversation, before more questions came up.

He gestured to the kitchen door. "It's still quiet in there; I am beginning to understand your concern. Perhaps we ought to make them aware of our presence?" He pushed back his chair.

"But if the wind and the thunder are not enough to deter them ..."

"I'm also thinking that we need a reason for being here, what our espionage agents call *cover*. I'll be right back." When Jack returned, he carried a branch of candles and a deck of playing cards.

Lightning flashed; thunder rattled the window panes.

"My nerves are not steady enough for piquet."

"Nor are mine." He passed her the deck of cards. "Shuffle these while I set the scene."

He returned with a bottle and two glasses. Charlotte's surprised expression brought a smile. Jack took possession of the cards and began dealing the entire deck.

"What in the world are we playing?"

"You'll never guess." He waited, anticipating her response. "War."

She clapped her hands in delight. "I've not played war for years. I am thought to be an expert at this game. Prepare to be vanquished, sir."

"You cannot cheat at war. It is a game of chance."

"I do not cheat—much."

He laughed. "Do we count to three before turning over our cards?"

"Yes, definitely. It makes more noise."

Jack won the first round; Charlotte won the second.

"I've been thinking. When Fleur and Captain Ord come out, we might be the ones with explaining to do."

Jack blew a cloud of smoke toward the kitchen door. He turned over a card, and so did Charlotte; she won the round.

Charlotte listed her reasons. "It is after two. Your men and my brother are at the Rest; my aunt and uncle are asleep. And here we are, whispering and playing cards, not to mention swilling down rum."

"Who's swilling? You haven't taken even one swallow. And this isn't rum."

"Grog, then."

He propped his chin on his hand. "What do you know about grog?"

"Wasn't it mentioned in *Robinson Crusoe*?"

"No."

She burst out laughing. "You are not an easy man to tease. Goodness, I am tired."

"I'll not let you off so easily. We are on mission, remember?" Jack tipped his head toward the kitchen.

"Then you'd best stop talking and get back to playing."

On the next draw, they each put down a seven. "War!" cried Charlotte. "Let's see, it's three down and one up. Are you ready?"

Charlotte won the round.

"It's as I told you," she said, collecting her pile of cards. "You are going down. I'll need to have Gibby come in with his fiddle."

Jack took a sip of wine. "Why would that be, Diana?"

"To play *Rule, Britannia*, of course."

"For me? I am touched."

"No, for *me*, when you are sent to the bottom. Scuttled."

"Not scuttled, dear girl, taken for prize. We do not sink ships unnecessarily."

She dimpled. "That assumes I would want you for a prize."

"Not *want* me?" With delight, Jack feigned heartbreak.

She laughed, and so did he. Truth to tell, this game was more amusing than any he'd played in years.

"You've won one battle only. Never underestimate Jack Blunt. Many are the men who've done so, to their peril."

Jack won the next round. He smacked his palm on the table. "Vindicated!"

The kitchen door creaked open; Captain Ord's head appeared. "Sir?" he said.

"What's all this?" teased Jack.

Ord gave him a measured look. "I could say the same, sir."

"Where is Miss Fleur?"

"She went up to bed, sir. I'm finishing my accounts."

"No Miss Fleur?" Jack exchanged a glance with Charlotte. "Very well, Ord. Carry on."

"What's he done with Fleur?" whispered Jack, as soon as the door swung shut. "She's got to be in there."

Charlotte brought a hand to her forehead. "Good heavens. Why did I not think of this sooner? Jasper, do you have a back staircase? For servants?"

"The servants' quarters aren't in use; I've never fitted them up, not having a need for—" And then he remembered. "Confound it! There *is* a stair, concealed behind a door. We don't use it."

"Apparently Fleur did."

Jack began to laugh.

"I am so sorry. I've kept you sitting here all this time, concerned for Fleur, when there was no need."

"Drink your wine, Diana. It will help you to sleep." Jack began to extinguish the candles. "It sounds like our storm has just about blown itself out."

She took up her candlestick with a sigh. "I'd forgotten that it takes forever to finish a game of war. We could have been here until breakfast."

"Which is why it's perfect for children. Keeps them busy."

As they passed the main salon, Charlotte darted inside. She came out with a pillow from one of the sofas. "May I borrow this? Mrs. Allen needed my pillows for her bed."

Jack followed her up the stairs. "Standing every watch and issuing the crew your own supplies, are you?" he said softly. "This is not the way to win a war, my girl."

Once upstairs, Jack lifted a pillow from his bed. Softly he padded to Charlotte's room and tapped on the door, praying that neither of the Allens would choose that moment to emerge.

The door opened a space, revealing Charlotte's surprised face.

Jack passed the pillow. "Sleep well, Diana."

16 At the Captain's Table

The force of habit was a curious thing. Charlotte had slept only a handful of hours, and yet here she was, wide awake before dawn. The wind no longer buffeted the house, and the sea was quiet. Just as Jack predicted, the storm had passed. If only the storm inside her heart would do the same!

Charlotte clutched his pillow to her heart. She must be sensible. There was no hidden message here. His pillow was kindly offered, simply because she had a need. Jack Blunt was like that. He could be brusque, almost fierce, in his opinions, but he was also considerate.

How in the world had such a man become her friend?

For he genuinely liked her, a thing that was entirely unique. Gentlemen were polite to her, or else they overlooked her or, like her father and brothers, they relied upon her. But Jack enjoyed her company. He sought her out in order to talk with her.

Instead of talking *at* her, as Mr. Collins had done.

Charlotte sighed some more and pressed his pillow to her cheek. These days away from home had become the sweetest of her life.

Jack, bless him, was chivalry itself. Never did he try to kiss her or hold her hand. Had he ever so much as offered his arm to her? Perhaps once or twice, but without romantic intent. This was disappointing, but Charlotte's aching heart rejoiced. He offered no false hope.

Outside the bedchamber door came a scuffle and a metallic clank, which announced the delivery of the canister of hot water and a small lamp. Kindling and firewood were here in her room; all she need do was start her own fire. In most houses this would be unmannerly, but there was no housemaid here. Jack's crewmen were surprisingly modest.

A short time later, dressed for the day, Charlotte descended to the vestibule. On the seat of a chair was a lantern, cheerfully burning. What else could she do but smile? Dear, considerate Jack! He had ordered this done for her. The tin cups and his pipe were missing, an indication that he was unable to join her today. However, he did not wish her to miss her walk. Still smiling, she drew on her gloves.

From the dining room came a scraping sound, as if chairs were being moved. At once Charlotte remembered the playing cards left out on the table—and heavens, the wine glasses and the bottle! Was she in time to clear them away?

Alas, no. A man she did not recognize was adding leaves to the table. "Good morning," she said, a little shyly.

He looked up. "Top o' the morning to you, miss. We'll have a crowd at the Table today and no mistake. Pushing the boat out, the Cap'n is, what with the party and all."

Was Jack going somewhere in a boat? She watched the man bring additional chairs from the kitchen. As the door swung open and shut, there came the unmistakable scent of bacon and fried potatoes.

"All hands on deck," the man added. "That be the way of it this morning."

So Jack was either occupied elsewhere or asleep. She would not presume. Charlotte returned to the vestibule, put on her knit toque, and took up the lantern. Quietly she let herself out of the house.

The air felt warmer today, if such a thing were possible. In the east the sky grew light, but without the angry red of yesterday. It would be a beautiful day.

It was not until Charlotte was halfway down the beach stair that she heard a shout. She turned to see Jack, coffeepot in hand, descending. "You did not wait for me?" he called.

"You're awake?" was all she could think to say.

"Of course I'm awake." He came level with her. "Do you think me a shirker, lying abed when there's work to be done?"

"Work? So that is what you think of my company!"

He laughed with her, and together they resumed the descent. "I was hoping to show you the Wayfarers' farm and the outbuildings, after you have filled your pocket with shells."

"We can go up now," she offered.

"And miss a prime opportunity for beachcombing? Let's see what the wind and waves have brought you."

Charlotte steeled her heart against the beauty of his smile. "I thought you were sleeping," she confessed, "because I kept you up so late."

"The storm kept me up. You kept me company."

When they reached the bottom of the stair, he paused. "I'd like you to stay for the Table today, instead of slinking away, as is your habit."

"Did you say *slinking*?"

"I did, and it is what you do. We have business to discuss, and I'd like to hear your ideas."

"Why? You are the Captain; you give the orders."

"Do you think me so stupid as to disregard good advice?"

"Will this be before or after you push the boat out?"

"Come again?"

"The man in the dining room said you were *pushing the boat out.*"

Jack's face cleared. "Ah. That would be Wiggy. And he means that I am spending money freely."

Charlotte stepped onto the sand. "Indeed, I think that's all you do here. How can you afford to support all this?"

Jack fell into step alongside her. "I wonder that myself sometimes. Cliff House and the Wayfarers fritter money like a wife. Here's hoping the war will ramp up again so that I can replenish our coffers."

It was as if a cold hand closed around Charlotte's heart. "W-what do you mean?"

"On a beautiful morning like this? Not a blessed thing. We're not out of money yet, my girl. Look, here comes our friend, the sun. The sea will blue up, and if you can ignore the cold, you'll have a taste of summer."

Breakfast was crowded today; even her uncle was present. When Fleur came in, Captain Ord placed a chair for her alongside his. Charlotte would have laughed, except that Jack did the same for her. Was it proper to be placed so close beside him? He would be leading the meeting; surely someone else should have her seat. But here she was.

His nearness made it easy to ask questions. "When the men say *Captain*, why do they mean only you and not Captain Ord?"

Jack put down his cup. "Ord's proper rank is Commander. Captain is a courtesy title." He lowered his voice. "Tomorrow night, you'll see one epaulette on his shoulder. That is, if Ord doesn't take to wearing his dress coat sooner to impress Miss Fleur."

"He seems desperately smitten," she whispered back. "Do you think they are holding hands beneath the table?"

Jack quirked an eyebrow.

"I read about that in a novel."

"Not the one with the sinister baron!"

Charlotte dissolved into giggles.

"You read too many romances, Diana."

If he only knew the truth.! This was anything but so!

Jack rapped on the table. “Will everyone be so kind as to take a seat?” Captain Ord placed a ledger before him, and Jack opened it. While stragglers came in and the last of the plates were being cleared, he turned to Charlotte. “Do all your romantic ideas come from books?”

“What other source is there?” she whispered back. “Certainly not Mr. Collins.”

She was rewarded with a wink. Jack turned to Captain Ord. “Let’s get down to business, shall we?”

“Aye, aye, sir.” Captain Ord raised his voice. “You heard the Captain, gentlemen. Captain’s Table is hereby called to order.”

This meeting was a new experience for Charlotte. So much of her time had been spent among women, but now she was surrounded by men. These were weathered fellows, many deeply tanned by the sun; men from every corner of the Empire, who had labored under hardships that Charlotte could never imagine. One wore an eye patch; several were missing teeth. But this she only noticed because of the smiles. Cliff House was not a perfect place, but its residents shared a happy spirit.

Roll was called, and the day’s activities were listed. Damage from the storm was catalogued, and assignments for repair were given out. An impoverished seaman by the name of Payne was submitted for consideration. There was even a report on the newest resident, John Lucas.

"Jono is making fine progress, Cap'n. It's a pleasure to have a boy with a bit o' mathematics lodged in his brain-pan."

The man speaking must be Flynn, the navigator. Was Johnny's nickname *Jono*? How Richard would laugh!

"Is there any discussion?"

Someone else spoke up. "We'd like to borrow the model of the frigate from the Great Cabin, sir, to help him learn the rigging."

"Permission granted."

Another man said, "If the weather holds fair, Cap'n, we're keen to take the sloop out. On New Year's Day, that would be, sir. Me and some of the crew, as Jono's never been to sea."

Jack had no objection. "Have you room to include Mr. Allen in your number?"

"Aye, Cap'n. That we do, if he's willing."

"Oh, but I am," said Mr. Allen.

If was something to see her uncle grin like a schoolboy. Apparently his gout was much improved.

Assignments for the New Year's Eve party were given out. Johnny was part of a group that would wash the dishes. The meal would be a simple one, as all the crew-men were invited, and no one wished to be confined to the kitchen for the entire night. There followed a friendly dispute over decorating the rooms, a thing called *dressing ship*. Apparently this was a popular assignment.

Jack then announced that today Mr. Allen would be formalizing a transfer of property. "Congratulations to our own Elijah Sims, not only for taking on a difficult apprenticeship, but also for excelling so handily."

At the far end of the table, a dark-skinned man was beaming. "Kirkby Quay now has a competent blacksmith, and Simmy, through your diligence, you have acquired the smithy and a fine house."

There followed applause and shouts of "Huzzah!" and "Good old Simmy!"

"Also, I have learned that Edward Gibson—Gibby—has not only sold the skiff he's been working on, but has orders for two more."

Now it was Gibby's turn to grin, as congratulations poured in.

"Are there any other concerns?"

This time, no one said a thing.

Take a risk, he'd said. Very well, she would. Charlotte put up a hand and was recognized.

"First of all, I would like to thank each of you, most sincerely, for the care you have given to my brother and to Mrs. Allen, my aunt. Bringing that heavy chair up to her room was not an easy undertaking. Mr. Griffith, you have been tireless in preparing beef tea and poultices and who knows what else. Words alone are not adequate to convey my thanks."

One of the men spoke up. "Well, miss, if it comes to thanking us, we'd like to hear the rest o' the story. The one as you were reading out when we brought in the chair. About the evil baron and the lassie."

Charlotte was taken aback. "Why, certainly, if you like. We can finish the book this afternoon. I'll have it sent down to my brother. He can read it to you on my behalf."

She heard Jack cough; was he laughing? How Johnny would dislike reading a romance to a crew of hardened seamen!

"Is there any discussion?"

"No indeed, sir," said someone.

"We loves a good yarn," said someone else.

Charlotte spoke up again. "There is one thing more. Fleur, we need to divide the duties of caring for Mrs. Allen. If we follow the example of our seafaring friends, it should not be too arduous. Four hours on, four hours off, just as they do at sea. Because of the easy chair"—Charlotte paused to give a friendly nod to Captain Ord—"she sleeps more often and more deeply, which provides a welcome respite for both of us."

"Very good, miss," said Fleur mildly.

Jack did not respond with a smile, and Charlotte understood it. Such a thing would not be appropriate. But there was a warm shine in his eyes just the same.

Was the meeting now at an end? Charlotte prepared to push back her chair. The men, however, sat quietly with bowed heads. To her surprise, Jack gave a short benediction, a prayer for the coming day.

Was this how he ran his ship?

Jack turned to his first officer. "I believe that covers it, Ord. We'll adjourn."

"Aye, aye, sir." Captain Ord raised his voice. "You heard the Captain, gentlemen. Captain's Table is now adjourned. Off you go."

There followed a scraping of chairs as the men rose to their feet.

"Simmy, Allen," called Jack, "we'll head out in twenty minutes, if that suits you."

He turned to Charlotte. "I'll not be seeing you until later this evening. We've a busy day ahead."

"Yes, and so have I. No doubt Mrs. Allen is awake and wondering where I am. Unless Fleur has already gone up."

Fleur was nowhere to be seen.

Jack's warm smile returned. "A timely reminder issued and received, without rancor. Well done, Diana. Carry on."

Surely this was the mildest of praise, the merest acknowledgement! Nevertheless, Charlotte sailed through her day with a smile and a song. She, who never sang save for in church!

17 Strike the Bell

New Year's Eve dawned bright and clear. Because there was much to be done, Charlotte offered to have their morning coffee in the salon.

"Forfeit our stroll along the shore? Not on your life," said Jack. "For too long I've neglected the beauty of the cove; I enjoy it as much as you do. Get your cloak and hat, and we'll be off."

Charlotte did not need to be told twice.

This morning he taught her to skip flat stones on the surface of the water, a thing Richard had once attempted. But unlike Richard, Jack Blunt did not give up. He stood behind her, speaking into her ear with a hand on her wrist to guide each toss. Charlotte's heart nearly burst with delight.

She ought to flirt with him, laughing and making use of her lashes. Lydia certainly would have done so. But

Charlotte did not know how to flirt. Instead, she concentrated on improving each toss. At last, a miracle. One of her stones skipped not once, but twice.

"Atta girl," crowed Jack. "You see? This is not so hard, once you know the way."

The sun came clear of the horizon, lighting the cliffs and making the water sparkle. Sea birds wheeled overhead. This was a memory Charlotte would treasure forever.

They returned to the house to find that the ceilings of the vestibule, dining room, and salon were now decorated. "They're old signal flags and number pennants, too faded to be used any longer," Jack told her. "No admiral would decorate with salvaged flags, but we prefer them. They've seen military action, just like us." He pointed. "That one, the letter P, has a bullet hole."

In the dining room, Captain Ord was working with a slate and a stack of place cards. Jack circled the table with narrowed eyes; he snatched up a card with distaste. "I shan't sit beside Mrs. Allen, Ord. Put her there, on the windward side of her husband." Charlotte then saw Jack take her own card and set it beside his place.

"You cannot do that," she protested. "Mr. and Mrs. Allen have precedence over the others, and most certainly over me. Mrs. Allen ought to sit to your right. On your left should be Mrs. Goodding."

"The vicar's wife may stay, but I do not intend to ruin my digestion by having to listen to Mrs. Allen's idiotic prattle."

Charlotte stood her ground. "This is proper social usage, Captain Blunt. We are not aboard one of your ships, where you have the freedom to seat your guests any which way. There are niceties to be observed."

"By whom? This is my house, and in my house I do as I please."

"Do not blame me when you offend Mr. and Mrs. Allen."

"Geoffrey won't care, and there is no pleasing Mrs. Allen. Everything I do offends her."

When his eyes held that icy look, there was no reasoning with Jack Blunt.

"Jasper," she told him later, "I cannot sit beside you tonight. Not again. People will begin saying things."

A frown descended. "What kind of things? Blast it all, do you mean about you and me? Don't sell me a dog! I am old enough to be your father."

"I *beg* your pardon? Only if you were fathering children when you were Johnny's age!"

He laughed at her.

"Jack Blunt, you are the most aggravating man!"

"Why, thank you."

"You are as stubborn as my *grandfather*!"

His eyes now held a twinkle. "I daresay I am worse. Where ought you to sit, Diana? According to the exacting rules of social precedence?"

She waved her hand. "At the other end of the table, among your lesser officers."

"With men you do not know and with whom you have little in common? That makes for heavy going when it comes to conversation."

"As if I am not skilled enough or well-mannered enough to make my way! I'll have you know that I am able to converse with anyone. And I often do."

"Egad," he said, smiling.

Charlotte was not finished. "Often at dinners I am seated apart from my well-born friends. My father might be a newly-made knight, but hostesses do not take that into account when it comes to me. If there is a dull or boring guest, he is sure to be my dinner partner."

"And you, naturally, make no objection."

"Why should I? I am the guest, subject to the will of my hostess."

"Thank you for making my point. You are *my* guest, and in this you are subject to *my* will."

Charlotte ground her teeth. How she longed to stamp her foot at him!

He folded his arms across his chest. "If I must *nail* your name card to the dining table, so be it."

"Oh very well. Have it your way. But do not be surprised when people begin linking our names and making horrid insinuations."

The twinkle was back. "Horrid, eh? You are making my points for me today."

"I did not mean to insult you, and you know it."

"I do know it," he said more gently, with a smile that tore at Charlotte's heart. "Won't you rescue me from Mrs. Allen? Please? You, of all people, know what she is like."

Charlotte's resolution was in tatters. "You once told me that you are known to be *ruthless*, Jack Blunt. I can now see why."

He spread his hands. "Has it taken you all this time to figure that out? And here I thought you were uncommonly perceptive."

"You, sir, do not fight fairly."

"I warned you not to underestimate me."

"It would serve you right if gossip about us were to *explode*! And my uncle, being concerned for my already-ruined reputation, were to insist that—"

His smile was provoking. "That what?"

"You know what."

"That I marry you? It is highly unlikely that Allen would plot such a course. Not many fates are worse."

"Worse for you? Like what? Prison? Being boiled in oil? Fed to lions?"

"Not for *me*, stupid girl," he fairly growled. "For you. I would make a detestable husband."

"But I—" Charlotte brushed away an angry tear.

"Come now, Diana, let's not argue any more. I take it all back."

She looked at him unhappily.

"I've upset you, which is the last thing I meant to do."

"I am only attempting to protect you from criticism."

"My dear girl, criticism from whom? My men won't care. Neither will the vicar and his wife. Allen will laugh." He paused. "Do you *wish* to sit at the far end of the table?"

"Of course not," she said in a small voice.

"Then sit beside me. There is no way to please everyone."

She sighed heavily.

"Diana, look at me."

Charlotte raised reluctant eyes to his.

"Is it so hard to please yourself?"

"Sometimes."

"Then let tonight be one of the times that you do."

That evening Charlotte came down to the vestibule behind her aunt and uncle. Mrs. Allen was looking better than she had in days.

"Is it not fortunate that my new gown was ready in time for our travels?" Mrs. Allen was saying. "Not to mention, in time for this party? A new gown for a new year."

Charlotte had a sudden, unreasonable yearning for a new dress. When she wore this blue gown to Mr. Bingley's ball, it did not matter that it was several years old. But tonight was different. How she longed to be pretty!

"Welcome to our humble celebration." The deep voice was Jack's. Charlotte slowed her descent, enjoying the rainbow of colored flags and the glow of candlelight. But it was Captain Blunt, as he made his bow to her aunt and uncle, who stopped her in her tracks.

His beautiful portrait paled in comparison.

Charlotte grasped the bannister rail, overcome by the golden glitter of his officer's dress coat, with its splendid epaulettes. And then there was the way the candlelight glanced off his tawny hair and beard.

Her heart was accustomed to pain, but the sight of him tonight took the ache to new heights.

And he thought he was old enough to be her father. This adorable man was anything but old! Was his hair graying at the temples? With a blond man, who could tell? Did he dislike the smile lines near his eyes? Who would notice those? Was it that he sometimes wore spectacles? Did he think spectacles aged him? Did he think she would care?

It was more likely that her own defects repelled him. But this was not right either. For too many years Charlotte had been rebuffed by young men. She knew the signs. Jack Blunt had never displayed even one.

And then Charlotte realized that Jack was speaking. "Our party lacks the magnificence of anything you would host, Mrs. Allen. We are simple men of the sea. But tonight, we have enough ladies for a little dancing. A few reels and the like, if you feel up to it."

"I just might, Captain Blunt, I just might." She and Mr. Allen passed through to the salon.

Fleur came down behind Charlotte. "Miss Fleur, welcome. Tonight you are our guest; I hope you will enjoy yourself. Captain Ord is in the kitchen overseeing things. I must confess, he looks rather lost. If you would care to take pity and lend a hand, I know he'd be grateful."

At once Fleur brightened. "Oh yes, sir! Thank you, sir. I'll go to him straightway."

"Captain Ord is not lost," said Charlotte, smiling. "He is one of the most competent men I've ever met."

"I merely said that he *looked* lost, as well he might, without her by his side. I must say," Jack added, "you are beautiful, Diana. Most girls wear white, but this shade of blue—"

"—is unusual, to say the least," she finished for him. "My mother chose it, as she thinks it is suitable for my age."

"Your blue complements mine perfectly."

Charlotte was still digesting the wonder of this when the vicar and his wife arrived. Another heart-rending moment! Here she was by Jack's side, greeting guests as if she were his hostess. As if this were her very own home.

Jack shook Mr. Goodding's hand. "I am so pleased that you are able to join us tonight."

Mr. Goodding turned to Charlotte. "You are in for a treat, Miss Lucas. Last year we were invited for the first time. This year, wild horses could not keep us away."

What a gathering! Officers all in uniform; crewmen looking their best. Mr. Griffith had prepared his famous stew with crumpets and various kinds of bread. Apparently seamen loved desserts, for the sideboard was loaded with cakes and pies.

Tables for the crew were quickly set up in the vestibule, a thing Johnny once would have scorned as *cousins' tables*. But not tonight. He looked happier than Charlotte had ever seen. Cheerful talk and laughter, as among friends, characterized this party. She could not help but compare the stiff formality of dinners in Meryton.

After the meal, everyone trooped into the salon, carrying chairs. The men arranged them not in groups, as in a Meryton drawing room, but in a large circle.

Jack placed his chair beside Charlotte's, as servings of pie were handed round. "Now we'll have stories," he told her. "Not that there is much truth in them."

At Jack's nod, a man jumped to his feet. Rubbing his hands together, he looked at each person in turn. "Settle in, ladies and mates, and gird up your loins. You're about to hear a tale o' the dread pirate Blackbeard."

"Ooh!" called several.

"This one's about the time he fell afoul of the Royal Navy—and me old grandad, Jerry Wright—off the coast o' Tortuga. It was like this, see—"

"Wiggy," complained a crewman. "We've heard that one a dozen times."

"Aye, but not our guests. And it gets better with the telling, lad."

"Ten pirates your grandad ran through the heart, instead of one?" Laughter.

"I like the mermaid story better," called someone else.

So of course they had to hear both, and many others as well.

Even Captain Ord joined in, with a thrilling tale of Trafalgar, the capture of the *Delphine.* "Too modest, Thomas," called Jack. "You're the hero of this piece." Needless to say, Fleur was beaming.

Gibby brought out his fiddle and announced that it was time for Commander Ord's famous jig. He launched into a sprightly tune.

"My dear," said Mrs. Allen, fanning herself, "I've had all I can take. Thank you for a lively evening, Captain Blunt."

Charlotte hadn't the heart to summon Fleur just yet. "I'll take you up, ma'am; Fleur can bring your hot water shortly."

With care, she guided her aunt into the vestibule and up the stairs. "Such an evening! I've not laughed so much in years. These rustics do know how to tell a tale."

"It's a pity you'll miss the stroke of midnight, ma'am."

"I've had my share of midnights, my dear. That Captain Blunt. What cheek! Expecting me to dance the reel with him. At my age!"

"It was a compliment, dear Aunt."

"He should save his breath for the young women." But Charlotte could tell that Mrs. Allen was pleased.

She opened the door of her aunt's bedchamber, and Mrs. Allen went in. "I expect I shall sleep the day away tomorrow," she announced, "while your uncle enjoys his sail. Thursday will be for packing, and Friday we'll leave for Bath."

Friday?

"How glorious it will be to celebrate Epiphany at the Abbey. If we're in luck, Mr. Allen will eat all the things he shouldn't, his gout will flare up, and we'll have a lovely long stay in Bath while he recovers."

"Very good, ma'am," said Charlotte quietly. But this news was not good, not at all.

A few minutes later Fleur came in with the water, and together they worked to get Mrs. Allen into bed.

"I'd ask you to read to me tonight," she said to Charlotte, "but the music below makes hearing difficult."

It was the word *Friday* that made everything difficult.

Charlotte fluffed her aunt's pillows, turned back the coverlet, and added wood to the fire.

"Is there anything else that you require, ma'am?" said Fleur, dropping a curtsey.

"No, my dears. Enjoy the dancing."

Fleur extinguished the candle and came out. Charlotte caught her by the arm. "I've only just heard the news," she whispered. "We leave for Bath Friday morning."

The dismay on Fleur's face mirrored the pain in Charlotte's heart. "So soon?" she faltered.

Gibby's fiddle had fallen silent, which was strange. Unless—

"I think they might be waiting for us to begin the dancing."

Fleur dried her eyes and put up her chin. "Then we dance, miss, and let Friday take care of itself."

At the foot of the stairs waited Jack and Captain Ord. "All settled? Good."

Jack held out his hand. A little fearfully, Charlotte placed her hand in his, savoring the sensation of his fingers closing over hers. She ought to be wearing gloves for dancing and so should he. But here he was, leading her by the hand into the salon, as if it were the most natural thing in the world.

"It won't be long before we're ringing in the New Year. Eight bells for the old, eight bells for the new."

Gibby played the first bars of the reel, and the dancers arranged themselves in a set.

"This is a new tradition for us," said Jack. "No wallflowers among our ladies tonight. You'll not sit out a single dance." He led her to the front of the line.

Charlotte had never opened a ball in her life, and yet here she was, standing opposite the most distinguished man in the room. Who also happened to be smiling at her.

Is it so hard to please yourself?

Not tonight. Her aunt was upstairs, and no one else cared. What did it matter if she dropped her guard a bit? If she returned every one of Jack's dangerously adorable smiles? If she laughed and twirled foolishly with him?

With all her heart she would dance this reel. Friday would have to take care of itself.

18 Like a Whetted Knife

Jack did not need to be told that something was wrong. This morning Charlotte was gazing at the cove as a condemned man might savor his final moments of freedom. This was such a change from yesterday. What had stolen the sparkle from her eyes?

"It is heartening to know that Johnny will be here with you," she said at last. Thereby implying that she would not be. That was the feel of it.

She added, "What you do here for your men is admirable."

Did she wish to converse about the Wayfarers? Very well, he would follow her lead. "So many are cast ashore without a safe haven. I offer that, if only for a time, to men who have served under me or who are known to my officers."

"And it is costly."

Jack took up a pebble and cast it into the surf. "I complain from time to time, but I shouldn't. The home farm is self-supporting. Your brother will work, same as the others, to feed himself. I have no truck with drunks or profligates, and so far we've been fortunate. These are clever fellows; they're always making improvements. The glass house, for instance, was something Gibby and Martin put up last year. I merely paid for the materials. Wiggy has us raising rabbits; Helms has plans to expand the poultry yard and pastures."

He sent a sidelong look in her direction, but she remained silent.

"Many take on odd jobs, find their feet, and move on, like Sims. Others are ashore on half-pay, like Ord. They're waiting to be called back, hoping for promotion." Jack paused. "I imagine Thomas has been rethinking the wisdom of that course."

"Because of Fleur?"

Jack smiled a little. "He now has a reason to remain ashore."

"Do you have a—that is, you cannot possibly help everyone, of course."

Now why did Jack have the feeling that this was not what Charlotte wished to say? Given her somber mood, it would be pointless to tease her about it.

"At present we house fifteen, plus your brother. A mere thimbleful in an ocean of need."

"But for the ones you help, it makes a great difference. You could have left your past behind; no one would blame you if you did."

"As a young man, this was certainly my intent. But I owe my life to men such as these, and to others who have passed on. I am an only son, but my years at sea have given me brothers."

"Will Captain Ord return to sea?"

"I believe so. Although if he plans to marry, he'd do better to sell out. Ours is a life of loss, with many partings and much hardship. I am the one to write the letters, you see. I greet expectant families, who are waiting for their loved one at the wharf, with the shattering news of death. Miss Fleur could one day be among them."

"Yet you will return to serve?"

"Once my foot is fully healed, I am eligible to be called up."

"Do you regret that?"

"Sometimes. Then I remember those who, even now, man our ships in all weather and manner of hardship, to protect us. How can I not do my part?"

The sun peeked over the horizon, lighting the cliffs "Look there. I didn't realize that they were leaving so early."

Sure enough, men were coming down the beach stair, carrying canvas bags and boxed supplies.

"They're taking on provisions. Then they'll scrub down the deck and rig the sails. Your uncle and brother will come aboard later. Would you like to help them shove off?"

Her interest was sincere, and she watched as Jack and the others half-carried the skiff to the water's edge. It did not take long to load, and soon Jack was helping push the skiff toward the breakers.

"This part is impossible to do without getting wet," he called to her. Sure enough, the next wave brought the water to his knees.

"Thankee, sir! We're away!" cried Martin, hoisting himself up and over the gunwale. Soon two pairs of oars were moving in concert. Jack retraced his steps through the backwash to Charlotte.

"Blast," he said, grinning at her. "That water is freezing!" His trousers were soaked from the knees down.

Charlotte's gaze, however, was fixed on the skiff. "But they must cross the surf! What if they become—I don't know the word."

"Swamped? Foundered? Not likely." He came to stand beside her. "Our cove is protected from the largest swells. Moreover, these fellows have been doing this for years."

Even so, he heard Charlotte catch her breath as the bow of the skiff crested a wave.

Once free of the surf, the men made steady progress. Soon they reached the mooring and began handing up the provisions and gear.

"It looks to be a beautiful day for a sail," Jack said. "The breeze is picking up."

"Will they remain out there until the others come?"

"Probably. A pair of them will run the skiff back. The *Flicka* sleeps four; five if the gear is turned out of the starboard berth. I imagine they might tuck in for a catnap."

"Why do you not go with them?"

"Well, you know, Allen will enjoy it more. He doesn't get out enough. To be honest—"

Jack dug the toe of his waterlogged shoe into the sand. To be honest, he did not go because he did not like to give up his stroll with her. Confound it, why was he reluctant to say so?

Instead he said, "Would you like to sit down?"

Jack retrieved the coffee pot, and together they picked their way over to the group of large rocks. Charlotte sat with a sigh, her gaze fixed on the sea. That longing look was back.

He filled her cup and passed it. "There's something on your mind."

She nodded.

He found a seat beside her. "Tell me."

She took a sip of coffee before speaking. "Mrs. Allen wishes to leave for Bath Friday morning."

Now it was Jack's turn to sigh. The day after tomorrow. What could he say? The last thing she needed was a trite condolence.

"It shouldn't come as a surprise, really." There was a catch in Charlotte's voice. "Our intent was to stay for a few days only. My aunt's illness changed all that. Now that she is feeling better, she is eager to be gone."

"I—we shall miss you." Jack stole a look at her. Was he imagining it, or were there tears in her eyes?

"I have loved every moment of my time here, please believe that." She hesitated and then added, "Even if I haven't been able to win a fortune at cards."

Jack caught her eye. "You could try tonight after dinner," he said with a smile. "Make a killing? Leave with your purse stuffed with pieces of eight?"

But Charlotte wasn't having any. "I'm no match for your ruthlessness today. In fact, I ought to go up and see how my aunt is faring. Fleur is probably with her now."

"But Diana—"

Charlotte returned the cup and rose to her feet. After a final look at the sunlit water, she turned and made for the beach stair. Up she went, without a backward glance.

Jack quietly gathered the cups and coffee pot. There was a word for the way he was feeling: *bereft.*

In silence he followed in her wake.

Allen, Johnny, and Flynn trooped in to breakfast, eager to be on their way. Allen remarked, as he filled his cup with tea, "There is nothing so fine, my boy, so worth doing, as messing about in boats."

An unusual way to put it, but true nonetheless.

"Hear, hear," called Flynn, raising his cup.

The Captain's Table, for which Charlotte dutifully remained, was brief today, as it included only the officers. Jack studied her wan expression. It would be easier to bear with petulance or pouting; perhaps he could have teased her out of the dismals. But to see her efforts to cover sadness with cheerful conversation cut Jack to the quick.

Fleur had Mrs. Allen ready in time to bid bon voyage to the sailors, and then she went into the salon. His salon. Blast the woman, she claimed it for her own use, prowling through his gear and rearranging items on the mantelpiece.

Jack decided to stay. Mrs. Allen needed watching.

Ord came in with a large basket. "Are these what you were wanting, miss?"

Charlotte thanked him and opened her work box. Confound it, these were Johnny's clothes! Did she intend to do his mending?

Meanwhile, Mrs. Allen talked on. "My dear, did I tell you about the time I attended the hunt ball at Melton Mobray, and General Clipton asked me to dance?"

"I've forgotten so many of the details," was Charlotte's patient reply. "Won't you tell it me again?"

Apparently, this was the right thing to say to Mrs. Allen. At once, she was off like a shot.

Jack took out his pipe but encountered a burning look from Charlotte. He frowned at her, but she held her ground, which was probably just as well. Even though this was his house, Mrs. Allen would give him a scold. Charlotte wouldn't like that.

Jack sighed and opened the newspaper.

Presently Mrs. Allen wearied of talking and asked Charlotte to read to her. "The lighthearted story, my dear, not the romance."

"Of course." She brought out a book and said, for his benefit, "This is Chapter 10 from *Illustrations and Obscurities by Messieurs Tag, Rag, and Bobtail.*"

Was she serious? Over the top of his spectacles, Jack gave Charlotte a look. "How's that again?"

She showed the title page. "*With an Illuminating Index.*"

With difficulty, Jack disguised a smirk. "You don't say."

He was rewarded with a genuine grin. This was more like it!

But after a half-hour of Tag and Rag, Jack was ready to consign both to the devil. As for Bobtail, he could go hang! No sensible man would put up with such bilge. He said pointedly to Charlotte, "I'll be in the Great Cabin if you need me."

But he knew full well how it would be. He would see her again only at dinner, and after that Mrs. Allen would monopolize her time.

At least there was their morning stroll to look forward to. Mrs. Allen could not interfere there. Jack planned to show Charlotte the cave.

It was a long dinner, and an even longer evening, thanks to Meg Allen. At last there was one final thing to be done before Jack blew out his candle. He was a day behind in his reading, not that it mattered much. He turned a page.

> *Give not thy strength unto women, nor thy ways to that which destroyeth kings.*

If only Geoffrey Allen had read this before courting his silly wife! Jack read a few more verses.

Open thy mouth, judge righteously, and plead the cause of the poor and needy.

A tall order. As he told Charlotte earlier, any help given to the poor was a mere thimbleful.

Next came this:

Who can find a virtuous woman? For her price is far above rubies.

The heart of her husband doth safely trust in her, so that he shall have no need of spoil.

She will do him good and not evil all the days of her—

A tapping at the door interrupted. Jack glanced at the clock. Ord was certainly up late. "Come," he called, closing the Bible.

The door creaked open, and then silence. Jack looked over the top of his spectacles. There stood not Thomas Ord, but Charlotte, holding a candlestick.

Jack drew a ragged breath. She wore a drab robe, tied temptingly in a half-hitch, with her hair tumbling over her shoulders. Her feet were bare.

He felt his lips curve into a reluctant smile. "Diana," he murmured. "When I told you yesterday to please yourself, I didn't mean—"

He was unable to continue. Desire, long buried, surged to life and took hold.

Confound it, she was beautiful.

Beautiful and desirable and here.

Alarm bells were sounding in Jack's head. This tactic had been tried before, without success. But never by someone so artlessly alluring. And never by someone whose company he so thoroughly enjoyed.

There she stood, angelic and trembling, with wide eyes. No wonder she stared. He was tucked up in bed with his nightshirt on.

He was about to speak when she interrupted. "Jack, I've been so worried."

She had reason. There was plenty to worry about. Especially with her aunt's room only two doors away!

"Blow out your candle and close the door," he said softly.

She did so.

"Did anyone see you come?" She shook her head. "This is important. Did you hear any sound, anything at all? A door opening and then closing?"

"I-I didn't notice."

Kiss her first, ask questions later.

As if Jack needed reminding that his baser self was alive and well!

The clock struck eight bells, which startled her. Midnight, the end of the watch.

"Come here," he heard his voice say.

She came. But instead of casting herself into his arms, she just stood beside his bed, looking forlorn.

He could not allow her to struggle. He must help her. Jack dropped his voice to a whisper. "What troubles you, my heart?"

She began to wring her hands. "I don't know what to do. I've been looking and looking for them. For hours."

Jack struggled to digest this. Who in blue blazes were *them*? Hadn't she come looking for, well ... him?

"I even went out to the beach stair."

"Dressed as you are? With bare feet?"

She nodded. "But I could see nothing. Has the sloop come in? Are my brother and uncle safe? What if they are still out there?"

Relief rolled over Jack like a wave, followed immediately by massive, irrational disappointment. She had not come for him; she was worried about her brother!

He took a shuddering breath. How could he have so thoroughly misread the situation?

"I know this has an odd appearance," she said, speaking in a rush, "and I am terribly sorry to disturb. But you see, your room has the best view of the cove. And when I saw a light under your door"—she paused to swallow—"I acted without thinking and knocked. I did not realize you had retired for the night. Gracious, I should probably go. Yes, I cannot think what I am doing here."

Jack found his voice. "Since you are here, we might as well have a look."

"But I should not be! This is terribly wrong."

He ignored this. "Can you see well enough to walk to the windows? Softly, on the balls of your feet. You must not make a sound."

"Yes, I understand. But truly, Jack, I ought to leave. What must you think of me?"

"What I think is that you are worried about your brother. Off you go. Softly, now."

While Charlotte began to make her way across the darkened room, Jack lifted his robe from the chair and put it on. He tied a reef knot, strong and secure. He met her at the windows.

Charlotte's whisper came out of the shadows. "Shouldn't you be quiet?"

"Why? This is my room; I am supposed to walk about. Now then, the spyglass is there on the chart table; will you fetch it? Let's discover the fate of the *Flicka.*"

"Should we go out?"

"It's cold, but we'll see more that way. But first, would you kindly do something about that knot?"

"The knot in my sash? What's wrong with it?"

"Diana, it is a half-hitch. That sort of knot is meant to be untied."

"It is not!"

"To a man of the sea, the message is loud and clear."

"Jack!"

"The next time you go creeping about in the middle of the night, wearing your robe, *don't* use a half-hitch."

She tied another knot over it. "Is that better?"

"A granny's knot will suffice. Not for use when your life depends upon it, but adequate." He opened the door.

"My brother and uncle could be drowning," she grumbled, "and all you care about is a knot."

Jack hid a grin. This was more like it. "Pay attention; this is important," he said. "When you come out, keep to the shadows. There isn't much of a moon, but it's enough for you to be seen. We don't want that."

Jack walked directly to the railing and opened the spyglass.

"Shouldn't you keep to the shadows too?"

"I am supposed to be here, it's expected. What we cannot have are two people on the balcony or two sets of footfalls. Or," he added, "two people talking."

A silence stretched between them. The cold air was a great help to Jack; he could think more clearly now. It was much better to have Charlotte hidden from view. The way her hair spilled over her shoulders, for instance, and her tempting figure, covered only by that robe ...

Plague and the devil take it! A single thought was enough to do him in!

With effort, Jack took himself in hand. His eyes scanned the horizon. Of the *Flicka* there was no sign. He closed the spyglass.

"Why are you giving up? Are they lost?"

He turned. "There is a clue that might not be apparent to a landsman. Mark the wind."

"But there isn't any."

"Exactly. They are having to row back. Not an easy feat in a sloop, as it is not designed for that. It's more likely that they'll set a sea anchor, wait for daybreak, and hope the breeze picks up."

"They'll stay out all night?"

"Is there something wrong with that? I've been at sea for a month without making landfall."

"But—"

"Diana, in the excitement of teaching your brother, they probably went too far. When the wind dropped at sunset, they were becalmed."

"So they are out in the dark somewhere, stranded."

"Not precisely stranded and not lost either. Flynn is along. Ten to one he's got his navigational gear. In fact, they might be staying out purposely."

"What?"

"Are you picturing them as suffering? It's nothing of the sort! There are blankets below, and if I know Griffith, plenty of food. They have lanterns for light and a bottle or two to break open. Not every sea story was told last night, and there are shanties for Johnny to practice."

"Do you mean they are out there *singing*?"

Jack allowed himself the luxury of a grin. "And eating and toasting one another's health, yes."

"Oh," she cried. "I made a fool of myself, bursting into your quarters, invading your privacy, terrified that they were perishing and in need of help. And it was all for nothing? I could die of shame!"

Jack passed her the spyglass. "Have a look at the stars. The sky is uncommonly clear for this time of year."

"I shall never live this down. Not ever."

"Well now, I don't know. Is this better or worse than riding double on that horse?"

"Jack!"

"There is no harm done, Diana. No one will ever know."

He heard her unhappy huff. "Yet another incident we must take with us to our graves."

"Uncanny how those keep happening, isn't it? Look." He pointed to the sky. "Due south, just there, is Orion; do you see? It is especially bright tonight. And to starboard—to the right—is the constellation Taurus."

But Charlotte did not answer.

"Here now, you're shivering. We ought to go in."

She was truly cold, and Jack's first instinct was to wrap her in a blanket. However, the blankets were on his bed, and the bed invited trouble. Every moment she remained was dangerous.

He sent Charlotte back to her room, unlit candlestick in hand, with instructions to build up her fire for warmth. Then Jack shut the door and returned to the windows. Back and forth he paced, wrestling with his thoughts.

There was a reason he did not allow women aboard, and here was a fine example. By God's grace he had dodged a bullet tonight.

Even so, he knew that sleep would be long in coming. He'd got himself into an awful mess.

19 Such a Man as This

Charlotte came awake with a start. Had she slept? How was this possible? Last night her fear had been so real, so overwhelming. The vastness of the dark and untamed sea, so wild and unpredictable, with her brother on it, lost and adrift. She had prayed and prayed, begging God for Johnny's safe return.

Had they made it home? She threw back the blankets, stumbled to the windows, and pulled back the curtains. In the east the sky was lightening, but the waters of the cove remained dark. Was the sloop at the mooring, or was that only the skiff? There was no way to tell. Jack would know.

Jack.

One thing she would not do; she would not burst into Jack's bedchamber with more questions. Charlotte felt her insides turn to jelly, not out of love for him but from shame. What had she done last night? He must think her a madwoman!

And what fine trust in God's care and sufficiency! Instead of relying on Him, she had run straight to a man. To her beloved Jack.

Charlotte rubbed the sleep from her eyes. It was strange; the sky seemed quite light for so early in the day. She peered down at the lane. Was that Jack's lantern below? It was! Was she late?

The clock confirmed this. Charlotte hurried to pull on her oldest dress and braid her hair. Down the stairs she raced, stopping only to put on her cloak and knit toque.

Sure enough, he was standing at the head of the beach stair, coffee pot in hand. "We've a change of weather coming," he called to her. "Mark the sky."

Dear, considerate Jack. Not a word about her tardiness, only a pleasant greeting. Was it any wonder that she loved him? The sweet aroma of tobacco came to meet her, and this brought another smile. Why did he bother with that pipe? Once he got to talking, it always went out.

Above the horizon hovered a scattered line of small clouds, just beginning to blush pink. Of its own accord, the corner of her cloak billowed and flapped. Was a breeze picking up?

"The wind!" she cried joyously.

Jack pointed to the distant clouds. "'*Mare's tails and mackerel scales make lofty ships take in their sails*,'" he quoted. "Good morning."

Any nervousness Charlotte felt at meeting him melted away. At his feet was the lantern, and as was her habit, she took it up. "Shall we have another ferocious thunderstorm?"

"I think not, although time will tell. We've a good eight hours before the rain arrives; our truant sailors should be back well before then. Shall we go down? Once the tide turns, our time to explore will be short."

Charlotte began the descent, and he fell into step beside her. "The cave is round yonder headland, where the darker rock juts out. All along this section of coast are arches and sea stacks."

As he continued to talk, Charlotte sensed a difference in his manner. Was it constraint? Hesitation? Jack Blunt was never hesitant. What was wrong?

But of course. Last night.

Last night, when she invaded his bedchamber.

Last night, when he was wearing only his nightshirt!

Charlotte had been too overwrought to notice then, but she remembered now, all too clearly. His dear hair was not in its braid, was it? Goodness, it was loose, caressing his shoulders. The golden candlelight was warm and embracing, as was his smile ...

He was not smiling like that today.

Did he think she had thrown herself at him? She hadn't, but he might not know this. Gracious, did he think her *wanton*?

Charlotte's feet stumbled, and she grasped the bannister rail to steady herself. It was cold like ice. She'd forgotten her gloves.

"The cave empties out at low tide," Jack was saying.

Charlotte now focused her attention on each stair tread. People could say what they liked about sailors, but Jack Blunt had a fine sense of honor. He was one man who did not take advantage.

On the other hand, perhaps she was not enough to tempt him.

She stole a look. Jack's profile was solemn, almost stern.

Of course she was no temptation! This was why he'd joked about that knot and invited her to look at the stars! Even so, it was a melancholy truth to face.

Now he was speaking of the sea life within the cave, something about periwinkles and whelps and limpets. He was making conversation, as if he needed to fill the silence. But why? Their companionable silences had always been delightful. What had happened?

What had she destroyed last night when she came into his bedchamber?

When they reached the stair's end, he led the way to wet sand. "Easier for walking, as it is some distance to the headland," he remarked.

She now remembered his foot. Had he experienced pain during their previous strolls together? If so, why hadn't he mentioned it? And yet she suspected that something other than pain was at work here.

Plainly put, Jack seemed nervous. Yes, and so was she!

What should she do? Apologize afresh for embarrassing him? He hadn't held it against her last night; why should he do so now? Moreover, would she do more harm than good by reminding him of it?

And so Charlotte kept silent, praying just as fervently as she had last night, but this time for courage and presence of mind. She would explore the cave with dear Jack, the man whom she loved more than any other, simply because he wished it.

Tomorrow, she would bid him farewell. It was possible that she would never see him again. But today he was her companion. That would have to be enough.

Presently they reached the end of the cove. When a wave pulled back and the way was clear, Jack led her around the headland. There, plain as anything, was the cave's mouth. What a delightful discovery!

Once inside, Jack commandeered the lantern. The cave was surprisingly tall and quite deep, with a pebble beach at the far end. Sounds were magnified here. The surf outside rumbled, and each wave that entered the cave pulled back with a sharp hiss.

"At high tide in calm weather, you can bring a small rowboat in, although it's treacherous for the novice. The power of the swells is amplified in here."

The light from Jack's lantern glanced off the high walls. He helped her locate sea stars and colorful marine algae. The lower rock walls were covered with a kind of rough white mollusk. "Barnacles such as these will coat a ship's bottom. We call them *crusty foulers.*"

Charlotte ran her fingers across the sharp surface, delighting in the novelty. There were living creatures hiding within the closed armor!

"Sheathing the hull in copper helps," he added, "but it's still a trial to keep clean."

"What would happen to us if we were caught by the tide?"

"As you can see by the high-water mark, the cave does not fill completely." He pointed. "We'd have to stand in that small space up yonder until the water subsided. A perilous business during a winter storm or when the tides are unusually high; we could easily be dashed to pieces or swept out to sea."

Near the end of the cave was a rock shelf ideal for sitting. Jack settled the lantern and poured out a cup of coffee for her. Charlotte did not like the taste of coffee any better than before, but she did not care. Always its welcoming aroma would remind her of Jack.

Again she glanced at him. How she longed to see one of his affectionate smiles!

A small crab scuttled across the face of the rock. "Here now, weigh your anchor," he said, but not unkindly. "I've something important to discuss. Interlopers are not welcome."

Charlotte studied the damp surface of the rock. Perhaps she ought to clean it with her handkerchief before sitting down? But when she hunted in the pocket of her cloak, a white folded paper fell out. She gave a cry and lunged for it.

Jack was quicker, and at once his gaze met hers. "What in blue blazes is this?"

What else could she do but feign nonchalance? "It's nothing, nothing at all. I meant to give it to Captain Ord to post."

"Ord, eh? But you've always given your letters to me."

Trust Jack to remember that! And trust him to turn her letter over and read aloud the direction. "*Miss Whitby, Headmistress, Rose Park Ladies' Seminary, Bath.*"

Why was her heart hammering so? And why did he suddenly look so suspicious?

"It's a school I attended for several years," she hastened to say. "From about the time I was Johnny's age."

"Curious that you should write just now." Even in the dim light, she caught the flash in his eyes.

"I'd like to call upon her when I'm in Bath."

Jack consulted the letter. "Is this Miss Whitby a friend of yours?"

It was useless to lie to Jack. "Not—precisely."

"I thought so." Immediately he broke the seal and unfolded the letter.

"Jack, no!"

Charlotte made a swipe for it, but he held it out of reach. Out came his spectacles. It did not take him long to read.

"If you must know," she said, "schools advertise for students at the first of the new year."

"Apparently they advertise for *assistant teachers* as well," he fairly growled.

He would make her explain it! "You were very right when you said I should not suit as Mrs. Allen's companion. The work is more arduous than I thought. Therefore, I am looking into other ways of earning my living."

"At a blasted school? Not on my watch you won't."

"You have no say in the matter! The decision is not yours to make! Take a risk, you said. So I am."

"Not this kind of risk. By the powers, you are plotting a course for shipwreck! I forbid you to call on that woman."

Charlotte squared her shoulders. "I most certainly shall."

"Does your uncle know about this?"

Of course Jack would notice that she flinched. "Aha," he cried. "He doesn't, does he? Nor does your father. Am I right?"

"No one knows. It is none of their business. And it isn't as if there is a position open. I daresay Miss Whitby won't want me."

"Of course she will want you," he grumbled. "You are young and intelligent and hard-working. She would be a fool not to take you on. For a slave's wages."

"A beginning teacher can earn as much as twenty pounds. If I can convince Father to give me my pin money—"

"You're out there. He won't do it. No caring father would wish to saddle his girl with that life."

Jack's eyes bored into hers. "It isn't as if you are destitute or orphaned and alone in the world. There are plenty of women who *are*. And you, being more qualified for the position, remove one such woman's opportunity. You could humble yourself and return home. You might be surprised at what comes your way."

"No, thank you."

Charlotte realized that she was trembling. Never had she seen Jack Blunt so angry.

"One of these days, my Diana, your pride will choke you."

"Pride? You're a *fine* one to talk!"

He gave a sharp, unpleasant laugh. "Aye, my girl. You've met your match in me."

"It makes little difference," she cried, "since you are determined to hate me."

"*Hate* you?" He gave a ragged laugh. "On the contrary, I—"

But Charlotte was not finished. "I thought you would be the *one* person to understand. You, who know about defeat and how loathsome it is to face pity. Yes, *pity*! A teacher's past life is her own. No one says of her, 'What a shame that she destroyed her one chance at matrimony.'"

"One chance? So you think that's all you'll have?"

"Because of Father's elevation, of course it is. I've an impossible ladder to climb. I've not enough income to tempt a gentleman, and yet my education intimidates a tradesman."

"Then swap ladders."

"Perhaps I shall. Perhaps a kindly schoolmaster will be looking for a wife."

Again Jack's frown descended. "To blasted *slave* with him in his blasted school! For the rest of your earthly life!"

"At least he would not turn up his nose at my paltry settlement."

Jack spoke through shut teeth. "You deserve to marry for love."

"As if I would know love when I saw it. All I know, as you recall, is Mr. Collins. And if he had not been *forced* to find a wife just then, he would never have proposed." Charlotte put up her chin. "If a decent man wished to so much as kiss me, I'd not know how to do it."

"You'd know, all right."

Charlotte put her hands on her hips. "Pardon my ignorance. I lack your vast experience."

"Ah yes, my vast experience with women," he said bitterly. "Here we go."

A wave entered the cave with a hollow thump and then withdrew, rattling the pebbles.

"Kindly put away that scowl and explain it to me. You are the only man I can ask about these things."

"You have brothers."

"As if Richard knows anything! And if he did, he wouldn't tell me. Not the truth, anyway! I can certainly rely on you for *that*, Jack Blunt." She stepped up to face him. "You once offered me a lesson. Is that offer still good?"

"W-what?" he whispered.

"A kissing lesson. Surely you remember."

"That was offered in jest, as well you know. If it's a kiss you're looking for," he added roughly, "there are a dozen Wayfarers who will gladly oblige."

"I am not asking you to kiss me. Given your frame of mind, that would be impossible."

He gave a sharp laugh. "Not to mention inadvisable."

"I simply want you to explain it to me in theory. What happens when a loving man—be he viscount or deck-hand—wishes to kiss me?"

Jack was pale with anger; his breathing was labored.

"Please, Jasper?" said Charlotte more gently. "I honestly wish to know. There is no one else I can ask."

He gave her a dark look, and then he sighed heavily. "Very well. Come here. When a man wishes to kiss a girl, he— Hold hard, what are you doing?"

Charlotte finished pulling the knit toque from her head. "In romances, when it is time for the kiss, the hero often complains that the heroine's bonnet is in the way. Therefore, although this is only a toque—" She cast it to the ground.

His expression was now openly suspicious. "You know more than you are letting on."

"That is the extent of my knowledge, believe me. What comes next?"

"He will stand before you, thus."

Charlotte narrowed her eyes at him. "You are rather far away."

"Very well, he'll move closer." Jack did so.

"He would have to be nearer than that."

With obvious reluctance, Jack drew nearer still. She could now put out a hand and touch his chest.

She tipped back her head and looked him in the eye. "And then what? He'll put his arms around me?"

"No."

"Mr. Collins did."

"Mr. Collins was a blasted—er, he was unwise."

"The man will just stand there?"

"He will just stand there."

"Shouldn't he stroke my hair or touch my cheek?"

"Not an honest man."

Charlotte gave an impatient huff.

"And may I take this opportunity to inform you that at this point, your eyes should be closed?"

"Why?"

He quirked an eyebrow. "Because, Diana, it is customary."

"If I am kissing Mr. Collins, of course I would close my eyes. Anyone would."

He choked back a laugh. "Will you be serious? I am trying to give you a lesson. And very difficult you are making it for me."

"I beg your pardon. I promise to close my eyes when the time comes. Then what?"

"Then a kiss either happens, or it doesn't."

"Your information is faulty, sir. In all the books, the hero takes the beloved into his arms—"

"The sinister seducer, yes! You asked about *a man who loves you*. He'll not force himself on you."

"So I stand like this, with my eyes closed."

"Yes."

"And I wait."

"Yes."

She heard him sigh. Now what was he doing? Charlotte took a peek.

Jack's eyes were closed.

This adorable man was standing before her *with his eyes closed.*

Could it be that he was hoping for a kiss? Jack Blunt was hoping for a kiss from *her*?

Impossible! He'd been so angry. Well, and so had she.

On the other hand, what if he were waiting?

There was no time to decide or even think, for this precious moment would not last. Once Jack opened his eyes, all would be lost.

Desperation made Charlotte bold. She stood on tiptoe, took hold of the lapels of his coat, closed her eyes, and deliberately pressed her lips to his.

His lips were warm and tender, and his beard tickled. She now knew the reason for closed eyes: enjoyment! This was nothing like kissing Mr. Collins.

Any moment now Jack would push her away, and who would blame him? She certainly wouldn't. The poor man! And then he would laugh and say *Blast!* and joke about the lesson being a disaster.

But Charlotte did not care. She loved Jack Blunt with all her heart. She could not go through life having kissed only Mr. Collins; she just couldn't.

But Jack did not push her away. His lips were soft and inviting. And then she realized that his arms had come round her, pulling her close. As if he meant to hold her and enjoyed doing it.

Charlotte let go of his coat and slid her hands to his shoulders. She had begun by kissing him, but now he was kissing her.

Could it be that he cared for her a little?

Or, perhaps, a good deal more than a little? She pressed against him more closely. Wonder of wonders, she felt his hold on her tighten.

With a soft boom, a wave entered the cave and then receded with a gentle hiss. Outside, the sun lifted above the horizon, as seabirds cried and wheeled.

Charlotte's heart went soaring with them.

20 Rugged Serenade

Surely this was a delusion born of madness! It had to be that, because he'd ruined the morning in every way possible. Instead of confessing his love, Jack provoked a quarrel. Yet in spite of everything, here he was, embracing his beloved Charlotte and kissing her.

Or, more properly, she was kissing him.

She'd asked for a lesson, but he was the one being schooled. For here were guileless kisses, innocent and true. He was Charlotte's first love, but Jack was beginning to realize that she was also his. No other romance came close to touching his heart. Not like this.

A wave rolled in, striking the wall with a skittering whoosh. Jack paid it no mind.

The seclusion of the cave heightened their tryst deliciously. He adjusted his hold and deepened the kiss. Charlotte's response was to press against him more closely.

That she was lonely he knew, but so was he. Charlotte's tender kisses were as water to parched ground. He had been alone for years. So many years.

What a good thing it was that he hadn't kissed her last night! Even this cold, damp cave gave opportunity to temptation.

And yet Jack refused to be like Collins. His hands did not wander but remained at the small of Charlotte's back. It was Jack's lips that betrayed him. Of their own accord they parted, increasing the intimacy of the kiss.

Blast, what was he doing? Even Collins hadn't made such a sensual move. She would surely hate it and him! Reluctantly he prepared to release her. But instead of pulling away, Charlotte shyly responded in kind.

That she enjoyed such intimacy was both shocking and thrilling.

Jack knew then that he'd be building a new wing to the house—for at least a dozen children!

A wave surged into the cave, sweeping across both the pebbled beach and his feet. The tide had turned and was rising. Jack's response was to lift Charlotte to higher ground.

"By this day, my love," he whispered roughly. "How did you *ever* think that you are unromantic?"

"It's because of you! I hadn't met you!"

A delightful answer!

She reached up to touch his beard. "How could *you* think that you are too old?"

"But we've fifteen years between us."

"There you go again, thinking the worst. It's only thirteen."

As if two years made an essential difference!

"I've seen May-December alliances in the navy," he said quietly. "The result is often unhappy. But let's not argue anymore."

She nestled against his shoulder. "It isn't arguing to have an opinion."

"Speaking of opinions, do you truly wish to teach in that school? If so, I'll not stand in your way."

"I only pursued it because—" She hesitated. "Because if I must leave you, it doesn't matter where I go or what I do. When one is miserable, it is preferable to be overworked."

His fingers caressed the softness of her cheek. "My dearest love, I've little to offer you save heartache and separation. My happiness should not rob you of yours. I hope you won't come to regret this morning's work."

She pulled back. "Do you regret it?"

"I regret nothing. God knows I've been looking for you, and waiting for you, all my life."

"Dear Jack, why has it taken us so long to kiss?"

Her innocent honesty was adorable. "We've been kissing for well over a week, my heart. But with words and with glances."

"I prefer lips."

What else could Jack do but kiss her again?

He'd seen men his age fall in love; they were fools. Now he gladly joined their ranks. A fool, lost in adoration.

Presently Jack was able to say, "Won't you consider returning to Lucas Lodge so that I may court you?"

"Aren't you courting me now?"

"Ah, this would best be described as *securing the battery.* I must call on your father, lay my prospects before him, and ask for permission to address you—"

Charlotte interrupted. "As if I am not of age!"

"—instead of showing up on your arm like some Captain Sharp."

"You are no Captain Sharp, Jack Blunt."

"I know that, and you know that, but do your neighbors and friends?"

"You are everything that is respectable."

"Not entirely. Nor, as you recall, are you."

Her eyes were wide with amusement. "Are you saying that I am notorious?"

"*We* are notorious. A matched set."

She gave a delicious chuckle and snuggled against him. "I find that rather delightful, Captain Blunt."

"It could be said that we deserve one another."

"I entirely agree."

"It could also be said that if we don't make a run for it, we'll be caught by the tide."

"What?"

At once Jack released her and set the lantern and coffee pot above the water's reach. "Hold tight; here we go."

He lifted her in his arms and, at the first opportunity, carried her through the cold backsplash. As they emerged from the cave's mouth, salt spray struck him in the face.. Laughing, he brought her to higher ground.

The breeze had stiffened; the sky was now cloaked with low clouds. Jack set Charlotte on her feet and studied the horizon; there was no sign of the sloop. "You'll have rain for your travels tomorrow," he remarked.

"Must I leave you?"

"My heart, what other choice have we? Were you thinking we'd run off to Scotland?"

"*Could* we?"

Her voice held such hope! "Honey, Gretna is four hundred miles away." Even so, Jack was happy to discuss how an elopement might be accomplished. As they made their way along the shore, they talked over every aspect of this journey.

To Charlotte's credit, she faced the truth squarely. "Four days of punishing travel, and then we'd have the return. I suppose it isn't worth it."

"A course I'd chart with regret. We'd be married over the anvil all right, but battered and bruised and in a flame of temper. Heaven help the highwayman who'd attempt to rob us."

"I'd scold him, and you'd shoot him, and then where would we be?"

"Hauled before the magistrate. Some honeymoon."

When they reached the beach stair, Charlotte looked up at the house with a sigh. "I suppose we are late to breakfast."

Jack consulted his timepiece. "Not yet. You go on ahead. After a decent interval, I'll follow. Keep a weather eye on the horizon. If you happen to see the *Flicka* come round the point, be sure to shout *Sail Ho.*"

"Very well." She made no move to go, but gazed at him unhappily.

He covered her hands with both of his. "Courage, sweetheart. We'll see this through. Off you go."

Charlotte began her reluctant ascent, and Jack leaned against the bannister rail to watch her. Halfway up, she paused and looked back at him. Was she missing him already? He was certainly missing her! Jack allowed himself the luxury of forming his lips into a kiss.

Charlotte saw this, and at once her resolve collapsed. Down the stair she ran to him. What else could Jack do but open his arms?

"Do you know how much I love you?" she cried. "Do you know that all this—your house, the cove, your position—does not matter to me?"

"I know, honey," he whispered. "I know."

She took his face between her hands. "I would live with you in a shack by the side of the road, Jack Blunt. With only my paltry settlement money between us."

He felt his lips curve into a foolish smile. "It may come to that, my heart; this is an uncertain world. Be it fair weather or foul, together we'll face whatever comes."

Jack now kissed her without restraint. He felt her fingers travel across his shoulders and tangle in his hair. Then came another shock. She was unfastening his braid.

"Here we go," he whispered, as his hair loosened and was caught up by the breeze. How he longed to unfasten her hair, and the tie of her cloak, and—!

It was a very, very good thing that the tide had chased them from the cave.

"I am a novice at kissing," whispered Charlotte, twisting a lock of his hair around her fingers. "I hope you have not been disappointed."

"How could I be? Blast, do you mean in comparison to other women? Diana, my reputation as the wicked sea captain has been greatly exaggerated. Do you think I have ever kissed another woman like this?"

"Of course. Because—"

"Because nothing! This is new territory for both of us."

"It is?"

He kissed her again. "Much as I'd like to continue this conversation—"

She interrupted. "You are *so* right. Kissing *is* a conversation!"

Jack brought his forehead to rest against hers. "So it is."

"I never knew it could be so wonderful. Kissing you, that is. I would never, ever wish to kiss anyone else."

Did she understand the power she had over him? It was a struggle to form a coherent sentence. "Unfortunately," he said at last, "we can no longer delay returning to the house."

"I'm sorry. That is my fault."

"As much mine as yours. This I will say: we know where we are. There are no boundaries between us; all the walls are down."

Her bashful delight was like sunshine.

"We also know"—Jack paused to share her smile—"that we are untrustworthy together, my darling. We dare not visit the cave tomorrow."

"But, Jasper."

He gave her a measured look. "I understand," she whispered.

A familiar sound—the faint squeal of block-and-tackle rigging—caught Jack's attention. Reluctantly he turned round. "And here are your uncle and your brother."

The question was, how much had they seen? Jack stepped away from Charlotte and shouted, "Sail Ho!" as the sloop came about and entered the cove.

"I'll just go up now," she said quietly. "I take it I'm not to kiss you ..."

"Later," he whispered. "When your aunt is not by."

21 Step Lively!

Jack watched the men pick up the mooring, and then he set to work on his appearance. His trousers were wet below the knees, his shoes were soaked, sand was everywhere, and somehow his cap had gone missing. Moreover, his hair was in hopeless disarray. It took some hunting to find where Charlotte had flung the tie, and the breeze was no help with the braiding.

A sharp whistle came from the top of the stair. It was Ord, waving to him. Something was up.

Jack took the steps two at a time. The breeze was stronger up top, and it set the lapels of his coat to flapping.

"There's trouble, Jack. A Royal Marine."

"For you or for me?" But Jack already knew the answer.

"Also, there's a bit of a change regarding the Allens. The missus is up and stalking about, and she's determined to leave today. Ahead of the storm."

Jack was stunned to silence.

"I took the liberty of suggesting that Miss Lucas not go up to her aunt in her present state, sir."

"Why? She is known to walk the beach each morning."

Thomas Ord's eyes were sympathetic. "Aye, Jack. But so are you."

Blast. He hadn't been as secretive as he thought.

Jack found the marine at the kitchen table with a plate of eggs and toast. Fleur appeared to be fighting tears, and Charlotte was somber.

Ord went at once to Fleur's side. "Now Flossie, pour the sergeant some tea, there's a good girl. As soon as Griffith has fried up those sausages, you give him a nice, generous serving, see?"

Jack quirked an eyebrow. Flossie, was it? This from a man who struggled to speak three words to a woman! And was it his imagination, or did Ord give her shoulder an affectionate pat?

He stepped up to the marine. "I'm Captain Blunt; I understand you have something for me?"

The man pushed back his chair and stood. "Sergeant Ives, Royal Marines, sir. It's an honor to meet you, Captain," he added. "I've heard stories about you, sir."

Jack signed for the packet; a stiff thing covered in oilskin. Sergeant Ives saluted and then returned to his breakfast.

A summons. God only knew what that meant. There could be a crisis brewing, or this might be news of his promotion. During his time ashore, Jack had watched his name advance up the list. His gaze shifted to Charlotte, who was standing quietly in the corner. She looked as if she might cry. The timing could not be worse. There would be no opportunity for courting. Unless—

"Thomas," said Jack sharply. "I need the gig poled up, on the double. Get someone on that, will you? Miss Fleur, fetch gloves for Miss Lucas and a bonnet; it doesn't matter which one. At once, if you please."

He turned to Charlotte. "Put up your hair as best you can and wait outside at the back of the house. It's vital that you are not seen, particularly by your aunt and uncle. I'll be out directly."

Fleur came back with the gloves and a bonnet, and Charlotte put them on.

Jack tapped a fingernail against the oilskin packet. It was best not to open this just yet. He'd rather not lie to Henry Goodding.

He stepped over to Griffith, who was busy with breakfast. "Tell Ord to give Mrs. Allen any assistance she requires. No doubt she intends to outrace the storm. Her husband might have something to say about the change in plans, but I doubt it. If anyone asks, I'll return within the hour."

Jack shrugged into his overcoat and put on a hat.

"But Captain Blunt," said Charlotte.

"The sailing party will be coming in shortly. You need to be elsewhere."

He could tell that she had questions, but she did as she was told. Just as the gig was being brought up, he joined her outside.

"Where are we going?"

"Up with you, honey," he said, handing her into the gig. "I hope Goodding is awake, because time is of the essence."

Whoever readied the gig was considerate; there was a blanket on the bench. Jack spread it over Charlotte's lap and gave her the oilskin packet to hold. He took up the reins and the whip. "Walk on, Pellew," he called.

The breeze tugged at his hat. Jack urged the horse into a trot, and they were off.

As soon as they were out of sight of the house, Charlotte tucked a hand under his elbow and nestled close. "Did you hear what Captain Ord said? I am leaving today. Today, not tomorrow!"

"As it turns out, I could be leaving as well. For Portsmouth, probably, or Whitehall. I'll read the particulars later. Chin up, Diana. We're going to call on Henry Goodding."

"Now?" she protested. "It is far too early! My hair is a fright, my shoes are soaked, this is my oldest, ugliest dress, and I am simply covered with sand!"

"So am I. Goodding won't mind. Vicars are accustomed to unconventional callers. He'll understand when he learns the reason."

"What reason would that be?"

"That summons you are holding. If I'm called back, we'll need a—oh, blast!" Jack drew the gig to the side of the road.

"What shall we need? Why are you laughing?"

"Of all the ramshackle suitors, I am surely the worst! I'm wretchedly out of line, my love, but I'll do my best. The trouble is, a gig is not designed for kneeling." Jack set aside the whip, shifted the reins to his other hand, and eased out of his seat.

"What on earth are you doing?"

"It occurs to me that we shouldn't be making this call until after I have proposed. Therefore—"

"Weren't you planning to speak to Father first?"

"I was. But his majesty's navy has a way of fouling things up."

The gig rocked as Jack went down on one knee. The horse was restless. "Settle down, Pellew," called Jack. "Give a fellow a chance."

Charlotte's eyes were shining. "Jack Blunt, are you proposing marriage to me *at the side of the road*?"

He took possession of her gloved hand. "Not precisely the stuff of girlhood dreams, is it?"

"You have no idea."

"Moreover," Jack continued, as if he hadn't heard, "it's indicative of our future life together."

"Yes!" she cried.

"Honey, I haven't asked you yet."

"I mean, yes, it is indicative. And I don't mind at all. And I think it's starting to rain."

"Blast, so it is." Jack winced. "Sorry, I shouldn't have said that. Here, let me get the umbrella."

"I am fine, truly." Charlotte clung to his hand. "You were saying?"

He sighed. "I ought to have done this days ago, but—as you are no doubt aware—in matters of the heart I am a confounded coward. I, er, shouldn't have said that either. Blast."

He saw Charlotte take her lip between her teeth. Was laughter during a proposal a good thing? And now his leg was starting to cramp. Jack shifted his position. Pellew took several steps forward.

"Will you—do me the honor of becoming my wife?"

"Yes! Yes, a million times! Now tell me, why are we calling on Mr. Goodding? I take it we are not headed for Gretna."

"Not in the gig, no. We need a license, my heart."

"A marriage license?"

"I am hoping to persuade Goodding to speak to the bishop on our behalf." He hesitated and then added, "Do you know, I believe it is customary to give one's future bridegroom a kiss."

"Jasper Blunt, I am surprised at you. We are on mission, sir. We must hurry, before Mr. Goodding goes out or anything else happens! I can kiss you later, as much as you like, but this is important."

With a grin, Jack resumed his seat. "Aye, aye, ma'am. You heard the lady, Pellew. Step it up, sir!"

Pellew, being eager for a trot, was happy to oblige.

22 Come, Let's be Merry

"The license will be good for three months," said Mr. Goodding, "but only in this parish. I'll call on the bishop, and if he can get it recorded today, the soonest you can marry will be the 9th of January."

Jack was holding Charlotte's hand. "That should suffice."

"The 9th," echoed Charlotte. Oh dear, she must not laugh!

Jack's eyes met hers. "No promises, mind. I'll come for you as soon as I can."

"The 9th is perfect," she said, smiling.

Meanwhile, Mr. Goodding was clearing a corner of his desk. He pushed forward the standish and presented a sheet of paper. "If you'll each list your current parish, the name under which you were baptized, and your date of birth, that should do nicely. I take it that neither of you have previous marriages to disclose."

"None," said Jack quietly. He dipped the pen into the inkpot and began writing.

"I cannot tell you how much this pleases me. Emma was saying just the other day that—in fact, do you mind if I share your news? In strictest confidence, of course."

Jack smiled at Charlotte as he handed her the pen.

Henry Goodding pushed back his chair. "I'll take that as yes." He went to the door and opened it. "Emma, my love, come quickly," he called. "You'll never guess what has happened."

Charlotte began writing. She heard scurrying footfalls and then a crash. "Oh dear. I'm coming, Henry!"

A few moments later Mrs. Goodding appeared in the doorway, smiling and somewhat out of breath. Her cap was askew, with golden curls escaping, and she wore a work apron. Charlotte had forgotten how pretty she was, and how young.

"Look who's come for a marriage license."

"You're to be *married*?" Mrs. Gooding's friendly smile became radiant. "We must celebrate! Martha has baked the loveliest seed cakes. And tea; we'll have tea. Martha is with the baby, so this might take more than a minute."

"I doubt there is time—" began Mr. Goodding.

Charlotte was on her feet at once. "That would be lovely, thank you," she said. "Please, let me help you."

Charlotte came into the kitchen in Emma Goodding's wake. "You'll think me impertinent," said Mrs. Goodding, "but when I saw you standing beside Captain Blunt at the party, I said to myself, 'Those two are perfect together.' And now, here you are. This is beyond delightful."

She hunted up the breadboard and a seed cake. "It has meant the world to Henry, having Captain Blunt here. He is so well read. Henry says he was meant to go to Oxford, before his parents died. But of course, you know that. And he has had to live out his faith. To truly depend upon God, as our fishermen do."

Emma paused, knife in hand. "You cannot know how much this means to a clergyman like Henry, who is serious about his work. To have someone actually listen to his sermons, instead of falling asleep. Not that I blame our fishermen; theirs is a hard life, and I daresay they are tired. Also, Captain Blunt is able to advise Henry about problems in the parish.

"And I am talking too much; what must you think of me? It's just that I was wishing, when I met you, that we could be friends. And now you are marrying Captain Blunt and are here in my very own kitchen. My wish is coming true!"

Emma Goodding's smile became confiding. "I know we shall be good friends, because this kitchen is in a dreadful state, as I am hopelessly inexperienced and have only Martha to help me. Yet you are not turning up your nose, as my sisters would."

"Of course not. I hope you will call me Charlotte. Or Lottie, if you prefer."

What in the world? Why had she suggested this? No one called her Lottie, not even dear Elizabeth! And yet somehow, it seemed right. Emma was her first friend as a married woman, or she would be on the 9th. Oh, the irony of that date!

Emma lifted the teapot from the sideboard. "Tell me how you met Captain Blunt, Lottie. Did you know right away, as I did with Henry, that he was the only man for you?"

"I knew of him, for he is my uncle's heir," said Charlotte slowly. "But we did not meet until Christmas Eve."

"*This* Christmas Eve? Not even two weeks ago?"

Emma was pleased instead of being horrified. Nevertheless, Charlotte felt a blush rise to her cheeks. "It has been rather sudden, yes."

"Then it is a love story, as it was for me with Henry! He was only a vicar and poor, for Kirkby Quay is an unprosperous parish. But I did not care. Father was not happy. My sisters did very well for themselves; Caroline married a baronet. But when Mama died last year, no one could be kinder than Henry. He was so good to Father and so helpful, that Father quite forgave him for being poor. He said that I had made the best match of all, which was very generous of him."

Emma opened the canister and began spooning tea into the teapot. "There I go again! Talking about myself. So tell me, was your introduction romantic?"

"Do you want the truth?"

Emma put down the spoon. "Oh yes, please."

"My brother and I were traveling on the stage and were attacked by highwaymen. Captain Blunt rescued us."

Emma's mouth fell open. "Did he come riding on horseback?"

"He did, just as one of the highwaymen was threatening to kill me. Jack shot him dead."

"Lottie! That is amazing! Did he sweep you off your feet? Did he carry you away with him on the horse?"

Charlotte brought her hands to her cheeks. "Yes."

"Oh! This is simply too wonderful for words!"

"It is not precisely like a fairytale, because at first I disliked Jack thoroughly. However, even then I had to admit that he was handsome and brave." Charlotte paused. "Jack Blunt could marry anyone. Why in the world does he wish to marry me?"

Emma took down a tray. "I think I know why," she said quietly. "You must stay with us when you come for the wedding. In fact, we—"

A door creaked open; in bustled an older woman with a baby. "Here's your little man, all ready for his breakfast."

Emma began loading cups and saucers on a tray. "Thank you, Martha. Lottie, could you fill the teapot? Or better yet, would you mind holding David? I daren't take him now, as he becomes so hopeful. Martha, could you take this tray into Mr. Goodding's study, please? Oh, and several of the chickens have escaped. That awful gate is loose again."

"I'll fetch 'em back, ma'am. Don't you fret."

Charlotte held out her arms for Emma's baby. He was quite young, perhaps three months. "What an angel."

"Henry says his name means *beloved,*" said Emma, over her shoulder. "I shan't be able to stay, as he wants feeding."

Charlotte gazed into his sweet face and was rewarded with a toothless smile. She would very much like to have a dear boy named David. She said as much to Jack when they were driving back to Cliff House.

"I'm hoping for a houseful. However, you must tell me what is wrong with the 9th. I doubt we can bring it about by then, but it's possible."

"Jasper, that was to be my wedding day."

"To Collins?" Jack gave a shout of laughter. "And what have you there?" He indicated the bundle on Charlotte's lap.

"I think it's a seed cake. Emma gave it me to convince Mrs. Allen that I've been here. The idea is that you brought me to call on her. On the spur of the moment, as soon as I heard about our change in plans."

"And so I did." He paused. "Do you like the Goodings?"

"Very much."

"I'm glad to hear it. Goodding has been concerned for his wife. The village is small, and as you can probably tell, she is somewhat out of her element. He thinks she has been lonely. Your presence here will be a great help."

"Speaking of help, can you spare Gibby for a day or two? Emma's kitchen needs a few repairs, and it sounds as if the gate to the poultry yard is falling apart. She won't like it, but if Gibby were to show up with his tools and that smile of his ..."

Jack shifted the reins, put his arm around Charlotte, and drew her close. "Yes, my love. We can certainly spare Gibby."

As expected, Cliff House was abuzz with activity. "Where have you been, dear?" were the first words out of Mrs. Allen's mouth. "Good gracious, just look at you!"

"I came up from walking on the beach, ma'am, just as I always do. When I heard that we were leaving today, I simply *had* to call upon Mrs. Goodding, the vicar's wife. Captain Blunt agreed."

"He would! For all his rank, he is utterly ignorant of social niceties."

"He insisted on taking me in the gig."

"A fine thing, to be calling at breakfast; it simply is not done! Your mother is greatly at fault. And I thought her to be so genteel."

"I am sorry I inconvenienced you, Mrs. Allen," said Charlotte humbly. "Are we ready to depart now?"

"It will be at least another hour, for a gown I particularly wished to wear has not been pressed. I don't know what has come over Fleur! You'd best spend the time attending to your attire and your hair, dear. As for this dress of yours, it is fit only for the rubbish heap!"

Charlotte kept her eyes averted. Her dress was suddenly precious, if only for the memories of the morning.

"Finish your packing soon, for I heard that Mr. Ord tell someone to bring our trunks down."

Charlotte did not need to be told twice.

Sometime later, with her hair pinned up in a severe style and wearing a dress that was crisply pressed, if not fashionable, Charlotte waited in the salon. The signal flags were gone from the ceiling, along with all evidence of the party, but memories were alive. God willing, she would return to this house and build a life together with Jack.

That thought was beyond wonderful.

Charlotte's gaze was drawn to the painting over the mantelpiece, a vivid depiction of the *HMS Valiant* in battle. Before, this scene represented Jack's heroic career, but now it pictured his future. It was a violent, dangerous future.

This was reinforced a few minutes later when Jack came into the salon, in uniform and wearing a sword. Under his arm he carried a cocked hat.

"You look very fine. You are armed, I see."

"For travel. We'll leave shortly after you do; it's easier that way. An empty house preys on the mind." Jack lowered his voice. "It also helps to think about future plans."

The only answer for this was a kiss, and Charlotte made a little move. She caught herself in time. With so many people about, kissing Jack here was unwise. "Is this what you wear every day?"

"More or less. Behold my undress coat; what we used to call a working rig."

"The hat is impressive."

"Ah yes, the best part of an officer's uniform." He fitted it to his head and struck a pose.

His boyish smile brought a blush to Charlotte's cheeks. This beautiful man was pleased to impress her. Then Jack laughed and removed the hat. Out came the oilskin packet. He drew out a page and gave it to her.

"I meant to go over this with you earlier. It could be considered confidential, although not in the official sense."

A little fearfully, Charlotte unfolded it. "This is beautifully written out. Quite impressive."

"The word I would use is *intimidating*. However, it is merely a summons, and as such it is typically obtuse. It could mean one of several things. I shall either be called back with my current rank as captain, or else my advice is needed in some way; these I highly doubt. The most likely option is promotion, with all the rewards and privileges."

"And obligations."

His eyes held an answering gleam. "And obligations, yes. I'd greatly enjoy the tactical nature of the job; I've always relished plotting and scheming, as you know."

"What sort of promotion is offered?"

"The next rung of the ladder would be either commodore or, as is hinted at here, rear-admiral. With a knighthood to follow within the year. The latter were offered thirteen months ago, before the infection in my foot became so serious."

"Being knighted is an honor; my father greatly enjoys his title. You will have a better seat at dinners and several social advantages. People will either fawn over you or sneer because you are a new creation. Trust me, I know."

"Wouldn't you fancy becoming Lady Blunt?"

"The only title I care to have is Mrs. Blunt, thank you."

Jack glanced to the vestibule, where men were coming in and out of the house. "My beloved Diana," he murmured. "If ever I wished to kiss you, it is now."

"I know," she whispered. "We are again reduced to words and glances."

He lifted a hand, as if to stroke her cheek, and then thought better of it. "While there are unsavory political undercurrents to being rear-admiral, the financial rewards can be staggering. Moreover, I would be stationed aboard a first-rate ship-of-the-line, so as to command a fleet. These are enormous ships, meaning much less risk of danger."

"Less danger? Then clearly you should become a rear-admiral."

"You, ah, will recall that while aboard such a ship, Nelson was felled by a stray bullet."

"Then you must thank them for the opportunity and decline."

But Jack did not laugh or even smile.

Charlotte returned the summons. "My beloved Jasper, this is an impossible choice. What shall you do?"

"I do not know; I honestly do not. If asked to return to the fight as before, my duty is clear. But this? As part of the admiralty, I could be in a position to do a great deal of good—or none at all. Or, I might be lending support to decisions contrary to my very character. Some of these fellows are a rum lot."

"Then I shall pray for discernment. Whatever you choose, no matter how arduous, I stand with you."

His fingers closed over hers. "Thank you," he whispered.

"But you should also know," she added solemnly, "that you are marrying a thief."

Instantly the gleam returned to his eyes. "Am I?"

"An unrepentant one." Charlotte put up her chin. "I have stolen and, if needs be, I would do so again."

He struggled to hide a smile. "Which possession have you purloined, my thief? I trust it is worth your while."

"Your bed pillow. The one you loaned me the night of the storm. You perhaps do not remember."

"Oh, I remember."

"Every morning I hid it in the bottom of my empty trunk, because I was afraid that whoever tidied my room would return it to your bed. Today, when Fleur packed my clothes, she did not realize it was there. I knew, and I did nothing. Now my trunk has been carried down and loaded. What do you say to that?"

"One more reason to marry you, my heart. To get my blasted pillow back." But Jack's smile was warm, and he pressed her fingers affectionately. "Come to think of it, I have space in my bag for a certain pillow ..."

How she was tempted to kiss him! "I shouldn't be holding your hand," she whispered.

"I suppose not." Jack gave a glance to the door and sighed heavily. He then transferred his hand to the mantelpiece. "Today we journey to Portsmouth, Miss Lucas," he announced crisply. "And then on to Whitehall. Commander Ord will accompany me. As you know, he is hopeful for promotion."

Charlotte turned. Her uncle and aunt were now in the vestibule. Apparently it was time to go.

Reluctantly she brought out her gloves and moved toward the doorway. Jack fell into step beside her. "Do I wish you fair winds and a following sea?" she inquired.

Jack lowered his voice. "Only if I am retiring, Diana. Or am being interred."

"What? Then I wish you a frightful journey, sir, in the worst weather imaginable!" She was rewarded with a gentle laugh.

Mrs. Allen caught the last part of this. "That we shall certainly have, dear, if we delay for even another minute. Come along."

23 The Back of Beyond

What should one say on such an occasion? "Good-bye and thank you for your kind hospitality" was woefully inadequate. As if she were an automaton, Charlotte stepped into the Allen's traveling coach. How could this be happening? How could she be leaving dear Jack? And yet somehow, she was able to settle into the rear-facing seat and adjust the lap robe. It was like Jack's men to provide hot bricks for their feet.

Captain Ord stood beside Jack; he also was in uniform and wore a sword. Because of the rain, both men wore their impressive cocked hats. She heard Fleur sigh.

"Good-bye," Charlotte said quietly, speaking through the window glass. What more could she say with others present? Jack responded with a smile and touched the brim of his hat in salute.

This was an image she would treasure forever.

"I never should have consented to visit Dorset," Mrs. Allen announced, as soon as they were underway. "What misery!"

Fleur pressed against the window, with a longing look at Cliff House. Charlotte sincerely pitied her. Would her future include Captain Ord?

"On the contrary, I am very glad we came," said Mr. Allen. "That sail was quite the adventure. Such splendid fellows, these seamen! Our Johnny is shaping up to be a fine midshipman, which is what Blunt has in mind. It is very good of him to lend a hand."

There was a pause. "It's curious that your brother has answered neither of my letters, Meg. I feel bad about leaving Johnny at Cliff House without Sir William's leave. I suppose it is easy enough to have him sent home. Has your family written, Charlotte?"

"I've received nothing," she replied, "which is odd because Maria is a faithful correspondent. I suppose that with the holidays and how much we've been shifting ship, their letters have yet to catch up with me."

"Dear Charlotte, you must be on your guard," said Mrs. Allen. "Captain Blunt has quite corrupted your speech. Never mind. Soon enough we shall be in Bath, among civilized creatures, where this naval cant will be cleansed away. I have had enough *sail ho* to last a lifetime."

Charlotte said nothing. Fleur dabbed at her eyes with a handkerchief.

"Now then, dear, would you read a little of that lighthearted book? The weather is so dismal; no doubt that is why we are downcast. We've no reason to be, considering our destination."

Charlotte brought out the book and opened it. "I believe we left off at Chapter 12."

Did Mr. Allen wince? Who could blame him? *Illustrations and Obscurities* was a very silly book.

"You needn't strain your eyes on our account," he remarked. "If you'd rather not read, we do understand."

But Charlotte did not mind at all. The coach swayed and jolted, the print was small, and after two days of this she would have a blinding headache. Yet stinging eyes were preferable to the aching chasm that had opened within her heart.

Jack had warned her about a life of separation. She was now beginning to realize just how painful a lovers' parting could be.

When writing to her family, Charlotte knew that she must use only one sheet so as to reduce the cost to receive it. Therefore, she took pains to write as small and as legibly as possible.

> *We arrived Saturday evening after a long and rainy journey from Dorset, broken only by a stay at an inn that, while clean, was anything but quiet. The poultry yard adjoined Mrs. Allen's bedchamber, and you can imagine the racket.*

If Charlotte had not been so sore and so weary, this would have been quite funny. But the inn was full and no change was possible. Mrs. Allen waxed eloquent about the agonies of this inn for the remainder of their journey.

Nevertheless, our aunt's wish to celebrate Epiphany at Bath Abbey was gratified. The Eucharist combined elegant liturgy, such as you enjoy, Mother, with glorious choral and orchestral music. Purcell's Be thou exalted, Lord *was especially fine.*

Here Charlotte paused. How she would rather sit beside Jack and hear Mr. Goodding's sermon! And enjoy the happy music of Gibby's fiddle! But Jack was either still in Portsmouth or traveling to London. Dare she hope that he was on his way to Meryton?

We have left the White Hart and are now established in comfortable lodgings in Pultney Street, within easy reach of everything. Mrs. Allen is recovered from her cold and has embraced a favorite pastime: shopping. As you know, dress is her passion. At the first opportunity she went straight to a leading modiste and ordered several gowns.

Charlotte never realized how many shops Bath had, or that her aunt would be eager to visit each one. Always, she must hear Charlotte's advice, whether it involved the perfect shade for a length of ribbon or the suitability of a hat that was said to be fashionable. How Jack would laugh at some of these! Charlotte's diplomatic skills were certainly put to the test. And invariably Mrs. Allen would say, "I simply cannot decide, dear. We'll come again tomorrow." And so they would.

Charlotte's interest was caught only by a spray of tiny white roses made of silk. Elizabeth wore silk rosebuds in her hair for Mr. Bingley's ball; how Charlotte had envied these! But surely she had a better use for her pennies. Then too, if she wore rosebuds, no one would notice.

But Jack would.

Charlotte bought the roses.

Maria, how I wish you were here with us, for Mrs. Allen is simply giddy to see all the sights, a thing I know you would enjoy.

Who would have guessed that her indolent aunt could have so much energy? Charlotte had ruined her most comfortable shoes on the beach—and for some foolish reason, she did not wish to have them polished and set right. Sandy and salt-encrusted, they remained wrapped in a handkerchief at the bottom of her trunk, along with Jack's pillow.

Our aunt's new ball gown should be delivered this afternoon, in time for the Assembly in the Upper Rooms. Meanwhile, we have had our hair cut in the latest style, and Mrs. Allen's maid has been taught how to dress it. You would stare to see how fashionable I have become!

The order included a very pretty muslin gown and pelisse for Charlotte. The price was beyond her slender means, but here her uncle intervened. It was his pleasure to give her a gift, he said. What woman would not enjoy something new to wear to the Assembly?

If only he knew that she would also wear it for her wedding!

Mr. Allen's gout is much improved. He and Johnny enjoyed an excellent sailing cruise with Captain Blunt's men, but I expect he will tell you all about it when he writes. None of your recent letters have reached me, but this is hardly a surprise because I have been traveling. I expect they will catch up with me soon.

Would Johnny remember to write? She hoped so. And now, she must offer an olive branch. This was not difficult, for she sincerely missed her family.

I have collected a box of shells and fossils. When I am able to return home, each of you shall choose souvenirs from the sea. I love and miss you all, and I trust this letter finds you well and happy.

Thus ended Charlotte's first five days in Bath.

There had been no letter from Jack, not even one addressed to her uncle. So sharp was Charlotte's disappointment, and so great was her fear for his safety, that each night, with Jack's pillow pressed against her breast, she struggled to hold back tears.

Bath's winter season was said to be popular, and Thursday's Assembly was proof indeed. There were so many ladies and gentlemen present that Charlotte and her aunt could scarcely move without bumping someone. Many red-coated gentlemen were present, along with a surprising number of naval officers.

Of course, Charlotte cherished the hope that Jack would step out of the crowd and ask her to dance. Alas, there was no sign of him.

Even more sobering was today's date: the 9th of January. On this day, she and Jack might have become husband and wife.

On the other hand, so might she and Mr. Collins.

Charlotte took herself in hand. In Kirkby Quay, Dorset, a marriage license waited. She was not without hope.

James Morland was with them tonight, as guest of her aunt and uncle. He seemed distracted.

Mrs. Allen worked her fan, for the air in the ballroom was stifling. This set her bracelets to jangling. "Good gracious," she said, observing him. "Mr. James ought to ask you to dance. I did not invite him to dinner to later be ignored."

"Perhaps he is looking for someone, ma'am."

"I hope not those dratted Thorpes. His friend, John Thorpe, is a perfect beast, and you know about the trouble with the sister. Such a fuss that vixen caused! We have had quite enough of them."

"He no longer appears to be heartbroken, ma'am."

Mrs. Allen snapped her fan shut. "I believe you are right. Just the other day, he said to me that he had taken to heart my advice about marriage. Quite encouraging, is it not? Now if only he would ask you to dance, he could get on with it."

"My dear Aunt," said Charlotte, smiling, "I have no intention of marrying Mr. James."

Charlotte's aunt sighed impatiently. "Then you must find someone else to dance with. An impossibility, for we are acquainted with no one here. It is all very difficult."

"It is, yes."

"And yet, Catherine Morland met Mr. Tilney in this very ballroom, and you know how nicely it turned out for her. She told me that they conversed about muslin, an odd topic to be sure. Young people have unusual ways of courting nowadays. You might fluff your skirts a little, dear. Perhaps there is another muslin-loving gentleman present."

"One never knows," said Charlotte solemnly, and she obliged her aunt by doing so. How Jack would laugh!

All became clear later in the evening when Mr. James brought forward a middle-aged man named Stuart and his wife and their lovely daughter, Juliet. When Mr. Morland performed the introductions, Juliet's eyes held an unmistakable light of admiration. Charlotte hid a smile. Her aunt would be very disappointed.

Mr. James made the prescribed bow. "Would you care to dance, Miss Lucas?"

Charlotte knew what was expected; she must either accept his invitation or forfeit dancing with anyone else. But she also guessed that his request was mere politeness. "Thank you, Mr. Morland, but I am rather tired. May I suggest that you dance with Miss Stuart instead?"

So happy was Mr. James to fall in with this scheme that he said nothing more, not even thank you.

Mrs. Allen gave a mutter of protest. Charlotte paid this no mind but instead conversed with Mr. and Mrs. Stuart. At the soonest opportunity she suggested that she and her aunt find seats against the wall.

"We might as well go home," grumbled Mrs. Allen. "I know no one here, and Mr. James has been a great disappointment. Twice we have hosted him to dinner, and now this. Daughter of his tutor, indeed."

"She is a lovely girl, and she obviously admires him."

"*Girl* is right. I'd like to see *her* hold household on four hundred a year! Let us find Mr. Allen. I have had enough."

When they arrived at their lodgings, they were told that they had callers waiting in the salon.

"Callers at this hour?" protested Mrs. Allen. "You have got to be joking."

"Apparently we do know someone in Bath," quipped Mr. Allen.

Charlotte allowed herself the luxury of savoring the moment. Callers, the attendant had said. This surely meant Jack and Captain Ord. Who else could it be?

With a ready smile she went tripping into the salon, only to be pulled up short by a couple sitting before the fire.

"Why, Mr. Brooksby," she cried. He rose to his feet and so did his unsmiling sister. Was something wrong? Then again, Miss Brooksby always looked mournful.

"Mr. and Mrs. Allen are my aunt and uncle. Mr. Brooksby is our curate, and Miss Brooksby is his sister." A disjointed introduction to be sure, but it was the best Charlotte could do.

Mr. Brooksby held out a sealed letter. "We come at the squire's bidding, miss," he said. "Your letter from Dorset said you would be coming to Bath."

"You must have had quite a search to find us," said Mr. Allen.

Charlotte broke the seal and spread the sheet.

"Is it good news?" said Mrs. Allen.

Charlotte read the message, but the words on the page began to swim.

"My father and mother are gravely ill," she managed to say. "So are the children, all of them. The squire bids me to come home at once, for they desperately need my help." She lifted her gaze from the letter. "I am to go with Mr. and Miss Brooksby."

"To a house filled with sickness?" Mrs. Allen was aghast.

"They need me, Aunt. Of course I shall go to them. Tonight, if possible."

"We leave at first light tomorrow," announced Miss Brooksby. "No dawdling, mind. We have many miles to travel, and we might not be in time."

"*Might not be in time?*" echoed Mrs. Allen. "My brother is at death's door?" She began to wail.

24 Between Wind and Water

Shortly before sunrise, the squire's coach came round to the Allen's lodgings. Charlotte waited with her uncle while her trunk was loaded.

"I do not like this," he said. "If your entire family has succumbed to illness, what is to prevent you from doing the same?"

"You needn't fear; I shall be careful. I have helped to nurse the younger ones many times."

"It sounds as if the servants are either ill or have fled."

"I shall do my best, sir. I promise to write as soon as I arrive. The situation mightn't be as bleak as we are led to believe." Charlotte paused. "If you happen to hear news of Captain Blunt, will you let me know?"

He looked surprised. "Should I hear something?"

"He was summoned to Whitehall. With military men one always worries that they will be sent into harm's way."

Mr. Allen patted her gloved hand reassuringly. "He said nothing of the kind to me; perhaps you misunderstood. Besides, if Blunt takes up a new command, I'll be the last to know."

He pressed a roll of something soft into Charlotte's gloved palm and closed her fingers over it. "Do allow me," he said. "You will doubtless have unexpected expenses, my dear."

Charlotte found herself blinking back tears. Until this visit, she never realized how kindhearted her uncle was. How much she had missed!

"Furthermore," he added with a smile, "if my solicitor forwards to me a letter from that knave Collins, I'll handle him as I think best."

"Oh. I was hoping you had forgotten."

"No such luck. A treat to see Captain Blunt in action, was it not? Farewell, my dear. I hope you will come back to us soon."

Impulsively, Charlotte threw her arms around her uncle's neck. "Thank you for everything. These three weeks have meant more to me than you will ever know."

There was nothing left to do but climb into the coach and settle in beside the formidable Miss Brooksby. Her brother, Charlotte noted, had the rear-facing seat.

Not until well after the sun was up and the horses were changed did anyone converse. Meanwhile, Charlotte's heart worked like a pendulum, moving from worried prayer for her family to concerned prayer for Jack. In either case, there was nothing to do but wait.

Presently Miss Brooksby roused herself. "Mr. Jones says 'tis scarlet fever, but what does he know? Your parents have no rash, according to common report."

Common report? Had such a private detail become a subject for gossip?

"Everyone's throats have been inflamed, and with some there has been fever, especially in young Robert."

Of all the children, poor Robbie was the least strong. "Then it's scarlet fever," said Charlotte.

"If you believe Mr. Jones. I daresay you know nothing about what an invalid should eat."

"Why, whatever he will tolerate: beef tea, chicken broth, apple compote, and weak tea with honey." Memories stirred Charlotte to add, "With application of a mustard plaster if there is cough or congestion."

Miss Brooksby sniffed.

"I haven't properly thanked you for following the squire's instructions so promptly. This is no small journey to undertake, and you enjoyed nothing of the pleasures of Bath."

"That White Hart was not as bad as the other inns," said Mr. Brooksby.

Charlotte was discovering that when his sister was present, he did not talk much. "When Father gets to feeling better," she told him, "I shall see that you are suitably rewarded."

"If we are not too late," said Miss Brooksby.

"He is in God's hands, as are we all," said Charlotte firmly. "*Let the day's own trouble be sufficient thereof.*"

"Amen," said Mr. Brooksby. There was a little silence. "You have been a good daughter to your parents, Miss Lucas," he said gently. "No matter what others say about the recent fracas that ended your engagement, I hold by my opinion."

"Fracas?" echoed Charlotte.

"A course of action that was both shameful and notorious," added Miss Brooksby.

But for that one word, Charlotte would have been highly embarrassed.

We are notorious. We deserve one another.

Dear Jack.

In spite of herself, Charlotte smiled.

Unfortunately, Miss Brooksby noticed, and she clicked her tongue in disapproval.

The best thing would be to let Miss Brooksby's comment pass, and three weeks ago Charlotte would certainly have done so. But now she spoke up. "Mr. Collins and I scarcely knew one another, ma'am. It should not be surprising that we decided that we do not suit."

"Not according to Mrs. Brock."

Trust Miss Brooksby to name Meryton's worst gossip!

And yet, what did it matter? The worries Charlotte now faced involved life and death. A snippy woman's opinion was just that: an opinion.

"Mrs. Brock knows *everything*," added Miss Brooksby.

"Perhaps more than even I," said Charlotte mildly.

Again Miss Brooksby sniffed. "I daresay her source was Mrs. Bennet, who had it from Mr. Collins himself."

Charlotte kept her chin held high. "All I have ever said is that we do not suit. Mr. Collins must have had plenty to say, which is hardly a surprise. Many men do not bear disappointments easily. I have enough brothers to know."

Miss Brooksby gave a crack of laughter. Her brother looked uncomfortable.

After the next milepost, Miss Brooksby spoke again. "Looking for another wife, that Mr. Collins is. That's what they say."

"I wish him well."

"Mrs. Bennet hopes it's her Mary. On account of the entail and all."

Charlotte did not respond. Silent prayer was more to the purpose than responding to deliberate jabs.

This silence lasted until the next change of horses. "You might like to know that the squire has summoned your brother home from school," Miss Brooksby announced.

"Richard?"

"A waste of time, if you ask me. A studious man is no good in the sickroom." Miss Brooksby gave a sidelong look to her brother. "I hear there are only Sally Keith and Ed Rollins, as works in the stable, at Lucas Lodge now."

"Dear Sally, what would we do without her? And you are wrong; Richard can bring in wood and help with some of the heavier household chores, such as the laundry."

"The bedding will have to be burned."

"I'll see what Mr. Jones has to say."

Another silence settled in. Miss Brooksby brought out her work bag and began darning socks. Charlotte gazed out the window and pictured the cove with its crashing waves and crying seabirds. In her mind's eye she could see Cliff House, standing sentinel, and Jack with his pipe, waiting for her beside the beach stair.

Oh Jack. Where are you?

He couldn't be at sea, not so soon. Then again, when that Mr. Wickham joined the militia, he was instantly sent to Meryton.

"So sudden your engagement was. A regular nine days' wonder."

With effort Charlotte returned to the present. If only Miss Brooksby knew the true wonder, which was her whirlwind romance with Jack! What would she say when this new betrothal was announced?

"Mr. Collins was eager to find a wife," said Charlotte mildly.

Mr. Brooksby opened an eye. "Nice for him to have a parish of his own. Not everyone is so fortunate. Not everyone is able to support a wife."

Again his sister sniffed.

"You are a steadfast and loyal curate, Mr. Brooksby. Your care for your parishioners is exemplary."

Charlotte was tempted to add that one day he would surely have his own parish, but this was not likely. "Our Johnny is being trained to become a midshipman, and his knowledge of calculus does you great credit." She gave him a sympathetic smile. "Johnny is not an easy student."

"Fond of sport rather than schoolwork, poor lad," said Mr. Brooksby. "Not everyone can be Richard."

Miss Brooksby looked as if she would say more, but Charlotte had had enough. She dug in her travel bag and pulled out her New Testament. Here was one activity that a curate's sister would not dare to interrupt.

She turned to the gospel of Luke. Why had she not thought of this sooner? An ancient Roman physician, working under the inspiration of the Holy Ghost, was a much better writer than Tag, Rag, and Bobtail could ever be.

Needless to say, it was a very long day. They spent the night in a coaching inn and the whole of the next day in travel. The sun was low in the sky when the squire's coach turned in at Lucas Lodge.

As it entered the yard, Ed Rollins came shuffling out. Together he and Mr. Brooksby managed to remove Charlotte's trunk. "It'll sit out here, miss, 'til I get somebody to help me haul it in."

What else could Charlotte do but consent?

It was very cold out, and she noticed that the fingers of Mr. Brooksby's gloves were worn clear through. Impulsively, she dug in her reticule, peeled off a five-pound note, and stuffed it into his hand. "For you."

"But Miss Lucas!"

"This is a gift from my uncle." She looked directly into his eyes. "You deserve a hero's reward, sir, after suffering such a journey."

Mr. Brooksby caught her meaning. "We each have our cross to bear."

"You carry yours with gentleness and grace. I trust that one day you shall hear *Well done, thou good and faithful servant.*"

He responded with a wry smile. "I must confess, there are times I make calls simply to be out of the house."

"Your secret is safe with me," she said solemnly. "Goodbye."

Charlotte came into the kitchen through the service door and surveyed it with critical eyes. It looked neglected rather than ignored, so that was something. On the hearth a pot of soup was simmering. Here was more good news. No one had starved.

Quietly Charlotte made her way through the rest of the rooms. They too looked neglected, and the air was stale. Here would be no holiday visit. She had been brought home to work, and work she would. What had she said to Jack during those sweet moments in the cave?

When one is miserable, it is preferable to be overworked.

She did not bother to change her travel-worn clothes, but went straight to her mother's bedchamber. Illness or no, she must learn the truth.

Lady Lucas, pale with circles under her eyes, was propped up in bed. When she saw Charlotte her face crumpled, and she began to weep.

Charlotte lit a candle against the gloom and came to sit beside the bed. "The squire had me brought home to you," she said, offering a handkerchief. With the back of her hand, she felt her mother's forehead. God be praised, it was cool. "All will be well now."

"Oh, Lottie."

Haltingly Lady Lucas spoke, enabling Charlotte to piece together the news. Her father was out of danger, although very weak. Maria was now able to sit up in an easy chair. Robbie was still very sick with an inflamed throat and fever; Susannah and Harriet were better, but experienced headaches.

And her mother still suffered the shame of Charlotte's broken engagement.

"There have been the most horrid things whispered about you. Your absence was my sole consolation. Oh, Lottie. How I have missed you!"

"I am sorry, Mother. I had hoped to spare you the worst by leaving. Miss Brooksby told me enough, and she would have said more if I allowed it. She is almost as bad as Mrs. Brock."

"That woman! She is a perfect menace."

"I've spent the past two days reading the gospel of Luke and have been reminded of things I thought I knew, but didn't. Do you know, even Jesus Himself would not have pleased Mrs. Brock. She would have found plenty of things to criticize in Him."

Lady Lucas was surprised into a wan smile.

"I've been thinking, Mother. Did He cower and fret about people's wrong opinions, as I have done? Of course not. He simply did what was right, and so must I. Mrs. Brock and those like her can go hang."

Charlotte's mother drew a long breath. "I did not wish the squire to bring you home at first, for you were well out of it. How glad I am that you have come!"

"Has—Father had any visitors?"

"Other than the squire? None that I know about."

So Jack had not come.

"I should go now. I need to see Sally about supper. Is she attending you without help?"

This brought on a fresh batch of tears. "What would we do without our Sally? She is not strong, but she serves us so faithfully."

Charlotte laid a comforting hand on her mother's shoulder. "God has been very good to us."

"He has indeed. Oh, the stories Sally told about the highwaymen! How our Johnny was made to go home with her as protector, even though he is far too young!"

"That was Jasper Blunt's doing. You remember him; he is Mr. Allen's heir."

Lady Lucas remembered. "Sally had much to say about him. Reckless as always, so typical for a sailor. How I have missed Johnny's bright cheerfulness! Perhaps after supper you can bring him up."

"I'm afraid Johnny is still in Dorset. He is well, Mother, and happier than I have ever seen him. Uncle wrote several letters to Father, explaining it."

Lady Lucas's voice faltered. "Johnny did not come home with you?"

"He shall come—presently. I'll just go down and see Father now. If I can find Uncle's letter, I'll bring it up to you."

Below stairs, there were more tears, this time from Sally.

"Never mind," said Charlotte bracingly. "God has brought me home to you in good time. We'll divide the work between us. When Richard comes, we'll set him to sweeping floors and dusting."

Sally smiled through tears. "Imagine that. Mr. Richard, with a duster."

"He can help with many tasks. Father's correspondence has been neglected; he can certainly sort through that. And then there is laundry. Shall we saddle him with it?" Charlotte shouldn't smirk, but she could not help herself. Richard had no idea. "It's all hands on deck, as the sailors say."

"Miss Charlotte, it does me good to see you here, back where you belong."

Did she belong here? There was so much that needed doing! Sally's words might very well be true.

Oh, Jack.

25 An Element of Surprise

The next morning Meryton was fogged, and it persisted well into the afternoon. Armed with a list and a marketing basket, Charlotte found Ed and told him to pole up the gig.

It was not until after she had placed her order at the butcher's and the green grocer's that she realized the extent of her mother's concern. She could not miss the whispering, the exaggerated politeness, and the stares. All the marks of scandalmongering were here.

Charlotte had once thought of gossip as a harmless way to pass the time, but now she knew better. As she watched Ed load her basket into the gig, she came up with an idea. It was a plan of action inspired by Jack.

Answer a fool according to his folly.

Jack had done so with Mr. Collins, and it silenced him. Mrs. Brock lived here in Meryton. Why not pay her a visit?

Then again, what was she thinking? Why invite trouble? Charlotte trembled at her own temerity. This would be like bearding a lion in his den! On the other hand, keeping silent and hiding behind a wall of pride had accomplished nothing. Her mother continued to suffer, and people continued to stare.

A brilliant maneuver. The element of surprise.

Jack's very words.

And there was something else, a text she had learned as a girl.

God resisteth the proud, and giveth grace to the humble.

Very well, she would humble herself and trust God to give her grace in the eyes of Meryton's most vicious gossip.

"Do you know where Mrs. Brock lives?" she heard her voice say to Ed.

Of course he knew. Everyone knew.

On the whole, Charlotte's call was not a disaster. Was it a success? Only time would tell.

"It was not so very bad," she told her mother, when she brought up her supper. "I did not call to upbraid Mrs. Brock, but to ask a favor."

"What in the world could that noxious woman do for you?"

"I needed a recipe for your mustard plaster, so I decided to humble myself and ask for help. If anyone knows a good recipe, it would be Mrs. Brock. She knows everyone and everything. On the whole, I think she was pleased."

"You took a dreadful chance."

"I did, and it was a move Mrs. Brock did not expect. She needs to see that I am not afraid of her. Also, our present neediness works greatly in my favor. She could hardly figure as one who refused help to the ailing family of a knight."

Lady Lucas looked unconvinced.

"She made quite a show of not having the knowledge herself, but in the end, she gave it me. Or rather, her cook did."

"That was meant to be an insult, Lottie."

"It was." Charlotte was unable to hide a smile. "According to her, I have a flawed character."

"What a cruel thing to say!"

"But it's perfectly true. I am flawed and sinful too. We all are. Is this not why we need a Savior?"

"You said *that* to her?"

"I did."

"Lottie, what has come over you?"

Charlotte sat on the bed. "Something happened while I was at Laurelhurst. If I tell you, you must promise to keep in mind that it ended very well."

Reluctantly Lady Lucas agreed, and the story of Mr. Collins's letter came out. Lady Lucas was horrified.

"I had no idea he was so base," she cried. "He was so cringing, so filled with fulsome compliments. This does not sound at all like him."

"I now wonder if the woman who provides his living put him up to it. At any rate, Mr. Collins did not reckon with Uncle Allen and Captain Blunt. They saw the letter, and Captain Blunt dictated my reply."

"Lottie, you wrote to him? You?"

"I did, with Uncle's full approval. He sent a copy to his solicitor."

"Oh my."

"Mr. Allen will stand behind me, if the matter comes to court. But it shan't. Captain Blunt was ruthless,. Mother; you should have heard the things he said. That letter shut Mr. Collins's mouth. Uncle sent it by express, and not one word has he heard in reply. In the process I learned that I must be brave in the face of criticism. This is why I called on Mrs. Brock. She needs to see that I am not afraid of her. Even though I am, a little."

"*I* certainly am," admitted Lady Lucas, "because I see the damage she can do. However, you have given me much to think about. How glad I am that you are home!"

On the following day Elizabeth Bennet came to call. There was no one else to answer the door, so Charlotte came down the stairs two at a time. Her hand was on the latch before she remembered to smooth her hair and remove the work apron.

How beautiful Elizabeth was, so carefree and smiling! She brought with her a basket of food prepared by Longbourn's cook.

Charlotte led her into the front parlor and noticed the film of dust everywhere. It couldn't be helped, but she sighed just the same.

Elizabeth's inquiries about the family were polite. There was constraint in her manner, and Charlotte understood it. The damage had been done, and what was worse, there was no way to apologize.

"You haven't been away for so very long," Elizabeth said at last.

"These three weeks seem like a lifetime." With a rueful smile, Charlotte found a seat. "While I have been absent, my name surely has not. No doubt our busy neighbors have been speaking of me."

"Well, yes. One can hardly expect them to do otherwise."

"Other than my infamous scandal—for according to Miss Brooksby, I am notorious—what else has been happening?"

Elizabeth was unable to conceal a blink of surprise.

"I may as well speak frankly," said Charlotte. "There is nothing to be gained by pretending that I did not invite catastrophe by accepting your cousin and then changing my mind."

Again Elizabeth blinked. "Well. Let me see. Kitty and Lydia say that Colonel Foster is to be married, much to Lydia's disappointment."

"Does she mind? He is a good deal older than the other officers."

"Yes, but Lydia prefers to have them *all* as suitors. Speaking of suitors, there is something." Elizabeth paused; her eyes searched Charlotte's face. "With my father's permission," she said slowly, "Mary has been corresponding with Mr. Collins."

The burden of sleepless nights, compounded with constant activity, fell heavily on Charlotte's shoulders. Suddenly she felt worn and old and weary.

And yet, this was good news. Surely Mr. Collins would be better behaved with a cousin than with a stranger. Mary might not show well alongside her more beautiful sisters, but Charlotte had always thought her pretty. Mr. Collins would respect that, too.

"How excellent," she said sincerely. "An epistolary courtship."

"With Mr. Collins, that would be preferable, yes. His letters keep Father amused. After all, how much can a man say in a letter?"

Charlotte knew exactly how much, but she was not about to discuss Mr. Collins's threats with Elizabeth. Even if she wished to, she hadn't the energy. "I trust he will be on his best behavior."

Elizabeth gave a gurgle of delight. "He is certainly that. Knowing Father reads his letters must give him added incentive to be clever. Only Mr. Collins would wish for an audience when writing love letters! It answers nicely. He remains in Hunsford, and we do not have to listen to him talk."

"Your mother must be delighted."

Elizabeth's smile became confiding. "Mary has now become her favorite daughter."

"I like that Mr. Collins is writing. There will be a limit to how many compliments he can think up, and then—"

Elizabeth interrupted. "Are you sure?"

Charlotte shared her smile. "What I mean is, eventually he and Mary will begin to discuss topics that are important."

"Which would be theology, her favorite subject. It's noble, but a bit dreary."

"And in him she has an avid listener. I like that." Charlotte paused. "This is an excellent foundation for friendship. And perhaps later, for love."

"Let us say that Mary is willing to marry him. Whether this stems from friendship or a desire to be the savior of the family—which amounts to martyrdom! —remains to be seen."

"I sincerely wish her well. Mary may surprise us yet."

"In the interim Mr. Wickham keeps us in stitches by imagining what could be written in their letters."

So Elizabeth's fascination with this man had not abated. Charlotte concealed a sigh. She had never trusted George Wickham. He confided in Elizabeth freely, but what were his true opinions? Sly like a fox he was. As unlike Jack Blunt as chalk was to cheese.

Charlotte spoke her thought. "Has Mr. Wickham ever spoken of the hardships he experiences as a militiaman? Of the sacrifices he is willing to endure?"

"Why, no. He would laugh at the idea."

Of course he would laugh; he was sacrificing nothing! "What about his willingness to fight to protect our coast from invasion?"

"After Trafalgar, is invasion even possible? Our navy rules the sea, does it not? Militiamen have little to fear."

"Perhaps the idea of suffering loss has never occurred to Mr. Wickham. It should."

Memories of Jack came welling up. How gallant he looked in his workaday uniform. His concealed sigh of frustration when he could not hold her hand. The way he touched his hat in salute as she drove away—

Dear, beloved Jack. Dutiful and honorable and good.

Charlotte worked to keep her tone light. "Mr. Wickham enjoys his fine officer's coat and the parties he attends. But for the military man, there is a cost. Namely, separation from friends and loved ones, not to mention the risk of danger."

"The only danger that our friends face," said Elizabeth merrily, "is being invited to Mapleton. Mrs. Mosley's new cook is a menace. Mr. Denny almost broke a tooth on an overcooked biscuit."

Elizabeth rose to her feet, and Charlotte did likewise. The call was over. And yet, there were things to be said.

"Thank you for telling me of Mary," she said earnestly. "She and Mr. Collins share many of the same opinions, just as you and Mr. Darcy do."

"Good gracious, as if I care for *that*! If I never see Mr. Darcy again, it will be too soon."

"Because he is not agreeable," said Charlotte.

"What?"

"You have been too long in the company of Mr. Wickham, a man who is always charming, always agreeable."

Elizabeth's chin came up. "He is just as he should be: pleasant and refreshingly unreserved."

"I wonder, is he never angry with you? Mr. Darcy has been angry; you told me so. It is important to see how a gentleman handles himself when he is crossed."

"Mr. Darcy becomes cold and withdrawn."

"Because you do not always agree! It's a unique experience for him."

"Oh, please. Are you again going to say that Mr. Darcy is in love with me?"

"No, merely that he respects you enough to be honest with you, instead of being placidly agreeable. Mary would tell you that *charm is deceptive.*"

Elizabeth's eyes were wide.

"I apologize; I am rather tired and have spoken too freely. The material point is this: if ever you meet Mr. Darcy again, I hope you will give him grace and a fair hearing. Sometimes first impressions are wildly inaccurate. I know mine were."

Elizabeth was frowning. "Your impressions of Mr. Darcy?"

"No, of someone else."

There was a pause. "Were there gentlemen at your uncle's house, Charlotte?"

Charlotte was betrayed into a smile, but she said nothing more. She did not dare!

There would be time enough for happy introductions when Jack came. She was now beginning to think that it would be a long wait.

Well, he had warned her.

26 The Moon Lies Fair

Gray skies, cold drizzle, and the unceasing demands of her family took a toll, but there was improvement. By the middle of the week, Harriet and Susannah were well enough to be up and about, although they easily became fretful. Charlotte spent time reading to them or telling stories of her travels. Eagerly they sorted through her box of treasured shells.

The minute they were content, Charlotte ran upstairs to see to Robbie. His fever had finally broken, and he was beginning a slow recovery. When she was not busy with him, there was mending to attend to or meals to plan. Now that people were feeling better, they were no longer content to eat soup.

Crabbiness was a sign of healing, or at least that was what people said.

Richard was now home, and much of the time he was with their father. The laundry Charlotte dealt with herself, or tried to. At last on Saturday the sun came out, and she got down to business.

How far she had come from being the carefully-behaved daughter of a knight! Her hair was closely braided and pinned up without reference to a mirror, the gown she wore was serviceable rather than pretty, and her work apron was anything but fashionable. After a morning spent washing sheets, her hands were red and chapped. There was something going on in the lane, but she paid it no mind. If callers were here, it was better to be out of sight. Surely Richard could receive them.

Out to the kitchen garden Charlotte went, lugging the laundry basket, mindful to avoid the mud. She began hanging sheets on the line.

Richard came out. "Lottie," he called, picking his way around the puddles. "Robbie is asking for something to eat."

Charlotte continued to pin up sheets. "There is always soup," she called back. "You'll find it in the kitchen."

"He wants toasted bread with cheese, poor fellow. I haven't the heart to refuse him."

Charlotte moved to the next section of clothesline. "Can you not figure out a way to do this?"

"Make toast?"

"You slice bread and then brown it over the fire. Honestly, Richard, I cannot attend to it now. Who knows how long the sun will be out? We are in desperate need of clean sheets."

She sighed heavily. "And then I must change the beds—all of them! The kitchen is simply overflowing with dirty dishes. Moreover, while the weather holds, I must order groceries or go for them myself. As if I have time for that. I am grateful for your help with Father, truly I am, but you might try to do something *useful.*"

Richard had the grace to go away.

Charlotte continued pinning sheets with a vengeance. "Thank goodness," she said between shut teeth, "that there are some men in this world who are not babies!"

"Well," said a voice. "I can hope that I do not belong in that category, but one never knows."

Charlotte froze, scarcely daring to breathe. Tears stung her eyes. She must not cry!

A beloved face appeared over the top of the clothesline.

There stood Jack, tall and beautiful and smiling. Charlotte covered her face with her hands and began to weep.

She felt his arms come round her, pulling her against his chest. Suddenly all was right with the world.

"My beloved Jack, where have you *been*?"

"Traveling," he said, with a sigh. "For almost a fortnight."

She pulled back to gaze at him. "You are too beautiful for travel." And he was. His dress uniform was spotless, and he wore his sword and the impressive cocked hat.

"Before coming here, we booked rooms at an inn. I could hardly present myself to your father in all my dirt."

Charlotte pressed against his cheek with a sigh. His beard tickled and his coat held the sweet scent of his pipe. How delicious it was to hear his voice rumble into her ear!

"After my meetings at Whitehall, I needed to travel to Taunton. From there, it was a short step to Bath, so I decided to surprise you."

"You found my uncle?"

"It took a bit of doing, but yes. Allen told me what happened."

"Then you came here?"

"Not quite. Your letter to him had just arrived, so I knew your family was out of danger. I also knew that the household was short-handed. What you needed was not sympathy, but reinforcements. And here we are."

"We?"

"I brought Griffith and Martin and Johnny."

"Oh, thank you," cried Charlotte. "Mother has been asking for Johnny for days. She will be so pleased."

"I brought him out of pure self-interest. I am not leaving Meryton without you. When your family is fully recovered, we shall return to Dorset to be married. Johnny has come to play chaperone to the bride."

Charlotte pushed a lock of hair from her eyes. "You do not return to sea?"

"Not for several months."

"How many—"

Jack interrupted. "Here now, you must be freezing." He removed his coat and put it around her shoulders.

Charlotte gazed up at him. Even in his shirtsleeves he was handsome. His fingers closed around the clothespin she held. "Let Martin handle the laundry, honey."

"It won't take but a minute to finish. I do not wish to saddle anyone else with—"

Again Jack interrupted. "Diana, we are paying Martin and Griffith to work. Johnny has already taken Griffith to the kitchen. You must introduce me to Richard, by the way. He has my sympathy."

Charlotte gave a gurgle of laughter. "Do *you* know how to make toast?"

She saw him bite back a smile. "It happens that I do."

"Thank goodness. I can now marry you without reservation."

Jack kissed her, right there in the yard. To Charlotte's aching heart, it was as if they were again in the cove, declaring their love for the first time. The breeze sent all the sheets to flapping.

"Come," said Jack, smiling down at her. "Introduce me to your father."

"I ought to take you in by the front door. Mother wouldn't like it if I brought you through the kitchen. You are dressed like a crown prince, or you would be if I were not wearing your beautiful coat."

"The better to be seen by all the neighbors."

"Yes, but I look like the scullery maid."

Jack's arm possessively encircled her waist. More scandal, more food for gossip! Together they came round the corner of the house in time to encounter a caller. Apparently he had just arrived.

Good gracious, this was becoming a farce! An introduction was in order, but Charlotte struggled to keep a straight face.

"This is certainly a surprise," she said. "I thought you were in Hunsford. May I present Captain Jack Blunt."

"Actually—" said Jack, with a twinkle.

Trust Jack to be in a teasing mood! Charlotte would have none of that, and she cut him off. "How kind of you to inquire after my family's health."

Jack released his hold on Charlotte and smilingly held out a hand. "Mr. Collins, I presume?"

William Collins's eyes were wide, and his lips curled into a sneer. Jack's hand he ignored. "What *have* we here?"

"Diana," murmured Jack, "you told me that you were desperate. I had no idea how accu—"

"Mr. Collins," Charlotte hurried to say, "it's such a surprise to see you here."

"I have come to share important news, ma'am."

"Have you?"

Mr. Collins puffed out his chest. "Miss Mary Bennet has consented to become my wife."

"I wish you joy, truly. You and Mary have much in common. Now everything is right."

"Not quite everything," cried Mr. Collins. "How dare you write that threatening letter!"

"The one in response to yours?" she countered.

Jack spoke up. "Perhaps this is a discussion for another time."

"On the contrary," said Mr. Collins. "This is the perfect time."

Jack shrugged. "Have it your way. *I'm* the one who spiked your guns, Collins. *I* dictated the letter Miss Lucas signed. I am happy to discuss it, in as much detail as you like. But not, perhaps, in the presence of a lady?"

Mr. Collins was shaking with anger. "I *demand* satisfaction."

"Do you now," said Jack slowly. "I'm agreeable. Swords or pistols? The choice is yours."

Mr. Collins's eyes became even wider. "D-do you mean a d-duel?"

Charlotte now noticed that Jack's hand rested suggestively on the hilt of his sword.

"I beg your pardon. This is generally what is meant by *satisfaction.* I don't suppose you prefer fisticuffs?"

Mr. Collins gave a gasp of horror.

"I didn't think you would." Jack sounded disappointed.

"Captain Blunt," said Charlotte, speaking low, "you must *not* fight Mr. Collins."

Jack spread his hands. "He is the one who asked for satisfaction, not me."

"What I meant," said Mr. Collins frostily, "is that I shall do exactly to you as you threatened to do to me."

Jack's smile reappeared. "Report me to my superiors, do you mean?"

"They deserve to know what a scoundrel you are."

"Be my guest."

"Your career as an officer will be finished." Mr. Collins paused to sniff. "If you *are* an officer, that is. How do I know that uniform is genuine?" He pointed a quivering finger. "I think you are an imposter! A rogue and a thief."

"Mr. Collins, really," cried Charlotte.

Jack's voice was unsteady with suppressed laughter. "You're not entirely wrong, Collins. Do you understand what I do for a living?"

Mr. Collins wrinkled his nose in distaste. "I haven't the slightest interest in your vulgar occupation."

"Blast and the devil take it, Collins, I'm *his majesty's pirate*! A professional scoundrel-at-sea! I chase down enemy ships and seize them as prize for the Crown. I'm rather like Robin Hood, if you consider the ordinary seaman to be the poor."

"I should think you'd be ashamed."

Jack shrugged. "If you'd rather be overrun by the French, that's your business; the majority of Englishmen do not agree. I suggest you contact Admiral Sir Edward Pellew."

"Pellew?" cried Charlotte. "But that's the name of your—" She stopped.

Jack smiled down at her. "The men name them after admirals. It's a classic reversal of roles. The horse does all the work, while the men ride. They like that." His smile twisted. "I suppose this means I'll have the next horse named after me."

Mr. Collins, meanwhile, had his hands on his hips. "I'll ruin you," he sputtered. "You just wait until—"

A shout interrupted. "Hallo, sir! There you are!" Johnny came loping round the corner of the house. "Well? Have you been to see Father?"

"Not yet, young scamp." Jack turned back to Mr. Collins. "I do not recommend writing to Admiral Cochrane, whom *The Times* fondly refers to as The Sea Wolf. Not that Cochrane wouldn't enjoy your letter; he would. It's just that Cochrane thinks I am too reserved, too law-abiding. Although," Jack added, "to be fair, I cannot see Pellew writing me a scold either."

"A scold?" cried Johnny. "Who would dare? Not when you've just been promoted to—"

"John," Jack interrupted. "Be quiet."

But Johnny would not be silenced. "*Admiral* Blunt," he announced, "is one of the heroes of Trafalgar. He won't tell you, being modest, but it's in all the history books. If you don't believe me, you can look it up yourself. The mates I'm staying with, they showed me. As for the other admirals, they *like* him."

Charlotte spoke up. "Mr. Collins has just become betrothed to Miss Mary Bennet," she said brightly. "Is this not good news?"

"Aw, Ed told me that when he took charge of the horses. Can't be here five minutes without hearing the latest chin-wag."

"Indeed," said Mr. Collins grandly, "in the service tomorrow—if you bother to attend, which I daresay you won't—you shall hear the first of the banns read."

"Banns?" said Johnny scornfully. "I say, that's rather scaly. What's wrong with purchasing a license? Not the sort of thing I'd like to see for a sister of mine, the banns."

"Johnny," warned Charlotte.

"It ain't gentlemanly, Lottie! Before, I did not know. But the mates talked it over with me, seeing as how Admiral Blunt is set to marry you. Banns don't cost money, and a license does. Which goes to show that when a fellow is sincere, he *pays*."

"Young man," said Jack. "If you do not shut your mouth this instant, I'll be rolling up my sleeve. And you know what'll happen then."

"Aye, sir, I get clonked," said Johnny happily.

"Better you than me," said Mr. Collins. "My errand of mercy has obviously been for naught. Good day!" He turned on his heel and marched back to the lane.

"Errand of mercy? What errand of mercy?" said Jack.

"I think he meant to comfort me with his happy news."

"Since when is rubbing it in comfort?" Jack paused. "That Miss Mary, whoever she is, is too good for him. She'd do better to marry Martin or Lt. Spaulding."

"You and your bachelor crew! I ought to warn poor Sally."

"Hang on, you called her—" Jack frowned in an effort to remember. "Didn't you call her Mrs. Keith?"

"If I did, it was as a courtesy. She is a spinster."

"She's not that much of a spinster. Confound it, Griffith's in the kitchen, playing rescuer." Jack's eyes brimmed with laughter. "Come along, Diana. We'd best see your father before Sally nips in to give her notice."

27 No Objection to Hearing It

Excitement broke over Charlotte's family like a happy wave. The sight of their wan and smiling faces, so sincerely joyful to hear Charlotte's news, touched Jack's heart. With his prospects presented and Sir William's blessing gained, it was time to celebrate.

"Let's treat ourselves to a bang-up high tea," crowed Johnny. "Martin and I can go provision at the shops." Everyone began to talk at once, offering suggestions. Within the family circle, this was quite a lively group. However, by the time Martin and Griffith were clearing away the tea things, it was evident that many of them needed to rest.

Jack stepped out to the yard and told Ed Rollins to ready the gig. "I know you," he said to Charlotte later, as he handed her up. "Unless I take you away, you'll work.

Therefore, show me Meryton. I want to see your haunts and favorite places. Please?"

This simple request delighted her. Jack stopped at the George Inn to exchange his dress coat for a plain one, and then they were off.

Longbourn House was a bit of a disappointment, for they were only able to see it from the lane. "Alas, Loud Lydia is nowhere to be heard," Jack lamented. "Ah well, there is always tomorrow's service. By Jove, we'll hear the banns read for Collins. That will be ... unusual."

"As we are each announcing an engagement, yes. How thankful I am that you are here!"

Jack next expressed an interest in the Netherfield estate. "What a shame that Mr. Darcy is not in residence," he remarked, as they drove through its imposing gates.

"It's Charles Bingley who has taken it, not Mr. Darcy. I daresay no one is in residence now."

"Excellent. We'll see if the housekeeper will permit a tour of the public rooms."

Charlotte hesitated. "Mrs. Nicholls is known to be disobliging."

"The woman has nothing else to do but watch over a spotless house. If it's too much trouble, she'll tell us no."

"That's what I'm afraid of."

He put his arm around her shoulder. "My love, if you'd rather not, we'll go elsewhere. On the other hand, after this week, you'll likely never see the woman again."

Jack was rewarded with a smile. "Very well, let's inquire."

Mrs. Nicholls admitted them, but only because Charlotte was Sir William's daughter. As they moved from room to room, she kept casting glances at Jack. "A stately place," he remarked. "It's a shame to see it empty."

Mrs. Nicholls gave a sniff. "The family has gone back to London, with no indication as to when they will return." She gestured to the grand staircase. "The ballroom is on the first floor."

Once inside, Mrs. Nicholls drew back one of the draperies to let in light. Jack caught Charlotte by the hand and led her to the center of the floor. "Is this where you danced with Mr. Darcy?" he said into her ear.

"It was Elizabeth who did that, not I," she whispered back.

"Better and better! And now you dance with me." Jack twirled Charlotte round, and she gave a gurgle of laughter. Mrs. Nicholls looked on with pursed lips.

Yet it seemed to Jack that the woman's reserve might be thawing. Presently she announced, "So you are the Admiral. We've heard about you."

"Already?" said Charlotte. "But he's only just arri—"

Jack interrupted. "Jack Blunt of the Royal Navy," he said, smiling. "I am at your service, ma'am."

Mrs. Nicholls looked him over. "According to what Mrs. Hill heard, you're a sham, a regular Captain Sharp. You don't look like a sham to me."

Jack did not dare look at Charlotte; he'd burst out laughing. "Ah, no, ma'am. I'm the genuine article, although I have no idea as to how I might convince you."

Without thinking, Jack rested a hand on the hilt of his sword. Charlotte gave him an uneasy look. Was she expecting him to use it?

"Thank you for showing us over, Mrs. Nicholls," she hurried to say. "You must have many other things to do. We really should be going."

"What were you thinking back there?" Jack wanted to know, once they were underway again. "That I would give a demonstration of swordsmanship to prove my worth?"

"I never know what you will do. You are not exactly safe, Jack Blunt."

"I know," he admitted. "I'm afraid you're stuck with me, my girl. It's a comfort to know that Careful Charlotte wouldn't dare end another engagement."

After that, they doubled back and drove through Meryton itself. Charlotte was pointing out various shops along the main street when a modest placard caught Jack's eye. "Clarke's Subscription Library?" He promptly reined in. "Is this where you and Loud Lydia borrow your books?"

"Hush, Jack, someone may hear! It is indeed, but—"

"That settles it," he cried. "We're going in."

Once inside, Jack had Charlotte take down *The Sinister Baron's Prey* from its shelf. He balanced the open book in his hand. "So here you are," he said to it. "Behold your handiwork."

"Handiwork? What handiwork?"

"Why, you and me. Your journey to romance began right here in this book, did it not?"

"No!"

Jack hid a smile. "I stand corrected." He shut the book, but did not return it to its place.

The library was deserted, save for a round little woman in a ruffled mobcap. She looked as if she would like to cluck.

"Is that the proprietress? I'll just step over and have a word." Jack walked up to the desk, with Charlotte hard at his heels.

"You are Mrs. Clarke, I take it? Excellent. You are just the person to help me. Might I have a list of romances that are similar to this one, please?" Jack presented *The Sinister Baron*. "My men are prodigiously fond of it."

"They are what?" demanded Charlotte.

Jack grinned. "*Prodigiously* is the word Wiggy used; I defer to his judgment."

"Men, did you say?" stammered Mrs. Clarke, cradling the book. "Men *like* this novel?"

"They're my crew," explained Jack. "John Lucas read this aloud, chapter by chapter, every night for a week. These are battle-hardened fellows, but they hung upon every word. Now they want more, and I am at a loss. Will you help me?"

Out came a banknote, modestly folded. "If I might make a contribution to the replenishment of your stock?"

Naturally, Mrs. Clarke was delighted to oblige.

"Just wait until word of *this* gets round," said Charlotte later, as he returned her to the gig. "Did you give her a five-pound note? She'll be over the moon."

"I did. I'm a dab hand at managing scuttlebutt, my sweet. The old girls in Meryton need more to talk about than your scandalous engagement, don't you think?"

"I don't know what to think. Except that here is yet another example of your high-handed determination to win every battle."

Jack waited, with a smile hovering. Would she say it?

Charlotte did not disappoint. She gave a sigh and tucked her hand under his elbow. "You are altogether *ruthless*, just as you said."

Charlotte never realized that Sunday morning could bring such a struggle. Why wouldn't her mother listen to reason? "It isn't necessary that you attend," she said. "You and Father ought to remain quietly at home. Think of how exhausting it will be."

"If I am prostrated for a week, so be it. I wouldn't miss this morning's service for the world. It's our proudest moment as a family, aside from your father's elevation. Are you certain that dear Admiral Blunt knows to wear his regimentals?"

"Yes, Mother. You told him several times."

"Good. I cannot wait to see Mrs. Bennet's face. After all, you are not marrying just anyone, but an admiral. Moreover, he's a hero."

"Mother! You are not to lord it over Mrs. Bennet."

"That woman was just *awful* when you became engaged to Mr. Collins. It was as if you were counting the days until you could cast her from her home! I daresay you did not hear everything she said."

Unfortunately, Charlotte had.

"And when you ended it, nothing could match her delight and scorn. She was the one who sent Mr. Collins here yesterday, I guarantee it."

This was probably all too true.

"I know just what I am going to say," continued Lady Lucas. "If I happen to encounter Mrs. Brock or Miss Brooksby, so much the better."

Lady Lucas lived up to her promise. Pale but determined, she clung to Richard's arm as they entered Meryton's parish church. Sir William followed, with Johnny and the two older girls behind. Charlotte and Jack brought up the rear. No one could mistake the many whispers of surprise.

It was not long before Charlotte heard her mother say, "Yes, we gave our blessing to the match just yesterday. Admiral Jasper Blunt is Sir William's brother's heir. Whose extensive properties are *not* entailed, I might add." There was a pause. "The Admiral has his own estate by the sea in Dorset."

Charlotte set her teeth. Cliff House was hardly an estate, as well her mother knew! "I am so sorry," she whispered to Jack.

"There is no contradicting the pride of a mother. My own mother, God rest her soul, would do the same."

Fortunately, the organist began the introit, and Lady Lucas was silenced. Yet Charlotte knew that after service there would be more to come.

Surprisingly, it was Elizabeth Bennet who approached first. Her lovely eyes were wide as she gazed at Jack. "So there *were* gentlemen at your uncle's house," she observed, smiling. "Mr. Collins told us of your engagement. I wish you joy."

"And Mary's happy news? I kept waiting for the banns to be read."

"Mr. Collins surprised us all by announcing that he will instead purchase a license. In light of what has come before, this is the happiest solution."

Lydia pushed her way forward. "Is this the sham admiral, Lizzy? I've never met an imposter before."

"Good morning, Lydia," said Charlotte politely.

But Lydia was too busy staring to reply. "Bless me," she said at last. "I shall always prefer a red coat, but I must say, the blue does catch a girl's eye. How do you do, sir?"

Jack shook the hand she offered and was rewarded with a flirtatious giggle.

Lydia then turned to her companions. "Why don't you have a coat like that, Wikky? With all the gold braid? It's a good thing you came to service after all, for seeing is believing. You must get busy and keep up. Charlotte Lucas cannot be allowed to have the handsomest man."

Smiles were exchanged, and then an artful division occurred. Charlotte suspected that this was engineered by Jack. "Who was that?" he said, once the Bennets were out of earshot.

"Lydia?"

"No, the smiling militiaman with the knowing eye. He's what I'd call a parlor snake."

"That's Mr. Wickham, the Bennet girls' favorite admirer."

"They'd best have a care."

Mr. Collins emerged from the crowd. Charlotte had the distinct impression that he was being prodded by Mary. Apparently, the betrothal had given her confidence.

"Best to get over the awkwardness at once," Charlotte heard her say. Mary put out a gloved hand. "I'm pleased to hear your news about Admiral Blunt," she said, smiling. "How do you do? All's well that ends well, is what I say."

"I am delighted to meet you," said Jack, shaking her hand.

Charlotte saw Mr. Collins's fingers move to clasp Mary's wrist. Instantly Mary turned. "Now, Mr. Collins, none of that," she chided. "You'll have people thinking that ours is a love match, when it is no such thing. It is infinitely superior." Mary smiled at Charlotte with simple pride. "A marriage of true minds is much to be preferred."

"If you say so, miss," said Jack politely. "Several of my men have settled near Hunsford and Weston. If you do not mind, I'll ask them to look in at the parsonage from time to time. Men of the navy are handy fellows to have about, should anything go wrong."

Would Mary understand Jack's direct look?

On the other hand, would such help be needed?

Mr. Collins was looking remarkably cowed and humble. Was he already living under the cat's paw?

"That is kind of you," said Mary. "Yes, very kind. It is a pleasure to have helpful friends and neighbors. We've been making such plans. Father and Elizabeth will fetch Jane from London, and then they will come to Hunsford for Easter."

"Your father is to travel?" said Charlotte. "That is a compliment indeed."

"He does not make a long stay, but Elizabeth and Jane will." Again Mary smiled. "They shall be our very first guests."

Out into the winter sunshine they came. Sir William, Lady Lucas, and the girls did not linger for long, but Charlotte, Jack, and Johnny stayed on to greet well-wishers. It seemed as if everyone in Meryton wished to shake Jack's hand.

At last the crowd dwindled. "If I hear *the hero of Trafalgar* one more time from your rascal brother ..."

"But, sir. Did you see Mrs. Brock's *face*? And Miss Brooksby's?"

Charlotte gave a gurgle of laughter. With one hand she took hold of Jack's elbow and with the other, Johnny's.

"We've had quite enough for one morning. It's time to take you men home to dinner, before anything else happens."

"We've certainly given people something to talk about," agreed Jack. "Do you know, Diana, I'm going to enjoy being part of this family."

28 As You Are Mine

Six days later, Jack and Charlotte were again in a parish church, this time in Kirkby Quay. Emma Goodding was Charlotte's attendant; Lt. Martin and Johnny stood up with Jack. Much to his credit, Commander Ord remained in Bath, as he had a courtship of his own to pursue. The rest of Jack's crew were at Cliff House, where a bountiful meal was being prepared.

"My first event as hostess is my own wedding breakfast," whispered Charlotte to Emma, just before the ceremony.

"Isn't that delightful? And there's not a cloud in the sky," said Emma. "It's the perfect day for a party."

And it was. The men had dressed the house, using the signal flags Charlotte loved, and Griffith outdid himself in the kitchen. After the meal, Gibby fiddled while Charlotte danced with Jack. Next came speeches and toasts and stories. The pale winter sun graced the afternoon, until at last the shadows lengthened into evening.

The Gooddings were the first to depart, on account of young David. Martin trimmed the lamps, and one by one the men resumed their duties. Chairs were returned to the dining room, plates were cleared, floors swept, and the parlor rug unrolled. Talk came from the kitchen for a time, but at last all was quiet.

Charlotte stood at the parlor windows and peered down at the cove. The sun had just set; it was becoming difficult to see.

Jack came in. "That's it for the night. I've locked up."

Charlotte turned. "It has been a perfect day."

Jack joined her at the window and drew her close. He said into her ear, "I quite agree." His beard tickled, a delightful sensation.

She leaned into his embrace. "And now we are husband and wife."

"That we are, my heart," he murmured. She felt him draw in a long breath and release it. Here was a sigh of contentment. They were home.

"I have known you for a month and a day," Charlotte whispered, "and yet I feel as though I've known you all my life."

"We were meant to be together."

"I waited long for you, husband. But then, you waited just as long for me."

"Longer, because I am older." He paused, with a smile pulling at his lips. "Are you looking for someone, honey?"

Trust Jack to notice! "I'm trying to see whether the tide is out. Do you think it is?"

His gaze held hers. "It looks that way."

"Some help you are! The tide table said half-past four would be the time."

Jack brought his forehead to rest against Charlotte's. "I couldn't care less about the blasted tide table."

"Yes, I know. It's just that ..."

His smile was warm. "That what?"

Charlotte hesitated. Suddenly her idea seemed rather silly. "It's nothing."

"No, it isn't. Tell me."

"I was thinking of—but it doesn't matter."

"Thinking of what?"

Charlotte sighed. "If you must know, I was hoping to revisit one of our old haunts this evening. I thought it might be a romantic thing to do."

"I am all for romance," he murmured. "What's in your mind?"

"Well," she said slowly, "we cannot return to Laurelhurst, which is where I first knew that I loved you."

"Dear Laurelhurst. Do you happen to recall which day that was?"

"It was when you took your hair down," she whispered.

"But you are miserably behind-hand!" cried Jack. "I began well before that, although I was loath to admit it at the time."

"Never tell me it was while we rode that horse together. Jack, it *wasn't*. It couldn't be."

"I'm not made of stone, Diana. It'd been a long time since I'd held a woman in my arms, and you are uncommonly lovely."

"But I was altogether unwilling! I disliked you thoroughly."

"That served to greatly heighten the appeal. But you were saying? About old haunts?"

"I thought," said Charlotte slowly, "of visiting our first romantic spot, a place I've remembered often during these weeks."

He grinned. "Not the cave."

"Now Jack, the tide is out. And it hasn't rained all day."

"But honey, if we go down there, we're sure to get wet. You'll ruin your new dress."

"Yes, but you keep saying that we have plenty of money. You'll buy me another."

"That and a dozen more, if you wish it. You are aware that it's beastly cold out?"

Charlotte was prepared for this objection. "You've a warm greatcoat, and I've got my fur-lined cloak. Do you see?" These garments were waiting, draped over the back of one of the sofas.

Jack's eyes were bright. "You've planned this. Very well, my love, I'm game. I'll just get the lantern."

"And perhaps," she whispered, "you might fetch a knife as well?"

He turned back. "Come again?"

Oh dear! Charlotte hadn't meant to speak this thought aloud.

But there was no hiding from Jack. "I know that look," he said softly. "Tell me."

She sighed. What was it about Jack Blunt that caused her to say whatever was in her mind?

"If you must know, it's from *The Sinister Baron's Prey*. The villain encountered a troublesome knot in the lacing of the heroine's stays. The story takes place in olden times, when bodices were laced in the front. So, he used a knife."

Jack's brows went up.

"Now you must admit," said Charlotte. "A knife can be good to have on hand."

"*He cut the heroine's clothes off?*"

"Of course not! Well, not all of them. He'd managed to cut one or two of the lacings when—"

Jack interrupted. "*This* is the kind of thing you girls read to one another? As you sip tea from flowered cups?"

"Now, Jack."

"Men like me risk life and limb to protect our shores, so that you can sit around and read *claptrap*?"

Charlotte dissolved into giggling.

"Great Scott," he marveled. "No wonder my men want more."

"Jack, it isn't like tha—"

"Some heroine! She just lay there and let this happen? She didn't fight him off?"

Laughter made speaking difficult. "She couldn't. She was tied up. On a table. In the attic."

"Like beef on a spit?"

"Nothing untoward happened. Before the villain could cut more laces, the hero came in through the window—"

"An attic window? How'd he *fit*?"

"I don't know. He came bursting through the window and then—"

Again Jack interrupted. "It was open? Where's the element of surprise? The villain would have seen the grappling hook catch on the sill. Then the hero would have to climb three or four floors up. That takes time."

"The book said nothing about a hook. And the window couldn't have been open, because there was a ferocious thunderstorm. Rain was lashing against the panes."

Jack gave a shout of laughter. "Oho! So, the hero bursts through the window, like a confounded rock launched from a sling. Somehow he manages not to cut himself on the broken glass."

"Exactly. And then he impales the villain through the heart with his sword."

"He's got to fit *a drawn sword* through a small attic window?" Jack cast up his hands. "Who writes these books?"

"Jack!"

'No, love, he'd have a knife, not a sword. He'd carry it in his teeth as he climbed."

"How do you know?"

"I've done this kind of work, boarding ships. He'd pull his lips well back, too, so as not to be cut with the knife's blade. Looks rather gruesome." Jack demonstrated.

"Ew."

He laughed. "Not exactly a kissable face, is it?"

"That's not the point. The sinister baron died, and the heroine's virtue was saved."

"That's romantic? There'd be blood all over the place."

Charlotte put up her chin. "The book didn't say anything about blood. It was heroic."

"You didn't think it heroic when that highwayman fell dead at your feet."

"That was different."

"Moreover," Jack went on, "after climbing hand-over-hand, during a blasted thunderstorm, and then killing the villain, the hero's blood would be up. That heroine had best beware. He might take up the knife and finish cutting the lacing."

"Jack!"

"I am just saying." His eyes were alight with laughter.

"Shouldn't you fetch the lantern? Oh, and before you go, could you help me with these buttons?" Charlotte presented her back.

She could not see Jack's face, but his surprise and delight were palpable. "I am always happy to help with buttons," he murmured as he unfastened them. "My only question is, why am I doing this now?"

"I've decided that you are right. This is a beautiful dress, and I don't want to ruin it." Charlotte slipped the gown from her shoulders and stepped out of it.

"You are going down to the beach *in your shift?*"

"One might as well be practical. As for the cold, I'll have my cloak."

"Well then, I jolly well don't want to ruin this coat," cried Jack, shrugging it off. "Or the waistcoat." He cocked an eye. "What about the breeches? Shall I leave these here too? And go down to the beach in my smalls?"

Charlotte brought her hands to her hips. "The lantern, sir?"

His grin widened. "Aye, aye, Mrs. Blunt. I'm a-going."

While he was in the kitchen, Charlotte pressed her palms to her cheeks. She had not meant to confess all this to Jack. How was it that her confession served to make the evening more exciting?

Once she and Jack stepped outside, they were met by the distant rumble of the surf. At the head of the beach stair, Jack halted and looked back at the house. "It's nigh unto freezing out here," he observed cheerfully.

"Yes, but we shan't mind that. Besides, didn't you once tell me that you are inured to cold weather?"

He grinned. "What happened to *all I ask is a comfortable home*?" He gestured. "Behold, there it is."

"That was because I hadn't yet discovered your comfortable arms."

"There is no arguing with that." Jack adjusted his hold on the lantern and offered an arm. "If you will permit another question, Mrs. Blunt. Am I to play the role of Jack, the honest seaman? Or the sinister seducer?"

Charlotte gave a gurgle of laughter.

"Right. Seducer it is. Ought I to carry you down to my, ah, lair?"

"*Could* you?"

Jack gave a cry. "Of course I could. Easily."

"You are not too old?" she teased.

"Old? I'll give you old!"

Charlotte found herself seized at the waist and unceremoniously thrown over his shoulder. "Not like a sack of potatoes," she protested, laughing.

"How else does a villain carry his victim? Quit complaining." Down the beach stair Jack went.

Charlotte continued to laugh. "Don't drop me!"

"I won't," he grumbled into her ear.

"Have a care! That lantern is hot. You'll burn yourself."

Jack set Charlotte on her feet. "Now see here," he said sternly. "The victim is not supposed to mind if the villain burns himself."

"But I don't want you hurt."

He sighed. "Would Careful Charlotte prefer to walk?"

"No, but it might be safer."

"Come along, then. Better take my arm, as the treads are rather slick. As a matter of fact," he added, as they resumed the descent, "the stair is the least of our worries. It will be dark and cold in the cave. Moreover—"

Charlotte interrupted. "Can't you start a fire? You have your tinderbox."

He smiled. "With what fuel, my love?"

"Why, driftwood. Castaways always burn driftwood."

"Ahem. Did you see any in the cave? Or anywhere on the beach? This isn't British North America, where the shores are littered with timber."

"Oh."

"It's just as well. Lighting a fire in there would bring out creatures. Spiders and crabs and the like."

Charlotte halted. "*Spiders?*"

The light cast by the lantern now assumed a ghoulish aspect.

"The real worry," said Jack, "are the seals. I should have brought a stout cudgel with me. Ah well. We'll find out soon enough." He resumed the descent.

She glanced anxiously at his face. "Seals might be in the cave?"

"It's their domain. If there is one, I can probably get him to weigh anchor. On the other hand, if it's a mother with her pup ..."

Again Charlotte halted. "I cannot have you fighting with an angry seal." Her voice dropped to a whisper. "This is turning out to be a very bad idea."

"I disagree. It's adventurous. Like you."

"Gracious, I am anything but adventurous!"

"You were brave enough to marry me."

"I couldn't *not* marry you!"

Jack set down the lantern and gathered her into his arms. "Ah, just a minute, love," he murmured.

Why, Jack was unbuttoning his overcoat! "There," he said, and he pulled her close against his chest. "That's better." He was deliciously warm. The wool of his coat held the faint scent of his pipe.

Jack's lips found hers and he kissed her, right there on the stair, under a wide and starry sky.

Here was everything Charlotte's romantic heart craved.

"Do you know," he said presently, "if we are looking to recreate a romantic moment, I have one that answers nicely."

Charlotte raised her eyes to his.

"It's a cherished memory, one that has been much on my mind."

"When I stole your pillow?"

"You're close. I was in my cabin, tucked up in bed when, just before the stroke of midnight, there was a little knock at my door."

Charlotte gave a sigh. "Must you remind me?"

Jack ignored this interruption. "I figured it was Ord. Instead, an angel with a candle came in. Barefoot and dressed in a robe with the sash half untied."

"Jasper," whispered Charlotte.

"You cannot imagine my disappointment when I heard why you were there. I was hoping that you came for, well, me."

"But I—"

"Even if you had," he went on, "I would've held the line. But a fellow can dream."

"Do you dream of me?" she said wistfully.

"Every night."

"I do the same, always."

Jack answered with a kiss. "Do you know," he said presently, "this morning I ordered a fire in the Great Cabin; it's been kept up all day. It should be nice and warm in there by now."

"A definite advantage over the cave."

"What say you? Will you come to my door with your little candle?"

"With my robe half untied?" she whispered. "Yes. Oh yes."

His smile was tender. "Come."

Arm-in-arm, they ascended the beach stair. "We'll try your cave idea in the summer. I've become rather fond of the role of sinister seducer. I might have to read that rubbishy book."

Charlotte gave Jack's arm a playful thwack. He laughed.

As they crossed the lane, their steps slowed to a halt. "I love this house," whispered Charlotte, gazing up at it.

"I've always thought of it as my life's work. But the building of it was only the beginning. It will be empty no more. When I come home from the sea, you will be waiting for me."

There was a small silence. Charlotte said quietly, "What you told me in Meryton, about having *a few months* before you're called back; that wasn't altogether true, was it?"

Jack did not reply.

"It could be as soon as tomorrow. Am I right?"

Again he said nothing. This was answer enough. Charlotte pressed her cheek against his; Jack's hold on her tightened. "I'm sorry," he whispered. The quiet was broken only by the sound of the surf.

Presently Charlotte found her voice. "Take me with you."

There was a pause. "To Portsmouth?"

"Yes! No! Aboard your ship, or wherever you go."

"But, honey—"

Charlotte pulled back to look him in the eye. "I'm no hothouse flower. I don't mind discomfort or danger."

"I knew that the moment I threw you into the saddle," he said quietly. "It's one of the things I love about you."

"Then you'll consider it?"

Jack sighed heavily. "Life at sea can be brutal. It can also be slow. You might not like it."

"There are plenty of things I can do to be helpful," she cried. "You'll see. I'll knit socks for the crew. Or jerseys. I can roll bandages. We did that at school for the army hospital. I can help the young midshipmen with their lessons."

Jack's expression was hard to read. Was he pleased? "Women use too much water," he said at last.

"I know, and I'll try to be good. Please, Jasper. Please don't leave me behind."

"Honey, it might not be up to me."

"But you're an admiral now. Won't you be the highest-ranking officer aboard?"

In the lantern's light, she saw the ghost of a smile. "Listen to you," he said fondly. "You're already talking like a navy wife."

"Please?"

"Maybe," said Jack.

Charlotte squared her shoulders. "I can live with maybe."

"But I cannot," he said suddenly. "Blast! Maybe, nothing. *Probably.*"

"Do you mean it? I would love that above all things!"

"My dearest Diana, so would I. I hope you won't regret this decision."

"Never!"

"Very well, Mrs. Blunt. Now that that's decided, shall we go in out of all this confounded cold?"

"Not until after you kiss me, sir."

"Alas for the life of a married man," lamented Jack, as he gathered her into his arms once again. "He's always being ordered about."

But Jack did not seem to mind. Neither did Charlotte.

The End

Epilogue ~ 1818

Charlotte's suspicions were proven correct. Tensions in the Atlantic did escalate into war, pressing Jack into active service sooner than anticipated. His rank as rear-admiral enabled Charlotte to live aboard the flagship *HMS Cavalier* for two years. She was able to see the shores of North America, including the (unsuccessful) shelling of Fort McHenry.

Shortly before the birth of their son, Benjamin David, Charlotte returned to Cliff House. The boy has his father's blue eyes and golden curls.

Some months later the war ended, putting Jack ashore for good. He and Charlotte reside at Cliff House, where they are expecting their third child. Plans are now underway to enlarge the house.

Henry and Emma Goodding now have five children and are fast friends with the Blunts. Henry supplements his income through the writing of mysteries and adventure stories, which in recent years have become very popular. Jack serves as his accuracy consultant.

Thomas Ord received his long-awaited promotion and took command of the *HMS Tyrant.* Before returning to sea, he and Flossie (Fleur) were married. They have one child and are expecting a second.

John Lucas is a lieutenant in the Royal Navy and has excellent prospects for advancement. His younger brother, Robert, recently signed on as midshipman. Richard Lucas is a solicitor in Fullerton, Wiltshire, where he oversees his uncle's business concerns.

Mr. and Mrs. Allen live quietly at Laurelhurst Manor, where Mr. Allen's fondness for acquiring investment property is thriving. Most summers he enjoys a week-long sailing cruise with Jack Blunt and Henry Goodding.

After a three-year engagement, James Morland married Juliet Stuart. He stepped into a living provided by his father and is now a rector.

A humbled William Collins gratefully wed Mary Bennet as planned. Mary's father and her two oldest sisters visited Hunsford at Easter, where Elizabeth became reacquainted with Mr. Darcy. Charlotte's advice did not fall on deaf ears after all. Elizabeth and Mr. Darcy were married in the December and have three children.

As of this writing, Mr. Bennet lives on as master of Longbourn. His heir, Mr. Collins, looks to have a rather long wait. Mr. and Mrs. Collins have one child, a daughter.

Oh dear.

Thanks so much for reading

If you enjoyed *So This Is Love*, an honest review at Amazon is very welcome.

The more reviews an independently-published book receives, the easier it is for new readers to discover.

For news of my new releases, follow me on my Amazon author page.

Other books I've written

Darcy By Any Other Name
The Mercy's Embrace Trilogy
A Very Austen Christmas
A Very Austen Valentine
A Very Austen Romance

May I recommend ... More to Love by Robin Helm

A lovely Pride & Prejudice Regency Romance

About Laura Hile

I live in the Pacific Northwest with my husband and a collection of antique clocks.
My job as a middle school teacher keeps me on my toes.
There's never a dull moment with teens!

Visit me on-line at LauraHile.com.
Do stop by. I'd love to meet you.

All of my titles are enrolled in Kindle Unlimited.

Made in the USA
Las Vegas, NV
02 May 2023